The Life She Wants

A GRANITE SPRINGS NOVEL

Maggie Christensen

To my wonderful husband and soulmate who proved
to me that it's never too late to fall in love.

Also by Maggie Christensen

Oregon Coast Series
The Sand Dollar
The Dreamcatcher
Madeline House

Sunshine Coast books
A Brahminy Sunrise
Champagne for Breakfast

Sydney Collection
Band of Gold
Broken Threads
Isobel's Promise
A Model Wife

Scottish Collection
The Good Sister
Isobel's Promise
A Single Woman

Granite Springs
The Life She Deserves
The Life She Chooses

Check out the last page of this book to see how to join my
mailing list and get a free download of one of my books.

Prologue

Ben was dead?

The words echoed around in Fran Reilly's head. It wasn't true. It couldn't be. The doctor, his blond hair falling over one eye, looked at her, a sympathetic expression on his face. 'I'm sorry, Ms Reilly.'

Sorry? He was sorry?

Fran turned her head away. She couldn't bear to look at him – this man who was alive, who was telling her that her lovely Ben, the love of her life, her future… was gone forever.

'But,' she began, only to feel his cold hand on hers.

'We were unable to save him,' he continued as if she hadn't spoken. 'Your own injuries are severe. You were lucky to…'

But Fran had stopped listening. Maybe this was a dream. If she closed her eyes, when she opened them again, she'd be lying beside Ben in their king-sized bed overlooking the ocean and Coogee beach. They'd make love, get up, have coffee on the esplanade, then plan their next adventure. She could see him there, on the beach. His smiling face. His dark hair all wet. Touching, laughing and joking. Her arms wrapped around him so tightly. So warm as she slipped into the darkness. A darkness filled with beautiful dreams that made all the pain go away.

But when her eyes opened again, she was still in the same hospital room, hooked up to various pieces of equipment that hummed and hissed. This time there was a nurse sitting by her bedside.

Ben!

Fran's eyes filled with tears. They ran down her cheeks and she tasted their saltiness as they trickled into her mouth. What had happened? She tried to remember but her head ached something terrible.

Then she remembered. They were on the bike, Ben's pride and joy. They were flying along a country road, her arms wrapped tightly around Ben's waist. The bike had skidded.

'Where... where am I?' she asked in a cracked voice, her throat aching as if it had been scratched.

'You're in Granite Springs Base Hospital. There was an accident,' the nurse said. 'You've been here three days.'

Three days. Ben had already been dead three days, while she'd been lying here in this town in the middle of nowhere.

She and Ben had been celebrating one last trip before the baby. They were due back at work a few days later and were powering through the New South Wales countryside when...

The baby!

She tried to see the baby bump they'd laughed about only a few days ago. A dreadful thought struck her. 'My baby?'

'I'm so sorry,' the nurse said.

One

Fran Reilly gazed down as the familiar outline of Granite Springs took shape below her and her heart began to thump wildly as she remembered what she'd vowed to do.

It was good to be home, but with her return came the decision she'd made. The past six months had been stressful, saying farewell to her mother in England, then having to close up and arrange to sell the house she'd grown up in, a house full of memories, both good and bad, but mostly good. Then there were the regrets. Regrets she hadn't been a better daughter. Regrets she'd left her mother when she was in her early twenties to forge a new life in Australia. Regrets she hadn't visited more often.

The time spent by her mother's bedside had been an emotional rollercoaster. There had been the good moments when the older woman had been lucid, and they'd reminisced about the good times. Then there had been the hours when her mum had been asleep or unresponsive. Those were the times when Fran had taken time to reassess her own life; to decide what she wanted from the years she had left.

Her thought processes had been fuelled by her turning fifty while there. Fifty was a milestone, an opportunity to take stock. And Fran didn't like what she saw.

When she'd met Ben Holland in her local pub in London, she'd fallen head over heels for the handsome Australian backpacker, and it had seemed like the most natural thing in the world to return to Australia with him. She didn't have any regrets about that.

But here she was, more than twenty-five years later, having left her native land again, this time for good. England didn't feel like home anymore, and the protests in the streets made her uncomfortable and eager to return to the place she now thought of as home.

Except… There was something she had to do.

It wouldn't be easy to turn her back on the relationship that had sustained her for the past ten years. But, sitting at her mother's bedside, hearing tales of her parents' life together, seeing how her mother's face still lit up as she spoke of the man who'd been her husband for over forty years, Fran knew what she had with Richard wasn't enough. If she was honest with herself, she'd known it all along. But it had been so easy to fall into the habit of having dinner together a couple of times a week, to spend the odd weekend together when they'd end up in his or her bed – usually his, as he rarely came to Granite Springs.

She could hear him now, his precise, modulated voice, 'It's a country town, Fran. What is there to do there? Much better you come to Canberra.' And she had; she'd spent so many weekends in the nation's capital, she could lead you through it blindfold. But it wasn't somewhere she could live.

Fran had made a life for herself here in Granite Springs. After the accident that took her lover and left her with ongoing back and neck pain, unable to face returning to her former life in Sydney, she'd stayed on in the country town. It was a place that had healed her, then made her welcome.

The plane landed, and a strange mix of excitement and trepidation took hold of Fran.

A blast of cool air greeted her as she left the aircraft. Fran pulled her windproof jacket tighter around her, glad she'd taken it with her on board, glad too she'd brought her roll-necked sweater to change into on the plane. It was cold here after the warmth of the summer she'd just left. She breathed in the familiar atmosphere. Her heart lightened. She was home!

Walking out of the airport, Fran felt the town enfold her just as it had all those years ago when she'd been a wreck, both physically and emotionally after the accident that stole her future. It would be true to say Granite Springs had saved her life back then. Here she'd discovered a caring community whose warmth had wrapped around her like a cloak, protecting her from her demons and helping her move forward.

Finding a job at the university, Fran had joined a local choir and become a friend of the local art gallery. As the years went on, she'd joined a book club, a Pilates class, and volunteered at the local hospital in appreciation of their treatment of her all those years ago.

Now she hailed a cab. As soon as she had settled herself and given the driver her address, her phone pinged with a text.

Welcome home. Dinner on Sat? Rx

Fran sighed. She'd have to tell him her decision then.

*

Next morning, Fran opened her eyes and gazed around the familiar room in her little townhouse. She lived close to the centre of town, within walking distance of most of the amenities, and overlooking the lagoon which provided her with a peaceful outlook.

Today, she intended to go to the university to check in. Six months was a long time to be gone, but she knew that Kay Jackson, the woman acting in her position, would have done a good job. She'd been in touch with her from England and knew Kay was expecting her. A coffee with her would help ease Fran back in gently, then she'd be more prepared to return to work next week.

She took her breakfast of coffee with toast and marmalade out into her courtyard to enjoy the early morning sun. The ground was a carpet of purple, the jacaranda on the other side of the fence was blooming early this year. It had been a warm, dry winter bringing on the early blossoms. When she finished eating, Fran sat for a few more minutes in the small courtyard facing the lagoon. She watched a few ducks and moorhens swimming past, a solitary heron landing on an outcrop of rock. A young woman pushed a pram along the path which stretched between the courtyard and the water, laughing as the young child waved his hands madly.

A wave of nostalgia for all she'd missed threatened to overwhelm her and was quickly quashed. Why did she feel as if…? Fran tried to analyse her feelings. What did she want?

She loved this town, this house – two things she certainly didn't want to change.

Rising stiffly to take her cup and plate inside, Fran put her hand to her back. One of the consequences of her accident was ongoing back pain due to the spinal injury she'd sustained when she was thrown from Ben's motor bike. She'd learned to live with it, through a cocktail of painkillers combined with regular physio and massage. The long flight hadn't done her any favours. Maybe she'd be able to fit in a massage before she went out to the campus.

Picking up the phone, she dialled her faithful massage therapist.

*

'Feeling better, now?'

Fran nodded as she struggled to rise.

Magda handed her a glass of water. 'No need to get up just yet. Your muscles were pretty tight. Have you an appointment with your physio? Remember – a massage can only do so much. I'd be willing to bet you've neglected yourself while you were caring for your mother. It's no good if you let yourself down like this. You were lucky not to be paralysed with the tumble you took.'

Magda was right, of course. The old woman was always right. Fran had discovered her soon after she was released from hospital and had been utilising her services ever since. Over the years they'd developed a friendship and Fran had found her a useful confidante, one who'd never gossip or reveal secrets.

'You're looking to make changes,' Magda said, nodding sagely, while serving Fran a cup of soothing camomile tea. 'You think you want something different.'

Fran had often wondered if this was a regular feature of Magda's service, or one she only offered to certain clients. Regardless, she valued this time which helped her recover from the massage and – sometimes – unburden herself. Magda had an uncanny knack of being able to determine exactly what was worrying Fran.

'I don't know what I want,' Fran said, honestly.

*

As she drove along the familiar road in the early afternoon, Fran began to sing along to the golden oldies on the local radio. As she warbled the words of *Moon River*, she thought they could have been written for her.

She reached the campus in plenty of time and spent five minutes walking around, noticing that not much had changed while she was gone, except... Wow! She stopped in front of the almost completed building that was to house the new School of Music and Drama. Construction had barely begun when she left, now it looked very impressive. And the adjoining theatre – to be named after the Australian conductor and music educator Richard Gill – would prove a useful addition to the town's entertainment venues.

Entering the university café – commonly called Banjo's – Fran immediately spied Kay sitting in the far corner. She ordered, then weaved her way past tables of chattering students to greet her.

'Hello, Kay. Thanks for meeting me. I know how busy you must be.'

'Hi, Fran. Welcome back.'

'It's good to be back.' Glancing around the room at the familiar scene, Fran knew it to be true. She belonged here. 'How have you found working with the prof?'

To Fran's surprise, Kay blushed and looked down at her hands which were loosely clasped on the table. 'It's been fine,' she said.

Their coffees arrived before Kay could say more. Fran gazed quizzically at her companion, then she remembered something Ann Baird had written her. Ann managed the education office. It had been she who'd arranged the temporary secondment and in one of her emails to Fran, she'd hinted at what she called a *liaison* between Kay and the dean of the faculty.

Reading between the lines, Fran suspected it was more than that, much more. She was happy for Kay. She knew she'd had a difficult time before coming to the university and deserved to find happiness again. Although the dean, Professor Nick Kerr, was a very attractive man, Fran had never been tempted to have anything other than a professional relationship with him. But she'd heard rumours about his marriage – the university thrived on such rumours – and knew how much he loved his two children.

'So, it's true? You and Professor Kerr?'

'What have you heard?' Kay fingered the rim of her cup. 'We… we've become… I'm moving in with him and putting my old place on the market.' She looked up as if daring Fran to disapprove.

'I'm so pleased.' Fran smiled. 'Ann Baird has been in touch and kept me up to date. She did mention… It's a big step – to take on two teenagers.' She gave Kay an enquiring glance.

'Oh, I know!' Kay's laugh rang across the table. 'The very idea gave me more than a few sleepless nights. My two are all grown up and I thought those days were behind me. But I think he's worth it.' She gave a secret smile and, for a moment, Fran envied her new-found happiness.

Fran decided to say nothing more about this, though she was curious. Nick Kerr was a very private man and she knew Kay had lived like a recluse since her husband's death. How had they managed to drop their guards enough to form a relationship?

'So,' Fran said, 'are you ready to step back to working with Ann again?'

The pair smiled knowingly.

Fran knew Ann had the reputation of being unapproachable, too formal in her manner, even gruff at times. But Ann had been a good friend to her over the years, and Fran knew that underneath the brusque manner, beat a heart of gold.

'Yes and no,' Kay replied. 'I've enjoyed working with Nick, loved the responsibility and the degree of independence it gave me. But it's become awkward now that people know about us.' She blushed again. 'Nick thinks – I think,' she corrected herself – 'it would be best if I found a similar position in another faculty. I think he'll be glad to have you back,' she admitted. 'We may have become too close to work effectively together.'

Fran felt a warm glow. It was good to be appreciated and it had taken her years to achieve her position with the dean. 'Is there anything available?' She thought that unlikely as those positions were at a premium and most, like hers, had been held by the same person for years.

Kay grimaced. 'Not really. They'll be appointing someone to work with the new head of the School of Music and Drama when it's established. But Ron Harris is pretty certain to get the position – he's been banging on about it for ages – and I'm not sure I could work with him.'

'Oh, dear.' Fran could sympathise with Kay's dilemma. Ron Harris had been teaching music education in the Faculty of Education for as long as she could remember. He was a crusty old bachelor, loved by students, but someone who found it difficult to relate to other adults. He'd be hell to work for. 'Well, maybe someone will choose to resign,' was all she could offer.

'Hmm. Maybe.'

'Now, what else has been happening while I've been gone?'

They drank their coffee while Kay filled Fran in on the various projects the dean had been working on and the usual round of university politics. Fran was pleased to note Kay's account didn't include any faculty or university gossip. As someone who abhorred gossip herself, Fran warmed to anyone else who took the same point of view. Though, given what she knew of Kay's background, it was exactly what she'd have expected.

'You'll want to catch up with Nick now,' Kay said as they rose to leave.

'If that's all right with you?'

'Of course. He's expecting you.'

The two women walked across to the education building together, passing several staff members who greeted Fran and offered their condolences. Each time, she flinched. 'I knew it would be like this,' she said. 'People either don't know what to say or they overdo it. I thought I might have been done with the sympathy card back in England.' She sighed, then realised she might have hit a hot button with Kay. 'I'm sorry. For a moment, I forgot…'

'No, it's okay. I'm over it now. Nick's helped me a lot in that regard – and this place.' She glanced around the campus. 'Anyway, I didn't have to put up with much sympathy when David died.'

Hell, Fran thought. *I've really put my foot in it. How could I have been so careless? Of course, losing my mother is nothing like what Kay had to go through when her husband committed suicide.*

By this time, they'd reached their destination.

'I'll just have a word with Ann first,' Fran said, in an attempt to regain her equilibrium.

'Come up when you're ready.'

Fran poked her head into Ann's tiny office. 'Hello, Ann.'

'Fran! Good to see you back. I didn't expect you till Monday. Couldn't keep away?'

Fran gave a rueful grin and spread her hands. 'You know me.'

Ann came around the desk and gave her a hug. 'I'm sorry about your mum.'

'Thanks.' It didn't feel so bad to accept sympathy from Ann. Fran knew it was genuine not just a meaningless platitude.

'So, you ready for the fray again?'

'Just about. I had coffee with Kay and she filled me in on what's been going on. I wanted to check in with you first, then I'll go up and say hi to Nick.'

'Kay's done a good job. We'd be sorry to lose her if she decided to look elsewhere. I believe…' She tapped her nose.

'She did say there might be an opportunity with the new performing arts school,' Fran said.

'The School of Music and Drama. Yes. They're interviewing for the head position tomorrow.'

'I thought it was a foregone conclusion. Ron Harris?' She raised her eyebrows.

'I believe there's quite a field. It may not go his way. I've heard there are some strong out-of-town applicants, one in particular.'

'Trust you,' Fran chuckled. 'You always did have a nose for the news.'

'It's actually a bit more than that, and something I wanted to talk with you about. Do you have a minute?' She gestured to a chair.

'Nick's expecting me,' Fran said, perching on the edge of the seat and hoping this wouldn't take long.

'He won't mind. He knows about this.'

Fran was puzzled. What on earth did Ann have to tell her?

'It's about the new school. The vice chancellor feels there needs to be someone there who understands the workings of the university really well.'

'Ron,' Fran said.

'Probably not. But if he is successful, he'll need to work with someone who has more people skills than he has. And if an out-of-towner gets the position, he'll need someone to steer him – or her – in the right direction. Aaron, our dear leader, hasn't put all that time and effort – not to mention dollars – into the project for it to fall down in a heap.'

'So there might be a chance for Kay there, after all? But she was dubious about working with Ron.'

'Not Kay.' Ann gave Fran a look.

'Not me! You're not trying to tell me the vice chancellor wants me to move? What about my position here?' Fran couldn't believe what Ann was suggesting.

'You're the most senior of the personal assistants we have. You've helped establish this school, worked successfully with two deans, you understand the regulations – written and unwritten. Who better? And before you start to object,' she held up her hands defensively, 'Aaron has discussed it with Nick and they've agreed Kay can continue with him despite their relationship, as they're handling it very well.'

'But I've just had coffee with Kay.'

'Kay doesn't know. Nick was under oath to say nothing to her until we'd spoken. It would mean an increase in salary, a change in job title. What do you say?'

Fran was lost for words. She loved her position here in the education faculty, but had to admit she also loved a challenge. She visualised the brand new building she'd walked past earlier, thought of the thrill of being part of the setting up of a whole new school, and felt a quiver of excitement run through her.

Ann didn't wait for a reply. 'The building's not completed yet, of course, but Aaron wants you on board immediately. There's a spare office here you can use in the meantime. Alec Wright's on sabbatical this semester so his office is free and…'

Fran held up a hand to stop Ann's flow of words. This was all going too fast. She gulped. Was she ready for this?

'I need to talk with Nick,' she said to give her breathing space. If her boss didn't like the idea – regardless of what the vice chancellor might think or want – she wouldn't even consider it. Fran was mindful of Kay's opinion that it was awkward to work for and sleep with the same man – though she hadn't exactly put it in those words.

'Of course.' Ann picked up her pen, a sure sign their meeting was over. 'But you will let me know when you've decided?'

Fran nodded.

When Fran finally left the campus, her decision had been made. Both Nick and Kay's encouragement had tipped the scales, especially when Kay laughingly said they could always swop places later if it didn't work out – and if Ron Harris didn't become head of the new school.

She recalled the odd feeling she had of wanting something more – maybe this new challenge was the answer. Not a new love, after all. But she was still determined to finish things with Richard.

Nothing that happened today had any bearing on her decision.

Two

Owen Larsen peered at himself in the mirror. His once dark auburn hair was now faded to a dull blond and was beginning to recede at the temples, defining the fine bone structure he'd inherited from his Scandinavian grandfather. If he failed to shave, the grey in his beard revealed his age more surely than the fine lines around his eyes and mouth.

How would the interview panel react to his hairstyle, the long locks tied back in a tidy bun reminiscent of the younger man he'd once been?

This interview was important to him, a chance to make his mark. He'd spent most of his life lecturing to teacher education students, many of whom had scant interest in the music education he was passionate about. The opportunity to set up a new School of Music and Drama in the regional William Farrer University in Granite Springs seemed like a lifeline.

The timing was good, too. His daughter, Pia, had recently flown the nest to share a flat with her boyfriend. Darren wouldn't have been Owen's first choice of a mate for his lovely daughter, but she vowed she loved him, and he appeared to dote on her. Owen just hoped it would last. His own foray into marriage with Brit had left him cynical about relationships, and he'd managed to avoid any serious commitments since they'd split when Pia was in her early teens.

Now in his mid-fifties, he'd become a solitary figure who haunted concerts, galleries, bookshops and libraries, and enjoyed drinking at home, alone. The prospect of living out a peaceful existence in a country town held a lot of appeal, even without the lure of the role.

And it would help him to put the past behind him. He'd been faced with several challenges in recent weeks and was keen to leave this city.

Driving into Granite Springs from the airport, Owen received a surprise. The town was bigger than he'd anticipated – more of a regional centre. He supposed the presence of the university here had a lot to do with that. Certainly, as he drove along the main thoroughfare, he could see groups of students milling around, loitering outside cafes and what appeared to be a well-stocked bookshop. He had a good feeling about this town, about the university. He mentally crossed his fingers the panel would like him. Granite Springs would be a good place to live, to put down roots. It was close enough to Sydney to enable him to catch up with Pia from time to time – when their workloads permitted – and far enough away for any differences to be forgotten.

Owen checked into a local motel, freshened up, and set out to explore the town. He wandered along the main street, into the bookshop he'd seen from the car, browsed in the window of a real estate agent, pleased to see the property prices here compared favourably with those in the city, and spent an hour or so in the local art gallery, impressed with the current display. Then, realising he was hungry and had barely had any breakfast before he set out, he found his way to a café called The Bean Sprout.

'Visiting Granite Springs?' asked a friendly voice.

Owen looked up from the menu he'd been perusing to see a cheerful woman who appeared to be close to his own age, her short hair forming a halo around her face. 'Yes. Seems like a lovely place.'

'We think so. Be sure to check out the local landmarks while you're here. The lass in the tourist information booth on the corner of Main and Alder can set you right, whatever your interests. Have you decided what you'd like?'

Having ordered a chicken salad with an accompanying black coffee, Owen took time to look around. The café was busy at this time of day, clearly popular with students, businesspeople and local shoppers. It had the look and feel of a family business, and Owen would be willing to bet it hadn't changed much for several generations.

After lunch, Owen knew he couldn't put it off any longer. His interview wasn't till tomorrow, but he had an urge to see the campus. Maybe it wouldn't live up to his expectations, maybe it would be an architectural monstrosity, set on land denuded of natural vegetation.

Having picked up a map at the information booth – along with several attractive brochures extolling the beauty spots of the surrounding area – he headed out of town to where the university sat on a wooded campus.

The long avenue of trees leading up to the entrance was impressive, as were the low buildings – none more than two levels, almost hidden among the trees – a mixture of gums and wattle with a sprinkling of cherry trees just coming into bloom. As Owen drove around in his hire car, he saw many groups of students lolling on manicured lawns, despite the coolness of the day. He felt a curl of excitement in his gut. He could work here.

Drawing into an almost full car park, Owen made his way up a gravelled pathway to where he could see a café. Drawing closer he read the name – Banjo Patterson Café. A café named after the famous bush poet who grew up not far from here was a good sign. Owen had grown up loving the bush ballads his grandmother read to him as a child and could still recite all of *The Man from Snowy River*.

Inside, he was greeted by the muted sound of music and the chatter of young voices. Although classes must be in progress, there were still clusters of students engaged in enthusiastic debate. It was all very familiar. But the atmosphere was different from the harsh city environment where he usually spent his days.

Ordering coffee and a slice of banana bread to assuage his growing hunger – despite the fact he'd just eaten lunch, Owen settled himself at a table by the window to observe what he hoped would be his new workplace.

He watched people come and go while he drank his coffee – more students, a couple of harried looking men he assumed were lecturers, an elegant woman who came in to greet another sitting in a corner to engage in what looked like a serious conversation. Then, deciding he'd see more of the campus on foot, Owen strolled along various pathways, ending up outside a partly finished building which bore the name School of Music and Drama. It was built of sandstone with a red tile roof and stood between the library – entitled Information Centre – and what appeared to be a large auditorium, perfect for concerts and performances.

It was as if it had been designed especially for him.

*

Next morning, Owen awakened to the sound of rain. Peering through the curtains, he could see it was lashing down and creating large puddles. He shivered. This wasn't a good omen. Why couldn't yesterday's sunshine have lasted for one more day?

He showered and dressed quickly, then made a quick dash across the courtyard to the motel dining room for breakfast. After two cups of reasonable coffee and a plate of scrambled eggs with toast and bacon, he felt more cheerful. What did the weather matter after all? This could be his big chance.

The campus didn't look as attractive this morning. The rain was still falling, filling the gutters, the overflow dripping down on unsuspecting students as they raced between buildings with umbrellas or holding bags over their heads for protection.

Owen managed to find a parking spot close to the building which housed the executive suite where his interview was to be held. He took a deep breath, picked up his briefcase, and walked in.

After what seemed like an interminable wait, Owen was summoned into a large meeting room where several people were seated around a long table. He was asked to take his place at one end and was introduced to the panel. He made smiling acknowledgements, sure he'd immediately forget the names, till a familiar face appeared.

Nick Kerr!

He'd known Nick years ago when they'd both been junior lecturers in Sydney – enjoyed a few beers together while complaining about the powers-that-be and the lack of academic freedom. Then Nick had left, Owen had stayed to build his career, and they'd lost touch. So, this is where Nick had got to, and done well if he was on this panel.

Musing about his old colleague, Owen neglected to pay attention to the subsequent names. He came to attention with a start when he heard the vice chancellor ask, 'Dr Larson, can you outline to the panel why you think you're the best person to lead our new school?'

The next hour passed in a blur. Owen thought he'd performed adequately, but was it enough to win the position he now craved?

As he flew back to Sydney, his heart felt lighter than it had for years. Granite Springs. He even loved the name of the place. It conjured up a peaceful oasis, a place where a man could live out his life in comfort.

Three

Fran dressed carefully in a pair of immaculate dusky pink pants topped with a wine shirt for her trip to Canberra to meet Richard. He was particular about how she looked – wanted his companion to show him in a favourable light to any of his colleagues and acquaintances they might meet. It was one of the things she'd admired about him when they first met at an art gallery opening – his fastidiousness, his determination to do everything correctly. But after a while it had palled. What was appropriate – maybe even essential – for a man in his senior role in the public service, could become wearing on a daily basis.

She guessed that was why their relationship had worked so well. They only ever saw each other at their best. Maybe it would have broken down earlier if they'd lived in the same town or shared a home.

What was she going to say? Richard was one of the good guys. He didn't deserve to be dropped for no good reason. They'd got along pretty well all those years. It was a true case of *it's not you it's me*, but she wasn't going to humiliate him with that cliché. He certainly didn't deserve that. She had to let him down lightly, allow him to retain his dignity.

Various scenarios crossed her mind, only to be rejected, as she drove along the edge of Lake George which contained hardly any water as a result of the long drought. The car entered the outskirts of the city before Fran reached a decision. She was still mulling over possible approaches when she drew up in front of the apartment Richard owned with its magnificent views over the blue waters of Lake Ginninderra.

'Fran! It's so good to see you. You were gone for a long time – too long. But I understand. I'm so sorry about your mother. It must have been difficult for you.' Richard greeted her with a warm hug.

It was easy to respond, to slip back into the effortless relationship they enjoyed. Fran wondered if she really wanted to end it. It was comfortable, predictable – boring. *Where had that word come from?*

'Thanks. Good to see you again too, Richard,' she said when he finally released her. She returned his kiss which, in typical fashion, was a mere touch of the lips. Richard kept all his passionate embraces for the bedroom, believing there was a place for everything. He liked everything in its proper place. *Why had that never irritated her till now? Why had she even respected it as one more example of his unique way of life?*

'I thought a celebratory glass of bubbly before we head out to dinner?' He gestured to the bottle of Moët sitting in an ice bucket on the coffee table along with two crystal glasses. Nothing but the best for Richard.

While he poured the wine, Fran wandered across the room to the window to admire the view she loved. She'd miss this.

'Fran?'

She turned and accepted the glass with a smile.

'To us. To your return.'

Fran swallowed. This wasn't the time to tell him it was over. Not when he'd gone to so much trouble, when he was being so caring. She clinked glasses with him and took a long gulp. He was so good to her. It would be easier if he was a bastard. But he was just a very nice guy, one who was easy to be with, who'd made her life comfortable. He didn't deserve to be dumped like some leftover lasagne.

Clearly ignorant of Fran's internal recriminations, Richard sipped his champagne and continued, 'I've made a booking at the Rubicon. We should get going soon if we're to make it. Then you can tell me all about your trip. I'm sorry it was such a sad one.' He drew her towards him and dropped a kiss on the top of her head.

The Rubicon was one of their favourite places to dine. Fran knew Richard had made a special effort to please, as he always did. It only made what she planned to do all the more difficult. Why couldn't he treat her badly? But if he did, he wouldn't be Richard.

'You're very quiet.' Richard glanced sideways at her as they drove across the city. 'Everything all right?'

'Yes,' Fran lied. 'It's been an odd week.'

'You're not back at work yet, are you?'

'Monday.' Back to a new position because, of course she'd agreed to accept the position. She'd had no option. 'I have news about that, too.' Fran wondered what Richard would think. He'd been encouraging her to make a change for some time now, but she strongly suspected what he meant by *a change* was a move to Canberra where she'd be more available to him for spur of the moment events.

No, that was unfair. Richard didn't do spur of the moment. He liked his life to be planned. She did, too. Though sometimes she wondered what it would be like to be more spontaneous. For her, any impulsive thoughts she might have had died with Ben twenty-eight years earlier. That was when she'd made the decision to take life more seriously. Her relationship with Richard had been one of the results of that choice.

Richard threw her a puzzled look but said nothing. Fran was grateful for his instinctive sense of knowing when to remain silent.

It was coincidence he'd chosen the Rubicon for their meal tonight. The very name of the restaurant spoke of her decision – a Rubicon moment being one in which a person commits irrevocably to a course of action. But, so far, she'd been too much of a coward to do what she'd planned.

As Richard ordered oysters to start, accompanied by another bottle of Moët, Fran studied the menu which she knew almost by heart. Deciding on the Pernod cured salmon, Madras spice, scallop mousseline, with summer vegetables, she put the menu down on the table.

'Good choice,' Richard said, 'I think I'll have the chargrilled beef rib eye. It's Wagyu.'

Fran smiled. He was so predictable. Always steak, Wagyu for preference, and always medium rare. A saying of her mother's came to mind – you could set your clock by him.

She was sipping the sparkling wine, when Richard asked, 'What happens Monday? Don't you have a job to go back to? Surely that professor of yours hasn't discovered he can manage without you?'

'No, though my replacement did pretty well. I've been asked to move to a new position in the School of Music and Drama. It's a bit of a mouthful. I'm sure the students will soon devise another name for it.'

Fran saw a crease begin to form on Richard's forehead.

'It's due to open next year,' she rushed on. 'They interviewed for the Head of School this week and…'

'And your interview is when?'

'I don't have one. No lesser person than Aaron Peters, the Vice Chancellor himself, has asked that I take on the position of assistant to the new man – or woman. But I expect it will be a man. It usually is. I start Monday.' She took a sip of the champagne which had been poured while she spoke and studied Richard's expression. It was unreadable.

'And how do you feel about it?'

Fran considered. It had all happened so quickly she hadn't had time to think about it, but now she did, she knew exactly how she felt.

'Excited, worried I may mess it up, worried about working for an unknown academic, I don't know.'

'I suppose it could be an opportunity,' Richard said carefully.

'Could be? It is,' Fran hotly defended her decision.

Richard leant his elbows on the table and steepled his fingers. 'You might come to regret it. These artistic types.' He frowned. 'They're a weird bunch – not of this world.'

Fran pictured Ron Harris, the only applicant she knew. Anyone less like an artistic type than stuffy, grumpy old Ron, she couldn't imagine. Though he did lack social skills. 'Well, we'll just have to wait and see,' she said.

The meal was delicious as usual, and no more was said about Fran's new position. Nor did she find an appropriate time to tell Richard her decision. He was being so tender, so attentive, Fran couldn't bring herself to utter the words that would bring it all to an end.

She still hadn't found the time when he bundled her into his BMW to return to his apartment, where the remains of the champagne he'd opened earlier was still cooling in the fridge.

It was so easy to slip into the familiar routine. Maybe she was overthinking this, maybe…?

'Penny for them?'

Fran raised her eyes to meet Richard's. They were filled with concern, concern for her.

'It's nothing.' Fran shook her head. One more night together wouldn't hurt. She owed it to him, though that wasn't how a relationship should work.

They drank a final glass of champagne, cuddled together on the sofa, a shaft of moonlight from the uncovered windows encasing them in its glow. Then, Richard took Fran's hand and led her to bed.

It was all so familiar, so comfortable, Fran thought, as she sank into his embrace.

He cared. She knew he did.

And she cared for him too – just not enough.

Four

This was it!

Owen slid the envelope bearing the embossed crest of William Farrer University out of the mailbox, twisting it in his hands. It had to be a rejection. Surely he'd have received a phone call to offer the position if he was successful. Taking it inside, he examined it carefully. Priority post. They weren't stinting if they sent out all their rejections like this.

Placing it on the table, he decided to make himself a coffee before opening it. Everything looked better with his morning coffee. He fussed with the coffee machine, his shirt tail flapping, his bare feet cold on the tiled floor that had seemed so leading-edge when it was laid. It wasn't suited to Sydney's cold winter mornings.

He was ready! It was times like this, Owen wished he'd never given up smoking. But he hadn't had a cigarette for years, not since a good mate developed lung cancer and scared him into quitting.

He took a long gulp of coffee and slit open the envelope.

Dear Dr Larsen,

We are pleased to offer you the position of Head of our new School of Music and Drama…

Owen didn't read any further. He let the letter drop to the floor as he raised his hands in thanks. He'd done it! This called for a celebration, but there was no alcohol in the house. And it was only nine o'clock in the morning. He'd have to wait till later. He drank the rest of his coffee and picked up the letter again to confirm he'd read it correctly. Yes, the words were still there. He was the successful applicant. They'd like him to start as soon as possible in order to be ready for the opening in January of the following year. Could he call to discuss a starting date with their HR section and arrange to liaise with a Fran Reilly who'd already been appointed as his assistant.

Owen grimaced at the last part. He'd prefer to have chosen his own staff. But he supposed it was a small price to pay for the opportunity it would give him. And he'd no doubt be able to select his own academic staff. He could get rid of their dull old admin person when it suited him. He remembered the buttoned-up woman in the executive suite who'd managed the interviewees and his heart sank.

He had to tell someone, but he had a meeting in just over an hour and another later in the day. Owen's heart lightened at the thought he could now write his letter of resignation, something he'd been looking forward to doing. It wasn't that he disliked his present teaching position and he enjoyed city living. But recently, he'd had a hankering for a quieter life and a different challenge. A move to Granite Springs and William Farrer University would provide both.

The day passed quickly. His meetings over, Owen printed out his letter of resignation and headed to the HR department of the university. He'd called William Farrer in his lunch break to notify them of his acceptance, to be informed the necessary paperwork would be in the mail today.

As Owen anticipated, he was able to give the requisite two weeks' notice and would be able to leave before the start of semester two. When he returned to his office he gazed at the overflowing bookshelves and filing cabinet in dismay. How was he to pack up a lifetime's collection of books, journals and lecture notes in two weeks, as well as arrange to move house? It was a pity he couldn't transplant his new personal assistant up here to help him out.

The phone call to Granite Springs had proved useful. The university were prepared to offer him a room in the student residences till he found somewhere to live. But he didn't expect he'd last long there. Students being students, Owen knew their noise would soon drive him out. But it would provide him with breathing space while he looked around. The idea of an acreage on the outskirts of town appealed to him, and he could hardly wait to start his search.

*

'What's up, Dad?' Pia sounded annoyed, as if his call was an interruption to her busy life which, Owen reflected, it probably was.

'I've had some good news,' he said. 'I've been offered that job I told you about. In Granite Springs. I wondered if I could take you and Darren out to dinner to celebrate.'

He heard a muttering at the other end of the line.

'When?'

'Tonight?'

There was more muttering.

'Sorry, Dad. Can't do tonight. Maybe next week? Can I get back to you?'

'Sure, sweetheart.'

Owen hung up, disconsolate. He'd hoped to share his good fortune with his daughter and her partner. Now he'd have to find someone else to celebrate with. He knew he'd find Chris and the rest of the gang in the local pub where they spent most of their evenings, drinking the local plonk and decrying the idiocies of the politicians. But tonight, he wasn't in the mood for their company.

Instead, he made his way to the Italian wine bar that had popped up a few months ago in the neighbouring suburb. They served imported Italian wines and did a nice line in freshly made Italian snacks, his favourite being *Pizza con Patate*. It had taken him some time to become accustomed to the idea of pizza with potatoes but once he'd tried it, he was hooked.

Owen ordered and looked around while he took his first sip of wine, enjoying its rich fruity flavour on his tongue.

'Owen!'

Feeling a hand on his shoulder Owen turned to see a colleague's smiling face. Andy Morris had an office along the corridor from Owen and, although they neither taught in the same courses nor were they close friends, the pair often took the opportunity to share their frustrations with the system.

'I hear you're leaving us?'

'Word gets around. I only handed in my resignation this afternoon.'

Andy tapped his nose. 'Friend in high places, mate. Actually, I bumped into your boss on my way out today. He couldn't believe you were leaving and wanted everyone to know what a loss you'll be to the department.'

'That's nice to hear.' Owen wasn't so sure Michael *would* be sad to see him go. They'd had their differences over the years, and more than a few run-ins recently over student grades. There had been an awkward meeting when one of the feminist members of staff had actually asked Owen what it would take for him to change the grades of one of her protégées. Owen had been struck dumb, more so when Michael had appeared to take her side, indicating that an assessment in music had to be subjective.

'Where are you off to?'

So, Michael hadn't revealed everything.

'William Farrer. They have a new School of Music and Drama. It's a chance to set up from scratch.'

'Half your luck, mate. Willian Farrer – that's in Granite Springs, isn't it? So, you're leaving the rest of us to rot away here in the city while you swan around in pastures new.'

'Don't know about the swanning around bit. But, yes, I'll be off before the start of next semester.'

Andy gazed off into space. 'Granite Springs. I think I drove through there once. Typical country town – red dust, gum trees, sheep. Would bore me stiff in less than a week. But there's no accounting for taste.'

Owen stifled a laugh. Andy had never spent any time out of the city. He had no idea of the rich community life to be found in an Australian country town. Outside the city, people tended to make their own entertainment, sometimes even more frenetic than that found in the city. But he wasn't going there for the social life. He was thinking ahead, looking forward to retirement, planning for a life after university.

The anticipation of a life without the hassles of city living was exactly what he found most attractive.

When Andy finally left him to catch up with a group of friends – Owen had politely declined to join them – Owen ordered another glass of wine to accompany the *Pizza con Patate*. He took both to a secluded table and opened his iPad. He might as well use the time to check out potential acreages for sale.

The pizza was finished, and Owen was on his third glass of wine. So far, he'd been unable to locate any acreage that met his needs.

His phone vibrated and lit up to show Pia's face.

'Dad. We finished earlier than we expected. Do you still want to get together?'

Owen checked the time. Nine o'clock on a Thursday night in Sydney. It was late-night shopping, so he presumed the city was still jumping. Pia and Darren's evening's entertainment had come to an end and they'd decided to take pity on the old man. Well, beggars couldn't be choosers and he sorely needed a blast of his daughter's lively company.

'Sure, honey. Where are you? I'm at the new Italian place off…'

'I know it. We're not far away. We'll be there shortly. See you soon.'

By the time Owen had closed his iPad and ordered more wine – a bottle this time – there was a flurry and loud voices at the door, and Pia and Darren appeared.

'Dad! Go you!' she said, hugging him with such warmth Owen wondered if he'd imagined her lack of interest earlier.

'Congratulations, Owen,' Darren said, shaking Owen's hand a shade too firmly. That was one of the things Owen disliked about his daughter's choice of mate. The younger man always seemed to feel the need to demonstrate his superiority whether it be with regards to career – Darren was a budding lawyer which in his mind was far superior to a mere university lecturer– or, as now, with the firmness of his handshake.

'Thanks,' he said, flexing his fingers to regain sensation. 'Wine?' He indicated the bottle sitting on the table with three glasses. There was a moment's silence and, for an awful moment, Owen thought Darren was going to dispute his choice.

Then he sat down, drew Pia down beside him and said, 'Thanks.'

Their glasses filled, the two young people toasted Owen and, for the first time since opening the letter, he felt a glow of happiness and contentment.

'So,' Pia said, wriggling with Darren's arm possessively around her shoulders, 'Tell us about this position. Granite Springs – isn't that out bush?'

'Not exactly. It's country certainly, but a fairly large regional centre. In addition to the university, there's a fruit processing plant, a wool mill, a fine art gallery and library, botanic gardens…' Owen listed the attractions he'd read about in the brochures but had yet to see for himself.

He could see from the glazed expression on Darren's face that he'd already lost interest. In his mind, no doubt the only thing worse than teaching in a city university was to move to one in the sticks.

'Sounds interesting, Dad. We could visit on weekends.' She nudged Darren who looked evasive. 'And you're to be setting up this new thing?'

Undeterred by Darren's lack of interest, and encouraged by Pia's question, Owen broke into a description of his new work environment and the new building which was close to being completed. 'We'll start out with a small cohort of students,' he finished, warming to his subject, 'and will probably use some of the existing staff to supplement those we can recruit before January. What's happening in *your life?*' Owen knew Pia had challenges of her own. Her career in recruitment had taken a battering when the firm she'd spent five years with had been taken over by a competitor. For a time, she'd feared her position would be one of the casualties but so far, she seemed to be surviving.

'Oh, you know,' she said dismissively.

Owen had the familiar sense of emptiness resulting from her refusal to share much of her life with him. He didn't know, because she didn't tell him.

He was about to question her further when Darren yawned and ostentatiously checked his watch, sliding his cuff back to show off the expensive timepiece. 'We should be going, babe. I have an early case meeting, remember?'

'Sorry, Dad.' Pia immediately reached for her bag. Owen winced. How had his lovely, intelligent and independent daughter managed to fall for such a superficial controlling man? He'd never understand women.

Five

Fran gazed around the office that was to be hers for the next month or so – the final completion date for the new building was still some weeks away and was dependent on the whim of the contractors. Despite her working there for a week already, the place was still in a mess and needed a good tidy up. Evidently Alan had assumed it would remain empty when he was gone and hadn't troubled to put his papers into any sort of order before he left.

Fran sighed. While she'd been trying to work around everything as she didn't want to destroy what might be his highly unusual filing system, she couldn't work in this chaos. Obtaining a bunch of boxes from Ann, as carefully as she could, Fran transferred the papers from the floor and the chairs into the boxes, which she then carefully labelled before piling them up in one corner.

The effort of tidying had taken all morning and she'd promised to have lunch with Kay, with whom she was becoming friends. After their initial coffee, the pair had met several times to discuss college business, and discovered they had a lot in common. It was the first time Fran had let her guard slip with anyone on staff other than Ann, and she was surprised to discover how much she enjoyed Kay's company.

'Ready?' Kay appeared in the doorway. 'Wow! You've certainly made a difference here. Alan won't recognise his office when he gets back.'

Fran shrugged. 'I couldn't work in it the way it was.'

She locked the office door and the pair set off across the campus towards Banjo's, chatting as they went.

'Did you hear the news?' Kay asked. 'About your new boss?'

Fran stopped in her tracks. 'Was there a memo? I must have missed it. But I've had my head in boxes all morning.' Fran realised she hadn't taken time to check her emails, something she normally did first thing. Her six months off had changed her in more ways than one. She needed to get back into her old habits.

'I'm not sure if it's actually been announced yet,' Kay lowered her voice, 'but Nick was on the panel.'

'Just don't tell me it's Ron,' Fran said with a rueful grin.

'No.' Kay laughed. 'You're to be spared that. It's an old mate of Nick's. Well, mate might be putting it a bit strong. They worked together in Sydney years ago and Owen – that's his name, Owen Larsen – stayed on when Nick moved here.'

'Owen Larsen,' Fran repeated. 'Sounds Scandinavian.'

'I think he's as Australian as you and I. But Nick didn't say.'

By now, they'd reached the café which was alive with students at this time of day.

'Oh, dear,' Fran said, 'we might have been quicker driving into town. It's time the VC built that staff dining facility he's been promising us for the past five years.'

'That would be nice,' Kay agreed, as they jostled their way to the only free table hidden away in the far corner.

When they had finally been served with salads and coffee, Fran met Kay's eyes across the table. 'I'm not sure how Ron's going to take this,' she said. 'He's been popping his head in almost every day trying to discover if I've heard anything. As if I'd hear before him. Although,' she grinned, 'I guess I just have. Unless he's already found out. I wouldn't like to be in this Larsen fellow's shoes if he has to work with Ron.'

'Will he?'

'That's one of the things I've been asked to look at. My new job description gives me more of a say in making staffing recommendations. Given the school will be starting small, it makes sense to utilise existing university staff where possible, which means…'

'Ron and Joshua,' Kay said, naming the music and drama lecturers in the Faculty of Education.

Both women grimaced. While Ron had a reputation for being antisocial, Joshua, who was in charge of the drama section, was the complete opposite, and had been taken to task on more than one occasion for becoming too familiar with his students.

'Oh, dear. The poor man. What's Owen like? Did Nick say?'

'Only that he'd worked with him and he was a good guy. But we both want you to come to dinner on Saturday. You can maybe find out more from him then.'

'Dinner?' Fran had never been on dinner terms with her former boss. She'd always managed to keep her personal life separate from her university life. The only exception was Ann Baird with whom she shared the occasional dinner, and now Kay Jackson.

'My friend Jo and her husband are coming too. I hope you won't mind odd numbers, or is there someone you'd like to bring?' Kay asked with a smile.

Fran thought of Richard. She still hadn't managed to break it off with him. To invite him to a dinner with this group would definitely give him the wrong impression, and she wasn't sure how he'd fit in with them, given his views on people who chose to live in a country town. With a start she realised that meant her, too. Was that why she always felt at a slight disadvantage with him? Not for much longer.

Kay was waiting for her answer.

'No, no-one. I'd love to meet your friend, Jo. I've heard you mention her. Isn't she the one who married an old friend?'

'A relationship I tried to talk her out of? Yes. I think you'll like her.'

*

Fran hummed to herself as she prepared for dinner with Kay and Nick. She'd managed to delay meeting with Richard, telling him she was too busy with her new position to travel to Canberra to see him. But she knew she couldn't put him off forever. Once she felt more settled again, she'd invite him to lunch. Maybe, on her own turf she'd find it easier to explain her decision, and with lunch they wouldn't end up in bed again. Richard was very proper about that, she knew. He regarded sex in the middle of the day the way some would regard a heinous crime.

Over the years they'd been together, Fran had come to accept his ways, ways some would consider unusual, even peculiar, telling herself it was just the way he was. But sometimes she couldn't help but remember the joyous coming together she'd experienced with Ben in her early twenties. Time and place had been no barrier to their lovemaking which had been passionate and frequent.

But she often reminded herself, she wasn't in her twenties any longer, and it was fitting for someone of her years to be more circumspect.

To Fran's surprise, she was looking forward to meeting Kay's friends. From what she could recall, they lived on an acreage outside town and Jo had three children – or was it Col? She'd no doubt find out. It was time she widened her circle of friends. Richard had taken up so much of her free time for the past ten years, her social life had been greatly reduced. She'd continued to be involved in the various groups in town and in her volunteer work, but dinner parties had been few and far between. She knew these gatherings – and the regular race meetings and balls – were the lifeblood of the community, but those social events had never appealed to her.

After Ben's death, her decision to remain in Granite Springs had been accompanied by the desire to make a complete change in her lifestyle. She supposed that was why she'd been attracted to Richard. He was the complete opposite of the happy-go-lucky larrikin she'd followed to Australia and missed so much. She'd never forgotten Ben, and it had taken her over fifteen years to let another man into her life.

As she walked up the path to the two-storey home which she knew Nick had lived in since he and his former wife arrived in Granite Springs, a young girl flew past her in a gust of expensive scent, chestnut hair flying.

'Hi, Ms Reilly,' she said, as she pushed past.

'Hi Sam,' Fran called to Nick's teenage daughter as she disappeared into the old car which had drawn up at the kerb behind Fran's little VW beetle in its signature shade of pillar-box red. She'd heard the company had ceased to manufacture them and it had made her love hers all the more. It was her one indulgence, her one concession to the girl she'd once been, before she became the correct, reticent woman she was now – the girl who'd answered to Franny and who hadn't a care in the world. Much like the one who'd just pushed past her. The accident had killed more than Ben and the life growing inside her. It had killed her youth.

'You must be Fran.'

Fran's thoughts were interrupted by a gentle voice at her elbow. She turned to see an elegantly dressed couple standing behind her. A black Subaru Forester now stood where the old banger had been. It must have driven up while she'd been lost in thought. The woman's silver blonde hair was on top of her head and she was wearing a loose jacket over a pair of tailored black pants. She was holding hands with a man who appeared to be about the same age. His thick white hair was swept back from a high forehead and he was dressed casually in well-pressed jeans and a pale blue shirt, a grey sweater tied loosely around his shoulders. Both looked vaguely familiar. They must be Fran's friends.

'Yes,' she said, smiling.

'Oh, you've met!' Kay appeared in the doorway, Nick behind her. A young boy Fran recognised as Nick's son, pushed past them wheeling a bike.

"Bye, Dad, Kay,' he muttered as he left.

'Don't be too late, Ryan, and watch out for traffic. Make sure you...'

But Ryan was gone.

Nick shook his head.

'You can only do your best,' Jo said, as the three followed Kay and Nick back inside. 'It *is* Friday night.'

'That's what I'm afraid of,' Nick said with a grimace. 'But Kay keeps me sane. I'm so grateful for her level-headedness.' He squeezed Kay's shoulder affectionately.

Fran wondered if tonight had been a mistake. Here she was, about to spend the evening with two couples who were clearly very much in love. Was it going to accentuate the absence of it in her relationship with Richard? One more sign she should take action while there was still time?

Time for what? The issue of time had never entered the equation before.

'Hi, Kay, Nick,' she said, following them inside. This was the first time Fran had been in Nick's home and she felt a bit awkward. He was her boss – had been, she corrected herself. It was strange to be on social terms with the man she'd kept a professional distance from for the past ten years. So much had changed since she returned from England.

When she'd decided that turning fifty was a watershed moment, this wasn't the sort of change she imagined.

Over drinks in the living room, Jo commented on the changes Kay had made. It appeared Nick had let the place go when his wife left, and it had taken all of Kay's cajoling for him to remodel the house into something resembling a home again.

'Kay's been the light that lit up my darkness,' Nick said with a wide smile. 'Even Sam and Ryan have accepted the changes she's made.'

Fran smiled politely and wondered again why she'd come. When the conversation moved on to children, she felt even more uncomfortable. Both Kay and Jo's children were grown and had children of their own. They were assuring Nick that the teenage years were the worst, but to enjoy Sam and Ryan's company while they could.

'Once they have families of their own,' Jo said, 'you'll still worry about them, but their lives are out of your control, so you can relax somewhat.'

'You don't have any children, Fran?' Jo asked, trying to bring her into the conversation.

Fran shook her head. 'No.' What more could she say? The accident that had robbed her of her love, had also taken the children she'd never have, damaging her body beyond repair. Maybe that was why she'd never managed to form another serious relationship. Part of her would always link a relationship to children.

But looking at the two couples beside her, Fran realised how foolish that was. Three of them might have children – she wasn't sure about Col – but not with each other. Their relationships were enough to sustain them.

'You may be lucky in that respect,' Jo said with a laugh.

Lucky? Fran's lack of children was a thorn in her flesh that tore at her whenever she saw mothers with their families. She always had to steel herself not to break down in tears. It had got better as she'd become older, when the offspring of women of her vintage were grown. But then, there were the grandchildren she'd never be able to enjoy.

Was that what had drawn her to Richard – his lack of children and with no desire to have any? He was so fussy about all aspects of his life, Fran couldn't imagine him coping with a child. It was lucky the question of children had never arisen.

Once dinner was served, the conversation became more general. Fran was able to share the dramas of selling her mother's house, finding common ground with Col who'd sold his home in Granite Springs only a year earlier, and Kay whose old place was still on the market.

'I may have to rent it out to students if it doesn't sell soon,' she grimaced.

'Or someone on staff,' Fran joked, thinking that was very unlikely.

'Hey, maybe Owen Larsen will be looking for a place,' Nick said.

'Owen Larsen?' Col asked. 'Sounds Scandinavian.'

'He's as Australian as we are,' Nick replied. 'I think his grandparents may have come from Denmark.'

'Who is he?' Jo asked.

'Fran's new boss,' Kay said, causing everyone to turn and look at Fran.

She squirmed before replying, 'I came back to take up my old position as Nick's PA but the VC had another idea for me. I'm now part of the new School of Music and Drama which the students are already calling The Mad House. Music and drama,' she explained, seeing Jo and Col's mystified expressions. 'Owen Larsen has just been appointed as the new Head of School. I haven't met him yet, but I understand Nick knows him.'

Fran was glad to get out of the limelight as all eyes turned to Nick.

'What's the SP on him, Nick?' Col asked.

'It's years since I knew him. Until I saw him at the interview, it must have been…' Nick scratched his chin through his beard, '…over ten years. Not since we left Sydney. We were both on the staff there. He stayed on when we came here.'

'You knew him well?' Col asked.

'Not really. We didn't move in the same crowd. I heard he led a pretty wild life when they were students – he and Brit – parties, alcohol, pot. They were married when I knew them. Owen seemed to have got his act together, toned down a bit. He's a brilliant musician, was in a band at uni – guitar and keyboard, very talented. I think he gave up performing when he started to teach. It's a pity. He composed a bit, too.'

'Sounds like you could find life interesting,' Jo said.

'Mmm.' Fran wasn't sure she liked what she heard. Where was

the information about his skills in communication, negotiation, organisation? She'd helped Nick with those when he was new to the dean's position, but the ingredients were there. She didn't imagine Nick Kerr had ever been wild, not even as a student. And he'd been eager to learn.

'He sounds like a bit of an aging hippie,' she said, wrinkling her nose.

'No, not anymore. He looked very smart at the interview – exactly what you'd expect of a Head of School.'

'He has a family?' Jo asked.

Fran could see her mentally adding him to the band of happy families and winced. Not another one.

Nick pulled on his beard. 'I think I heard something about a marriage split. But don't quote me on that. And there was a child – a girl I think – but she'd be grown by now. Anyway, he'll be here soon, and you'll all find out for yourselves. I don't think you need to worry, Fran,' he said, clearly sensing her apprehension. 'He's a regular guy, been in a senior lecturing position at Sydney for years. They don't put up with idiots. He'd never have lasted if he acted the fool. He was impressive at the interview. The entire panel agreed he was the man for the job.'

That made Fran feel better, though it was strange to have already taken up her new position before her boss arrived.

It was as they were leaving and standing by their cars at the kerb that Jo whispered in her ear, 'Fran, if you ever need someone to talk to – someone who's not part of the university mafia – give me a call. I can always provide an ear.'

'Thanks,' Fran whispered back, grateful for her thoughtfulness. Despite her misgivings, it had been a pleasant evening and Fran knew she'd found a new friend, one she might need.

Six

It was raining, the steady downpour Sydney was renowned for. It was a pity he couldn't take some of it to Granite Springs with him. The Australian countryside had been suffering from drought conditions for months with no sign of a reprieve.

Owen surveyed the pile of boxes containing all his worldly possessions. It didn't come to much when he looked at them sitting in what had been his living room and hallway. But at least he'd be able to sell his home to the developers who were eating up his suburb and had been hounding him for some time. He'd grown tired of their letters, phone calls and emails, but it was the acts of vandalism that had worried him most.

When he'd accused them – stormed into their head office in the city – they'd denied all knowledge of it, suggested it might be schoolkids or some homeless person. But Owen was sure the slogans on the front fence, the broken window and, worst of all, the threatening phone calls, had been the work of their minions. He wasn't easily intimidated, but these acts of vandalism had caused him sleepless nights and, when he did manage to drop off, he'd awakened at the slightest sound. There were many of those in his old terrace in Glebe where the slightest breath of wind caused the house to creak and groan, so it didn't make for a restful sleep.

The house had seen better days when he and Brit bought it back in the early days of their marriage. The plan had been to renovate, maybe even extend. Then Pia had arrived, and they'd been too busy – or too cash-strapped – and the renovations had been put on hold.

Now it was too late. Soon, the place would fall under the developer's hammer. It would join the others in the line of terraces in his suburb to disappear only to be replaced by a tower of little boxes which were the modern answer to the growing demand for inner city living.

He wouldn't be able to fit much into the student room he'd been allocated, only a few clothes and some personal items. The boxes of books could go into his office, albeit a temporary one till the building was finished. But he'd find a place for his keyboard and guitar. He couldn't live without those. And, as soon as he could, he'd search for something more permanent.

Despite looking forward to the move and the new challenges it would bring, Owen knew it would be a wrench to leave this place that had been his home for almost thirty years. He'd had happy times here, when he and Brit were first married, when Pia was growing up. But whereas he'd decided to leave his hippie past behind and conform to the image that was expected of an academic in a prestigious university, Brit had never accepted the need to change from her student ways.

Was it that which had led her to form a different relationship? Owen wasn't sure. They'd been drifting apart and he hadn't been completely surprised when she informed him that she'd prefer to live with her friend, Rosemary, who was *more simpatico*.

Pia had been in her early teens at the time and had taken it in her stride, moving effortlessly between home in Glebe and her mother's new house in Balmain. It had worked. They all still met for dinner from time to time and managed to remain civil to each other. But it had left Owen wondering if there had been anything he could have done to avoid the split.

He sighed and picked up his guitar, his go-to when things were getting him down, and after several minutes strumming some favourite melodies, he was ready to face the farewell dinner Pia had insisted on.

*

'Here he is!'

Pia's excited voice caused the other customers in the harbour-front restaurant to look around in surprise. She was seated at a waterfront table with Darren, Brit and Rosemary. A bottle of what appeared to be expensive champagne was sitting in a cooler in the centre of the table, but the two women were drinking what Owen recognised as their customary measures of gin mixed with only a hint of tonic.

Taking a deep breath Owen started walking towards them, glad the amused diners had ceased to be interested in the middle-aged man who was the recipient of the loud greeting. He wished he'd refused Pia's demand that they all get together "one last time". He was only going to the country. He wasn't dying or travelling to some far-off land.

'Hi, darling.' He greeted his daughter with a warm hug, before shaking hands with Darren and accepting air kisses from Brit and Rosemary. Whoever thought up that custom ought to be shot. It was so pretentious but was common in so-called polite society these days. What was wrong with a good old-fashioned kiss, be it on the lips or the cheek? Though he had no desire to kiss Brit or Rosemary on either.

'This is your seat.' Brit drew out a chair next to hers, and Owen slid into it to be immediately offered a glass of the champagne by Darren, who was full of an unusual bonhomie tonight. Perhaps it was the knowledge Owen would be leaving Sydney next day and he'd have no need to force himself to be polite to him to appease Pia.

'So, you're off?' Brit asked, taking a sip of her drink. Her slight slurring of the words might only have been noticeable to him. This wasn't her first drink tonight.

'Tomorrow.'

'What on earth possessed you to take a position in the back of beyond?' Rosemary asked, her lip curling. 'You wouldn't get me leaving Sydney to vegetate in the country.'

'I don't suppose I would,' Owen said mildly. He'd never had much time for Rosemary, even before she and Brit had announced their love for each other. He'd always felt that, if Brit did have to fall in love with a woman, she could have made a better choice. But what did any of us know about what appealed to others?

Pia had no problem with the woman and had often criticised Owen's antagonism to her as jealousy. But he knew it wasn't that. He had no issue with Brit finding another partner – man or woman.

He just wished she'd found someone more supportive, more caring, more… like herself, instead of this woman who always seemed to want to drag her down and criticise Owen.

The meal was delicious. The seafood chowder followed by grilled John Dory fillets in Doyle's special chilli plum sauce, all washed down with a wooded chardonnay. Pia then ordered two dessert platters to allow them to share a gelato trio, banana and caramel cheesecake, and a dark chocolate brûlée while they finished the champagne.

Owen would miss the delicious seafood so readily available in Sydney, and the proximity to the ocean. But, he reminded himself, there would be other benefits, and how often had he ever taken advantage of the nearby beaches in recent years?

At the end of the meal, as they were enjoying a final coffee, Darren surprised Owen by asking for the bill and producing his American Express card with a flourish. 'My treat,' he said in his most magnanimous tone.

Owen wasn't going to disagree. He was happy to let Darren play the generous host.

'He wanted to do this for you,' Pia whispered while her partner dealt with the payment. 'You can return the favour when we come to visit.'

Owen couldn't imagine the city slicker in Granite Springs, but nodded, hoping it would be Pia who'd be visiting – on her own. 'When I'm settled,' he said.

Everything considered, it had been a good evening. Pia had been interested to learn more about the new school and the town of Granite Springs. Leaving, Owen was glad he'd arranged to come by cab. He'd had an inkling he'd be drinking too much to risk driving. He hoped the others had been equally considerate. But, when they left, although he saw Pia and Darren entering a cab, Brit and Rosemary tottered off in the direction of a line of cars, Rosemary clicking on her car keys till one of the cars made the connection, beeped, and lit up.

*

Next morning, Owen regretted his indulgence of the night before. He had a long drive ahead of him and it would have been better to have a clear head. The car was already packed with his immediate needs, and his mate, Chris, had agreed to be there for the removalists later in the morning. After a lot of thought, Owen had decided to arrange for his belongings to be taken to a storage facility in Granite Springs where they'd be easy to access once he found a more permanent place to live, hopefully soon.

He was fixing himself a coffee prior to packing the coffee maker – he'd left out the breakfast essentials for last-minute packing – when there was a knock at the door.

'Thought you might welcome this, mate,' Chris said, juggling two take-away coffees and a paper bag which looked as if it contained croissants.

'Thanks. I have coffee, but this is a lovely thought. Come in.' Owen led the way through the narrow hallway, now made even narrower with stacked boxes, all clearly labelled, to the now denuded kitchen.

'We'll miss you,' Chris said, perching on one of the two stools which weren't covered in boxes. Chris was one of the other associate professors in the Faculty of Arts and the pair had formed a close friendship, as close as Owen had with anyone at the university. He'd always preferred to keep his social life separate from his professional one, something that might be more difficult to do where he was going.

'I'll miss the old place, too. And this house.' Owen gazed around the kitchen – its comfortable old table a reminder of many casual dinner parties. But seeing it like this – the bare surfaces, the empty fridge with the door standing open, the outdated cooktop and oven, he knew he was doing the right thing.

'So, it'll be Professor Larsen, will it?'

'I guess so. None of this associate stuff. Though I'm not a great one for titles. Happy to be Dr Larsen, or Owen. I'm hoping to develop a more informal atmosphere in this new school, one in which the students feel comfortable, where we can dispense with all the hierarchy nonsense.'

'Good luck with that.' Chris shook his head. 'You always were a bit of a rebel. Do they know what they've let themselves in for?'

Owen just grinned. 'What have you brought us?' he asked, pointing to the paper bag. 'It's not croissants from Sonoma?'

'What do you think?' Chris opened the bag to reveal the special croissant pastry scrolls sprinkled with cinnamon citrus sugar the bakery was famous for. 'One last taste of Sydney before you head off into the blue yonder.'

'Not another one!' Owen pretended to wipe his brow. 'Give us a break. I got that last night from Rosemary. You'd think I was heading off to darkest Africa, instead of taking the opportunity to wind down in the peace of the New South Wales countryside.'

'It may not be that peaceful from what I've heard.'

'What have you heard?' Owen was curious. He knew Chris was a more social animal than he was and had contacts all around the state, fostered by his regular attendances at the conferences Owen had always tried to avoid.

'Oh, just that a certain person's nose is out of joint.'

Owen sighed and took a gulp of coffee. He leant his elbows on the kitchen bench. 'I suppose one of the local guys thought he was a shoo-in? That's to be expected. Always happens. And probably more so in a small place where everyone knows everyone else and he – I presume it's a he – had his expectations raised. Ah well, guess I'll have to smooth some ruffled feathers. Wonder if he's any good. What have you heard?'

'Not much, to be honest. Just that your appointment came as a shock to some guy who's been there for yonks and thought it was a *fait accompli*. You might have your work cut out there. But you're good at that, aren't you – making friends and influencing people?'

Owen looked at his friend. He wasn't sure if he was being serious. 'Yeah, right,' he said.

When they'd finished the coffee and croissants, Owen checked his watch. 'I should be going,' he said, with one last look around. 'The removalists will be here soon. Thanks for taking care of this for me.' He handed Chris a bottle of Glenlivet knowing his friend was partial to a decent malt. 'Just lock the door behind you.'

'Thanks. You shouldn't have.' But Chris fondled the bottle with pleasure. 'I'll think of you when I drink it.'

'Not all at once, I hope.'

The two men laughed. Chris slapped Owen on the shoulder as they made their way to the door.

'Well.' Now the moment had come, Owen was reluctant to make the move that would take him away from Sydney, from his past.

'On you go,' Chris encouraged him. 'Do I have to push you into the car?'

Owen laughed again, slid into the driving seat of the old Mazda he'd been driving for years, and he was off.

Seven

'Can I help you?' Fran asked the dishevelled man who was standing at her open office door.

'I'm looking for a...' he studied a scrap of paper on which something was written in an untidy scrawl, '...a Fran Reilly.' He raised his eyes – the clearest blue eyes Fran had seen since... and her heart almost leap out of her chest.

'I'm Fran Reilly,' she said, 'And you are?' Fran was too busy to be interrupted if she was to finish this before the new Head of School arrived. He was due this morning. She didn't have time to waste with this disreputable-looking person.

He was wearing baggy army surplus pants, a chambray shirt that had seen better days had become untucked from the waistband and his bare feet were pushed into a pair of Birkenstocks. His long faded blond hair was tied back in what looked like a bun and a worn leather satchel hung from one shoulder. He must be a student, though a pretty mature one. He appeared to be around her age.

He held out a hand. 'Owen, Owen Larsen.'

Fran's eyes widened, but she had the presence of mind to rise and take his hand. As his warm fingers curled around hers, she could feel the callous which no doubt came from his guitar playing.

'Sorry,' he said, pushing a strand of hair back from his face and grinning – a wide grin that showed a good set of teeth. 'I must look a sight. I've been unpacking. It didn't occur to me to go back and change. I guess I'm not what you expected?'

'Not exactly.' Nick Kerr's words flitted through her mind. *Wild. Pot-smoking. Played in a band.* But Nick said he'd got his act together. *Could he have been wrong? Was her new boss really the aging hippie she'd feared? Had he somehow pulled the wool over the eyes of the panel to gain this position? What was she going to do?*

'Look, this was obviously a mistake.' His eyes ranged over Fran in her neat pants and tailored shirt, her makeup impeccable, her short blonde hair as neat as ever. 'I'm in student accommodation for the time being – until I find something more permanent. Why don't I go back and tidy up, then we can start again?'

Why did Fran feel he was laughing at her?

She nodded, and he disappeared. It was as if he'd never been there. Had she imagined it, or had the untidy man at her door really been her new boss?

An hour later there was a polite knock on the door and Fran looked up to see a different version of Owen Larsen. The hair was still the same, though tidier. He was wearing jeans, but they were neatly pressed, as was the white open-necked shirt which was covered by a black cord jacket. Her eyes dropped to the floor. The Birkenstocks had gone, and his feet were now encased in… Nikes. Fran couldn't suppress a grin. She had the distinct feeling her life was about to change.

'So, Fran. How about you show me around?' he asked.

Standing there, hands in his pockets, leaning back slightly and rocking on his heels, he looked so at ease. It wasn't difficult to imagine him being able to persuade the interview panel of his suitability to head up the School of Music and Drama. But what would he be like to work for? Suddenly, old Ron Harris was looking good. She swallowed. 'What would you like to see, Professor Larsen?'

'Everything.' Owen spread his arms wide. 'The grand tour. Treat me like a tourist. And, for God's sake, call me Owen. I'm not one for formality. Let's leave the Professor Larsen stuff for the powers-that-be, shall we?'

'Okay.' Fran tried to hide her amusement. If his appearance was anything to go by, Owen Larsen was a complete stranger to formality in any shape or form. But she was very aware of the university rules and protocols and could see some battles ahead. And, as his PA, the onus would be on her to see that he not only understood them, but conformed. She sighed inwardly, wondering if she'd made the right decision in taking on this position. She'd seen it as a new challenge, welcomed it, even. But that had been before she met Owen Larsen. She should have been prepared when Nick spoke about him. But hadn't Nick said he'd… "got his act together"? Well, if this was the result of him getting his act together, she wondered what on earth he'd been like before.

'Are you ready?' Owen's voice brought Fran back to the present. She blushed. He'd been waiting for her while she deliberated about him. Not a good start.

'Yes. Of course, prof… Owen,' she said rising quickly and picking up her keys. 'Who have you met already?'

'Apart from the interview panel, the HR bod and the accommodations woman, you're it. Is there someone I should meet?'

Fran thought of Ann, who'd no doubt have her own opinions about this unconventional professor, then decided against it. He wasn't going to be part of this faculty. He – and she – were about to set up an entire school from scratch. It was a heady thought. 'No, I guess not,' she said. 'Let's go.'

As she took him on a guided tour of the campus, Owen proved to be an amusing companion, though his more laidback ideas had her wondering exactly how he intended to put them into practice. It was all very well to say it was a School of Music and Drama, therefore couldn't be expected to be subject to the same restrictions as other faculties on campus, but Fran didn't feel comfortable with most of his proposals.

They stopped when they came to the building where the new facility was to be housed, and Fran saw Owen's eyes light up.

'Our new home,' he said with satisfaction and, for a moment, she thought he was going to give her a hug or at least take her hand. Fortunately, he did neither as she didn't know how she'd have reacted. She also didn't know why she felt a little disappointed.

'And, lastly the café, commonly called Banjo's,' she said, stopping in front of the building which was now empty of students.

'That was great, thanks. Helps me understand where everything is. Stop me getting lost too often,' he chuckled. 'Let me buy you a coffee.'

'Oh, I don't think…' It wasn't appropriate. What if Ann Baird was to see them? What if…? But Fran hesitated just a moment too long.

'As a thank you… from a grateful boss to a new assistant. No one could argue with that, surely?'

He'd read her mind. Now she'd appear to be a real stickler for the rules if she refused.

'We can talk about work if that's what's worrying you,' he added.

Rocking on his heels and hands in his pockets again, this time Owen looked as if he belonged there. More so than Fran in her smart outfit and perfect makeup. Before she could summon up an excuse, she found herself following him into the café.

'I'll have a long black. Let me guess,' he gazed at her for a few moments, making her feel uncomfortable, 'I'd say you're a latte lady. Am I right?'

Stunned, Fran nodded. How could he know, or was it just a lucky guess?

The coffees arrived and, true to his word, Owen was all work. But it wasn't what she'd expected.

'Tell me about the staff we can poach from education,' he said first, stirring two sachets of sugar into his coffee.

Mesmerised at seeing someone who actually still took sugar in his coffee, Fran didn't reply immediately. Then she said, 'Poach? You don't really mean that.'

'Well, it may be the wrong word. But if we're to get moving in first semester next year, we need to get a shifty on. There's barely time to recruit staff and have them prepare courses ready for the start of semester. I presume the outlines have already been done – had to be to get the degrees approved. So someone or other must have been involved in that process. Stands to reason they might be suited to joining us.'

He folded his arms on the table waiting for her reply.

'Well, I've been gone for six months, but I do know the proposals got started last year and, if I was to hazard a guess, it would be that Ron Harris and Joshua Martin from Education had a hand in them. Ron's music ed staff and Joshua's drama.'

'Ron and Josh, eh? What are they like?'

Fran found herself in a quandary. She'd never been asked before to comment on staff, to assess their capabilities, for that's what Owen was asking her to do. She looked down at her hands, picked up her cup, took a sip of the piping hot coffee before replying.

'I think they're good at their jobs. They've both been here a long time. I can get their CVs for you.'

'I don't want their CVs. That won't tell me what I want to know. They wouldn't be here if they didn't add up.' He paused. 'Fran, what I need to know is how they are to work with, how they relate to students, how they react to innovation – things like that.'

Fran looked down again. 'I think maybe you should speak with Nick about things like that,' she said primly.

Owen heaved a sigh. He took a long swig of coffee and ordered another, nodding towards Fran's half-full cup. She shook her head.

'Okay. Let's see what else we have. I presume the ads have already gone out.'

'That was the first thing the VC's office asked me to do. The closing date is next week.'

'So, little chance we can get anyone on board before the end of semester – unless they're currently unemployed.' He thought for a moment. 'You have the proposals with course outlines?'

'In my office.'

'Right.' Owen's coffee arrived and he gulped it down. 'Let's go. I can go over them this afternoon and we'll meet again tomorrow to work out the next step.'

When Owen left Fran at her office door, she was in a daze. He was unlike anyone she'd ever worked for, like a dynamic force that would forge ahead regardless of any obstacles in his way. Life with him might be challenging, it might be hectic, but it certainly wouldn't be boring.

But could she keep up with him? Would he consider her too prim and proper for what he wanted? And why did the thought of not being able to live up to his expectations make her heart sink?

Eight

Owen made himself another coffee in the staff tea-room, before settling down to peruse the various documents Fran had given him. He knew they'd be readily available on the web but, for this job, he needed the paper copy.

He grimaced at the taste of the instant coffee, reminding himself to get a takeaway from Banjo's next time. Maybe he could have Fran order a proper machine for his new office. That would certainly make life pleasanter. He knew he was addicted to the stuff, but hey, there were worse addictions. The image of Brit staggering towards the cab after his farewell dinner forced itself into his mind's eye. But that wasn't an addiction. He knew it was her choice – and Rosemary's influence – to overindulge on social occasions while, most of the time, she restricted her alcohol consumption to one drink of an evening. He had Pia's word for that, and he believed his daughter.

He ran a hand through his hair which was coming loose from the bun – maybe he should consider losing the bun now he was a full professor?

Why did he still feel some sort of responsibility for Brit? He had no idea. They'd been divorced for over ten years. She'd been in another relationship for longer. It might have been understandable when Pia was still a teenager, seeing her mum regularly, and there was the possibility she could be influenced or harmed by her mother. But now Pia was grown, lived an independent life, and she felt responsible for Brit, too. He had to face it. Brit was one of nature's victims and he and

Pia were the rescuers, whether they wanted to be or not. He'd never feel rid of her.

By the time Owen had studied the course materials and glanced over Ron and Josh's CVs, it was getting late, and the floor of his temporary office was strewn with papers. He was amused Fran had included the CVs despite his saying he didn't need them. She was an odd bird. He leant back in his chair and swirled it around and around while he considered the assistant he'd been assigned.

She was easy on the eye, that was for sure. And, he suspected she could be a lot of fun if she ever let go. It might be amusing to see if he could persuade her to change that prim manner of hers, see the woman who emerged.

He was about to pack up and head for his student quarters, intending to check out the local pub food for dinner when there was a knock at the door. Looking up, he saw Nick Kerr standing there. Although he'd seen Nick at the interview, he hadn't expected him to arrive at his door like this. He'd planned to arrange a more formal meeting with him to discuss staffing issues.

'Settling in?' Nick gestured to the papers on the floor. 'Looks like you've been busy.'

'It's a mess, you mean?' Owen chuckled. 'Just some preliminary work. Getting caught up on where we're at. Fran's been helpful.'

'Good. I was sorry to lose her, but my loss is your gain.'

Owen's eyes widened. 'Fran was *your* PA? I didn't know.'

'No reason why you should. Why don't you come to dinner tonight and I'll fill you in? It can't be much fun in the student residences.'

'Thanks. I was going to give the pub a try.'

'I'd hate to take you away from their pie and chips, but I think Kay and I can offer something a bit tastier – and healthier. Let me give you the address. We're out by the old quarry.' He found a blank piece of paper on Owen's littered desk and jotted down an address and phone number.

Back in his tiny room, Owen freshened up, then drove into town to find a bottle shop. Ten minutes later, with a bottle of Penfolds Bin 28 shiraz sitting on the passenger seat, he plugged Nick's address into the satnav he'd recently purchased and headed towards a part of town he hadn't seen before.

Outside the two-storey house sat an old Mazda – even older than Owen's – and the front door was wide open. Owen walked up the pathway carrying the wine, stopping just short of the door where a teenage boy with hair much the same length as Owen's, but tied back in a loose ponytail, stood. Nick was standing in the doorway having words with a teenage girl dressed in a short skirt and denim jacket.

'Yes, Dad. I know,' she was saying. 'We'll be back by ten, won't we?' She turned to the boy who was shuffling his feet and looking as if he didn't want to be there. He nodded. 'Yes, Mr Kerr. I'll make sure Sam gets back okay.'

The young pair pushed past Owen and got into the car which drove off with a blast of smoke.

'Not sure that's going to get them far,' Owen said, as he reached the door and Nick greeted him with a slap on the shoulder.

Nick gazed after the car, an unreadable expression on his face. 'Be glad you don't have teenagers,' he said, as he ushered Owen inside.

'Been there, done that,' Owen replied, following him through to a brightly lit living room where a young teenage boy was focussing on his iPad. A dark-haired woman wearing brown pants and a cream blouse appeared from the back of the house. She looked vaguely familiar.

'Kay, this is the new Head of the Music and Drama School – Owen Larsen. Owen, my partner and currently also my PA – Kay Jackson.'

There was a story here, Owen thought.

'Hello, Kay.'

'Lovely to meet you, Owen. Welcome to Granite Springs.'

They shook hands, then Owen handed Nick the bottle of wine. 'Hope red's okay,' he said.

'Perfect,' Nick said. 'I've been marinating steak for the barbecue– that's about my limit. And I think Kay has some roast veggies to go with it. This is Ryan,' he said, gesturing to the boy, who, barely raising his eyes from the iPad, gave him a wave. 'Teenagers! Now let's get you a drink.'

A can of James Squire 150 Lashes in his hand, Owen joined Nick by the barbecue, watching with admiration as he cooked the steaks to perfection. 'Never been much good with the barbecue, he said. 'I'm a dab hand in the kitchen though. Once I'm in a place of my own, I'll cook a decent paella for you and Kay.' He gestured towards the kitchen window where they could see Kay organising the rest of the meal. 'Serious, is it?'

'Can't do much till the divorce comes through,' Nick said with a shrug. 'But, yes. We'll get married next year. The kids are good with it.' He was silent while he turned the steaks. 'Michelle is eager to marry her toy boy too. No hold up there. This division of assets thing is dicey though. You're divorced. How did that go?'

'No problems. Brit moved into her friend's place. Rosemary already had a house in Balmain, inherited it from her parents. Pia spent her time between us. There wasn't much else to divide. It was all very amicable. We still see them on family occasions.' He recalled again that last evening, wished he could forget it.

'Pia – your daughter – how old is she now?'

'Twenty-seven. Living with the boyfriend.'

'Ow!'

Owen grinned. His feelings precisely.

'Good guy?'

Owen grunted.

'That bad?'

'Not really. Pia seems happy enough. It's just…'

'No one's good enough for our daughters, are they? You saw that long-haired lout Sam's with tonight.'

Owen touched his bun like an old friend. It was tidy, but… 'I'm wondering if I should get rid of this,' he said. 'Was there anything said after the interview?'

'No more than you'd expect. The chair of the board made some comment about "what you might expect from those creative types". But you're here, aren't you?' He checked the meat. 'These look ready. Give me that platter, mate, and we'll take them inside.'

'How are you finding our little town?' Kay asked, when they'd finished the main course and Ryan had escaped to the other room with a bowl of ice cream, his father shaking his head at Kay's indulgence.

'Not so little,' Owen said. 'It seems to cater for just about everything anyone would need.'

'We like it.' She threw a tender glance at Nick.

'Have you always lived here?' Owen asked. 'I know Nick's been here around ten years.'

'Yes, he's still regarded as a newcomer by the old timers. I grew up here, married and raised my family.' She faltered.

Owen saw Nick reach out a hand to cover Kay's on the table. 'Kay lost her husband under traumatic circumstances over three years ago. It hasn't been easy for her,' he said softly. 'But,' he added in a brighter voice, 'when Fran had to rush off to England to care for her mother, this lovely lady took her place. It was the best thing that could have happened to me. Michelle had gone north with her new fellow, and I was floundering with the two kids to look after.'

Kay blushed. 'It was a godsend for me, too,' she said.

'I didn't know that was why Fran was away for six months,' Owen said. For some reason he'd assumed she'd been on holiday, on long service leave, or some such thing. 'Her mother?'

'She passed away,' Kay said.

'I'm sorry. I didn't know.'

Was that why she seemed so prickly? He knew what it was like to lose a parent.

'No reason why you should,' Nick said. 'More wine?'

Owen nodded and held out his glass for a refill. 'So, she didn't want to return to your office?' he asked Nick.

He saw Nick and Kay exchange a glance.

'It's all a bit awkward,' Kay said at last. 'I was the one looking for another position. We…' she gave Nick a warning look, '…thought it could cause too much talk if we continued to work together once everyone knew… I actually had the position with you in my sights.' She gave a sigh. 'But it wasn't to be. According to Aaron – our esteemed vice chancellor – I wasn't familiar enough with university regulations and politics to steer a new man. Hence, you got Fran, and I got to stay with Nick.' She spread her hands wide.

'I think what Kay's trying to say,' Nick explained, 'is that the committee had already pretty much decided they wanted an outsider for the position and thought Fran would be a better person to steer him – you – through the minefield of William Farrer bureaucracy.'

'Right.' It was beginning to make sense to Owen. 'And how did Fran feel about this?'

'Fran doesn't give much away,' Nick said. 'But she's always been able to see things from the perspective of the VC and the senate, so they got no argument from her. I think she views it as a challenge. She probably views you the same way,' he chuckled. 'She's pretty conventional.'

'So I've discovered. I think I may have shocked her when I turned up at her door looking like a tramp – she may have thought I was one of the students.'

The rest of the evening was spent with Owen and Nick reminiscing about their days in Sydney. Kay went to bed leaving them sitting outside in the moonlight with coffee and a warning to Nick not to bend Owen's ear for too long. Ryan was nowhere to be seen.

When Owen finally left, it was with the strong impression he'd renewed an old friendship, and that Nick would prove a useful ally in – as Nick described it – the minefield that was William Farrer. Every institution had its own idiosyncrasies and he was sure this one was no different.

He was glad, too, to have scored a PA who understood how everything worked. He was looking forward to working with Fran Reilly – and to perhaps helping her become more relaxed. She was too uptight for his liking, but it couldn't have been easy for her to lose her mother, then have to come back to the other end of the world. He wondered what had brought her here – to Australia and Granite Springs – in the first place, and what had made her stay. He had the distinct feeling there was some secret in her past.

Nine

Fran leant on the kitchen windowsill to watch a small band of lorikeets feasting on the red spiky clusters of the grevillea outside the window, their bright red and green plumage making them almost invisible among the foliage. Although she couldn't hear them through the glass, she knew their screeching and squawking would be almost deafening. They were so different from the tuneful warbling and dull colours of many of the birds in Britain, and she loved them.

As Fran turned from the window, she reflected that, in the two weeks since Owen Larsen had arrived, there hadn't been a dull moment.

He'd taken to turning up in her office first thing each morning, bearing takeaway coffees from Banjo's – often with the added benefit of croissants or carrot cake – and settling down in a chair as if he belonged there. At first, she'd just wished he'd leave to allow her to get on with her work. Then, as she became accustomed to his presence – and his offering of what she realised were valuable suggestions – Fran began to look forward to his arrival and to his subsequent unheralded intrusions during the day.

Owen was certainly different to anyone she'd worked with before. Whereas Nick Kerr had been meticulous and left her alone to organise everything for him, Owen was like a whirlwind. He would arrive, throw around a number of ideas, then leave a maelstrom in his wake, expecting her to pick them up and run with them. And, while some of his ideas had undoubted merit, some left her gasping for breath and making her wonder what it would be like when the school actually got going.

But she wasn't going to worry about that today. Late last night, she'd finished her library book. *A Path to the Sea* was the latest by an author she'd come across when she was in England, and Liz Fenwick's books took her back to holidays in Cornwall when she was a child. With her mother so ill, it had been good to escape into memories of happier times. Today, she intended to check out the most recent book by Marcia Willett, another of her favourite authors who set her books in Devon, then she might treat herself to a coffee at the nearby cafe.

It was such a lovely spring morning, Fran decided to walk the short distance to the library so, shrugging a light denim jacket over her white shirt and slipping her bag over one shoulder, she set off.

To her delight, Fran found the book she was looking for. *Reflections* was sitting on the shelf of newly returned books as if it was waiting for her. She picked it up, anticipating an enjoyable evening getting lost in what was bound to be a heart-warming tale. She loved the way this author brought back characters from earlier books to make her readers feel they were meeting old friends, and wondered who she'd reconnect with in this one.

Having negotiated the self-checkout which the library had installed since she left for England, and had a brief chat with Donna, her favourite librarian who was also involved in researching local history, Fran walked around the corner to Mouthfuls.

She was ordering her latte, deciding between an apricot slice and a salted caramel brownie, and chatting with one of the owners about the upcoming Granite Springs Show, in which Melody was entering her famous pavlova, when a voice called, 'Fran!'

Turning quickly, Fran saw Kay sitting with her friend, Jo, in the far corner of the almost empty café.

'Why don't you join us? Unless you're meeting someone?' Kay called.

Too surprised to answer immediately, Fran hesitated, only to see Jo smiling across the room, too. She waved her acceptance and completed her transaction, deciding on the brownie.

'Ooh that looks good,' Jo said, as Fran slid into a seat opposite her and placed the brownie on the table.

'It's larger that it looked in the case,' Fran said eying the cake ruefully. 'I'll get a knife and we can share.' She hopped up to return with a knife with which she cut the sweet confection into three. 'There, now none of us need feel guilty,' she said.

At that moment, Melody arrived with her coffee and, overhearing, said with a laugh, 'No need to feel guilty, ladies. It's very healthy.'

They all chuckled.

'How are you getting on with your new boss?' Kay asked, when the niceties had been covered, and Fran had learned the two other women met here regularly every Saturday morning. 'He's a bit different from Nick.'

Fran didn't know what to say. She was very aware anything she might say would no doubt be repeated to Nick – that's what couples did, wasn't it? She remembered Nick and Owen had taught together in Sydney and she wasn't sure how well Kay knew him. 'Umm,' she said.

'Don't worry, nothing you say will go any further. We had Owen to dinner when he arrived and that's all I know about him, But he's certainly a very different kettle of fish from Nick. I'm not asking you to gossip, but sometimes it's good to have someone to let off steam to. We're here.'

Jo nodded sympathetically.

'You're right there. It's taken me a while to get used to him. No, scrub that. I don't think I'll ever get used to him,' Fran said.

'How is he different?' Jo asked.

Fran took a sip of coffee and a bite of the brownie before replying. 'Well, for one thing, he looks more like a student than a member of staff. I know academics are often accused of looking unprofessional, but he takes it to a whole other level. His hair! His clothes! His whole manner. He races through the corridor – and my office – like a tornado wrecking everything in his wake. No,' she picked up her cup, then set it down again, 'that's unfair. He does have some good ideas. They're just so different. Maybe I should have expected something like that, him being what I believe is called *a creative*. He even sits in his office strumming his guitar when others would be pounding away on their computer. Says it helps him think.'

'And does it?' Jo was interested.

'Maybe. He certainly manages to come up with some outlandish ideas.'

'Such as?' Kay asked.

Fran thought for a moment. 'One is that the student assessment needn't all be written. He wants to explore *more creative* ways of providing evidence that course objectives have been met. I'm not sure what the board of examiners will make of that.'

'Oh, Fran,' Kay said. 'Don't take this the wrong way, but Nick did mention you always tended to take the bureaucrat's view.' She hesitated before continuing in a kind voice, 'You're so conservative.'

'Someone has to be,' Fran objected, looking down into her coffee. *Had it been a mistake to join these women if they were going to criticise her?*

'Of course they do,' Jo interrupted. 'And I'm sure that's exactly why the vice chancellor wanted you in that position – so you could curtail some of his wilder flights of fancy.'

Her words made Fran feel better. 'Thanks,' she said.

'And to support those that could make a real difference and help him bring them to fruition,' Kay added. 'I'm sure the powers that be are aware some things need to change and that this new school can be a force for change. It all takes time.'

'And Owen doesn't demonstrate much patience. He wants everything to happen now, doesn't realise the planning and permissions required, doesn't want to accept the care needed to effect change. He's so spontaneous, just like…' She stopped short. She'd been about to say, '…just like Ben.' *What had made her think of Ben?* To hide her confusion, she picked up her cup again and drained her coffee.

'Like?' Jo asked.

'It's nothing. Just someone I used to know. And Owen drinks a lot of coffee. My coffee consumption must have tripled,' she said, looking down at her now empty cup and hoping Jo wouldn't pursue that line of questioning. She didn't want to bring Ben into the discussion, didn't want to think of him, not now. Maybe later, when she was on her own, she'd try to work out why he'd come into her mind at that moment. 'He brings some every time he drops into my office,' she explained.

'He stops in often?' Kay asked in surprise. 'I thought he'd have enough to do in his own.'

'He likes to… share, I suppose,' Fran said. She'd often wondered herself why Owen felt the need to run what seemed like every idea he had past her. It was as if he needed her approval, or maybe he was just trying them out for size before putting them up to the various university committees.

'Is he still living in the student residences?' Kay asked, changing the subject.

'Yes. It must be difficult for him. They're designed for young people straight from home, not for a mature man used to living with his household goods all around him. He's rented a storage unit in the industrial area till he finds somewhere. Didn't you mention you might be renting out your house?' she asked Kay, recalling an earlier conversation.

'I did. But I've since had an offer for it – a good one.' She frowned. 'I made the decision to sell even before Nick and I got together, but it's a big step to give up what's been my home for years.' Fran saw her bite her lip, then straighten her shoulders. 'But I have to do it. That place holds some bad memories.' Kay gave a shiver. 'So, I'm afraid I can't help. I'm sure something will turn up.'

They chatted for a bit longer then Jo looked at her watch. 'I need to be going, ladies. I have a husband who'll be wondering where I am. Col was getting a crash course in animal husbandry in relation to goats this morning and should be back home by now.'

'Goats?' Kay asked. 'Are you thinking of getting some?'

'No,' Jo laughed, 'though they're fun to watch, they can be a lot of work. Our neighbours kept theirs in our paddock before Col and I got together,' she explained to a puzzled Fran. 'John and Bernadette – the owners of the goats – have bought themselves a motor-home and plan to spend at least six months touring Australia. We've agreed to look after their livestock while they're gone, hence this morning's handover. As well as the goats there are two cats. Scout would never forgive me if they wandered onto our land. I don't suppose this new professor of yours would be interested in housesitting an acreage?' she asked with a chuckle.

Fran had been picking up her bag and library book and stopped with the book halfway up. She placed it on the table. 'That may not be as laughable as it sounds. I know Owen has been looking for an acreage for sale without success. And, even if he did find one, he wouldn't be able to move in immediately. This might appeal to him. But would your neighbours be willing to have someone live there while they're gone? I don't think I'd have liked to have had a stranger in my house when I was in England.'

The very thought of someone Fran didn't know living in her space, poking around in her belongings, made her shudder. But she knew there were lots of people who routinely swapped houses for their holidays and didn't have any problem with it.

'Why don't I ask them, then give you a call?' Jo asked. 'It would certainly make our lives easier. We've had to make the decision not to go on holiday while they're gone and, if anything happens to the animals… Col and I aren't so young anymore and goats can be fey creatures. It's quite a responsibility. Col seems happy with it, but I'm not so sure.'

'Okay.' Fran could see this might solve Owen's housing problem and it might get him out of her hair somewhat if he wasn't living on campus. 'Thanks for inviting me to join you both. It's been fun chatting.'

'Anytime,' Kay said, 'we're here most Saturdays. Feel free to drop by.'

'Thanks.' Fran was grateful for the offer. She wouldn't join them every Saturday, of course. That might prove too intrusive. But some weeks, if she was feeling down, it was good to know they'd be there, and she could find a friendly ear – two friendly ears.

But as she left to walk home, it wasn't her new friends who filled her thoughts, or the possibility of solving her boss's problem. Her mind went back to that memory of Ben and to the lunch she planned for tomorrow. She'd managed to put Richard off till now. But it had to be done. The memory of Ben had been so strong, she knew she could never settle for someone like Richard. If she was ever to let a man into her life again, it had to be someone more like Ben, someone the complete opposite from Richard with his fussy ways, his exacting thinking, someone more like…

Why did the image of Owen Larsen appear in her mind's eye? She immediately dismissed it. She couldn't possibly be interested in her boss in that way. It was unthinkable!

Ten

Fran nervously prepared the quiche and salad they were to have for lunch, the radio blaring in her ears in an attempt to drown out the misgivings she was having. Why hadn't she finished with Richard immediately she returned from England as she'd planned? Then it would be over, and she wouldn't have to suffer the dread she was experiencing at the prospect of seeing him again. She had no answer, other than she'd been too weak to make good on her decision.

But she knew she couldn't break her promise to herself. Thoughts of what she might say, how she might break it to him gently, had kept her awake almost all night. Now it was almost time for him to arrive and she still hadn't worked it out.

She poured herself a glass of the chardonnay designated for lunch. Maybe that would help give her the courage. Though, she couldn't tell him before lunch, could she? How would they manage to share a meal after she told him it was over? But could she go through an entire meal without saying anything about how she felt? Fran was torn.

She'd just finished her wine and rinsed the glass when there was a knock at the door. Taking a deep breath, smoothing down the loose long-sleeved turquoise dress she'd elected to wear and forcing a smile onto her face, Fran went to the door.

Richard stood there, looking immaculate as usual. Today he was wearing khaki pants with a pale blue shirt and dark blue blazer, his shoes polished and shining. He was carrying a large bunch of flowers – roses – and a bottle of what looked like champagne. Hell! This was going to be even more difficult than she imagined.

Both hands full, Richard leant forward to kiss her, the kiss landing awkwardly on her chin. He laughed. 'You'd better take these,' he said, handing her the flowers. He kept hold of the bottle on the side of which Fran could recognise the familiar logo. Richard and his Moët. But what did he think they were going to celebrate today? She felt a shiver run up the back of her neck.

'Can I pop this in the fridge?' he asked, holding it up like a trophy. 'For later?'

Fran nodded, unsure what else to do. She had to tell him before it was too late.

To gain time, she fetched a vase from the cupboard and filled it with water, glad she'd turned down the radio only minutes before. He hated the *Australia All Over* program she'd been listening to, much the same way he hated Granite Springs. She was about to arrange the flowers when a hand reached over to remove the vase and place it on the benchtop beside the flowers. Richard took Fran in his arms.

As he opened his mouth to speak, Fran knew. It was too late!

'I've been thinking, Fran. These past two weeks. Since you returned. You've been so busy with this new job you've taken.'

She wished he'd come to the point, though she was afraid she knew where he was heading and didn't know how to stop him.

'I feel I may not have made my true feelings clear to you. While we seemed to be going along quite happily with our occasional meetings and…' he coughed slightly. 'Recently, I've become aware that we might make it more permanent. Those six months you were gone made me realise…'

Fran tried to speak, to stop him, to prevent him saying something he'd regret later, but it was no use, Richard put a finger on her lips and continued. It was as if he'd memorised this speech and had to see it through. She felt an urge to giggle which she fortunately managed to suppress.

'Fran Reilly, will you marry me?'

At least he hadn't gone down on one knee was all Fran could think.

But he hadn't finished. 'We could fit into my present home, but I'm aware you're not too keen on apartment living so I'd be prepared to move, maybe find a house somewhere close to the city where we could…'

'No!' Fran finally found her voice. 'I'm sorry…' Her eyes filled with tears. What a fiasco!

'No, *I'm* sorry. I've rushed you. I was too precipitous.'

Fran almost smiled through her tears. Even in this situation, Richard could be his customary precise self.

'You need time. I understand. I should probably go and let you…' He waved a hand in the direction of the rest of the house, then stood looking at her for a moment. 'I'll be in touch,' he said and walked out the door.

Fran gazed after him in amazement. How could such an intelligent man be so obtuse? What did he think she'd said no to? Was she going to have to go through all this again? Did he have a ring in his pocket?

She was sitting gazing into space, a kaleidoscope of her years with Richard playing behind her eyes. The ringing of her phone brought her back to the present.

'Hello?' she managed to stutter.

'Fran? Are you all right? You sound strange. It's Jo, by the way.'

Fran grasped at Jo's name as if at a lifeline. 'Sorry, Jo. It's been a bit odd here this morning.'

'Morning? It's afternoon. What's been happening?'

Fran checked the time, wondering what had happened between Richard leaving and now. They were supposed to have had lunch. The quiche and salad were in the fridge – as was an expensive bottle of Moët.

'I don't suppose you'd like to help me drink a bottle of champagne, would you?' she asked unable to suppress a laugh.

'Are you sure you're all right? Would you like me to come into town or contact Kay?'

'No. Sorry.' Fran managed to sober up. 'I just had the oddest experience and I now have a fridge full of quiche, salad and champagne.' Jo must think her mad. 'But that's not why you called.'

Thankfully, Jo didn't ask any more questions. 'No. Col spoke to Bernadette this morning – the neighbour who's going off tripping around Australia. She says she'd be delighted to have someone stay while they're gone. But they're leaving at the end of this week. Do you think your professor could get out to see them before then? I can give you their number.'

Fran drew in a breath. She'd completely forgotten their conversation in the café yesterday, forgotten Jo's promise to check out a possible housesitting arrangement for Owen. All this stuff with Richard, the planning, the worry, then the reality of it, which surpassed anything she could have imagined, had blotted out everything that went before.

Oh, right. Good. I'm sure he'll manage that. He'll be delighted. Let me get a pen.' Fran scrabbled around in the mug she kept by the phone, her fingers slipping in her attempts to pick up a pen. *What was wrong with her?* 'Okay, I have one.' She jotted down the number Jo gave her and put the pen down, feeling a little more in control, the action of writing the number helping to calm her.

She needed a drink. It was only early afternoon, but Fran felt as if she'd gone through an entire day. When she opened the fridge, the bottle of Moët was staring her in the face, reminding her of Richard. As if she needed any reminding. She didn't think she'd ever forget the look on his face when he asked her to marry him, then when she yelled "No".

Ignoring the expensive champagne, Fran picked up the chardonnay she'd opened earlier and poured a glass, taking it through to the study where a sudden impulse made her open the bottom drawer of her desk and pull out the box that had lain hidden there for so many years.

When her belongings had arrived from Sydney all those years ago, among them had been all her mementos of Ben and their relationship. Unable to face them, she'd hidden them away and had never looked at them again. She had no idea why she had the urge to drag them out now.

She sat on the floor with her glass of wine, her legs curled under her, and opened the box. Holding her breath, Fran picked up the first photo – one of her and Ben on the bike – the same one that killed him. She let it drop, a tear sliding down her face, and picked up a card – the last Valentine's Day card she'd ever received from Ben – then another photo, and another.

Fran didn't know how long she sat there, only deciding to move when it became so dark she could no longer see clearly. Her glass was empty. She rose stiffly. With her back, she should have known better than to have sat on the floor, in the same position, for so long. She wiped the tears from her eyes.

Fran had no idea why Ben was back in the forefront of her mind, why she had this hankering to revisit that time. After the accident, she'd decided to consign it to the past, to close a door on everything that had gone before. And, until now, it had worked.

What had happened to bring it up now?

Eleven

'Did I hear you correctly? Did you really say someone would like me to housesit an acreage?' Owen gazed at Fran in delight. He'd spent the weekend chasing up places for rent without finding anything remotely possible, and there were no acreages for sale within his price range. Surely someone wanted to sell a ten- or twenty-acre block? He'd even settle for one acre or five though, in his mind, they weren't much better than a regular house block. Now here was his assistant offering him six months on a property outside town.

'You did.' Fran appeared surprised at his reaction. Maybe she wasn't used to anyone expressing enthusiasm quite as strongly. 'Their names are John and Bernadette. I'm afraid I don't have a surname. Jo didn't mention it. She's the friend who told me about it. I have their number here.' She fossicked in her bag, before bringing out a neat card bearing the details.

No scrappy bit of paper for her, Owen thought with amusement. She must be the tidiest person he'd ever come across. He wondered if her obsession with order hid some deep problem from her past, then mentally shrugged. But he would like to know, and one of these days he intended to find out.

Owen took the card and turned it over in his hands, feeling a glow of satisfaction. Things were beginning to work out for him. He'd call and see if he could arrange to meet them later this afternoon. It would be a relief to get out of the student residences before the majority of students returned from their semester break. Even the few who'd elected to remain on campus tended to wander home late, their boisterous, drunken voices keeping him awake. And, last night, he could swear he'd heard a skateboard rattling along the paved courtyard between the buildings.

He drained the coffee that had become an essential part of their daily morning meeting. 'Well, better get on, I suppose.' He rose, crushing the cardboard cup in his hand before dropping it in the bin.

'Don't forget you have interviews with Ron Harris and Joshua Martin today.'

'How could I? It's right there in my schedule.' Owen directed a grin at Fran, surprised to see her blush. It was amazing how a blush could change a woman. For an instant he saw Fran as she could be if she allowed herself to relax, then her professional persona took over again and she was all business.

At first, he'd been annoyed when Fran had seemed to organise him, entered appointments into his online calendar and insisted he maintain a regular schedule so she could monitor his comings and goings. Then, the annoyance had turned to amusement. Now, he was grateful for her timely reminders. He hadn't realised how demanding this job was going to be. If he'd thought about it at all, it was to imagine the students, the freedom of being in charge. What he hadn't anticipated were the meetings, the never-ending meetings – all with the same group of people – which never seemed to resolve anything, except the date of the next meeting.

'Would you like me to be there?'

Owen must have looked surprised, because Fran added, 'To take notes.'

'That might be a good idea. My office, then?'

She nodded.

Back in his own office Owen put the card down on his desk and called the number. A woman's voice answered. 'Kelly residence.'

Owen cleared his throat. 'Owen Larsen here. I've been given your number by a…' he checked the card again, '… Jo Ford. I understand you'd be willing to have me look after your acreage for some months?' He paused and held his breath. What if he'd got it wrong? Or if Fran had misunderstood, though she wasn't the sort of person to misunderstand anything. She was the most exacting person he'd ever met.

He released his breath again when the woman spoke. 'Oh, hello. I'm Bernadette Kelly. Yes, Jo mentioned you. Thanks for calling. We'd love to have someone here while we're gone. But there are goats to look after, not to mention two very superior cats who think they own the place. Are you sure you're willing to take that on? We're a fair way out of town.'

Goats, cats, out of town – it sounded ideal. 'I'm sure. Can I come out to meet you? Would this afternoon be too soon?'

'Perfect. I don't know if Jo told you we're leaving this weekend, so you could move in any time, if you still want to once you've seen us. Jo and Col are on the next-door property. You know where that is?'

'No. I don't actually know Jo. She's a friend of my PA. I'm at the university. I hope that…'

Bernadette gave a tinkling laugh. 'No problem. Let me give you directions. Got a pen?'

Owen noted down the directions, unsure if he understood how to follow them, but he could put them into his satnav, though it might be hard for Emma – as he'd named the disembodied English voice which gave him directions – to find the RMB address. Deciding to ask Fran for clearer directions, he thanked Bernadette and hung up, arranging to be there between four and four-thirty that afternoon.

Picking up the folder containing the CVs of the two men he was to meet, Owen leant back and put his feet up on a chair to remind himself of their backgrounds. On paper, they both looked good, exactly the sort he'd want to work with, to choose as part of his team. What was it Fran had said? One of them was difficult to deal with – was it the one who'd wanted his job? He racked his brains, then remembered. Yes, the muso – Ron. He was to meet him first, so he'd see if she was right, or if he'd managed to get over his disappointment.

'Ready?' Fran appeared in the doorway with a smile. Owen dropped his feet to the floor, embarrassed to have her catch him looking so slovenly and wondering why it bothered him.

'As I'll ever be. This Ron…' He didn't have time to finish the question.

'Professor Larsen?' The gruff voice held a sarcastic note. The man standing in the doorway where Fran had been only a few moments before, was older than Owen had expected. His greying hair was neatly trimmed, and he was wearing what seemed to be the academic uniform of a sports jacket and khaki pants with a white shirt and red tie.

Beside him, Owen felt underdressed in his customary jeans and cord jacket. At least he wore a proper pair of shoes today. He'd seen Fran's surprise and disgust at his Nikes on his first day. He stood up and motioned Fran to the chair which had recently held his feet.

She perched on the edge of the chair.

'You must be Ron Harris. Thanks for making time to meet with me. Take a seat.'

'Hrmph,' Ron grunted, but took the offered seat, giving Fran a glare. 'Is she going to stay for our meeting?'

'I've asked Fran to join us to take notes of anything we might need later.'

Ron didn't look pleased. 'I don't know what this is all about,' he blustered. 'You blow in from Sydney to cut us locals out of our dues, then you want to talk?'

Owen realised he was going to take a firm stand. 'The university has appointed me to the professorship to lead the new School of Music and Drama,' he began.

'The Mad House – that's what the students are calling it already. So be warned.'

Owen couldn't hide his amusement. He grinned widely. 'I knew they'd work out an acronym. They've done it sooner than I expected. I rather like it. The Mad House should be fun to work in, don't you think?'

His grin drew a restrained smile from Ron. 'You don't consider it disrespectful?'

'I'm not after respect without having earned it, and I don't think a name matters. Call me Owen, by the way. Now,' he pulled Ron's CV out of the folder, 'I understand you were one of the contenders for the position. For some reason, the committee preferred me,' Owen shook his head as if at a loss to understand their decision, 'but I don't see any reason we can't get along together, do you? You have a lot to offer.' He tapped the papers in his lap.

The conversation proceeded with many stops and starts but, by the end, Ron had agreed to be seconded to Owen's school for at least one semester, on the condition he could continue to teach some of his existing courses in the Faculty of Education.

'Thanks. Good to meet you, Ron. I look forward to working with you. And I'll be sure to check your contribution with Professor Kerr.'

'Wow!' Owen said to Fran when Ron was out of earshot. 'You weren't wrong about him. He sure has a chip on his shoulder. He has a strong background, but I can see why they didn't give him the position. Is this Josh guy going to be as bad?'

'No, he's very different. He'd have hated your job, prefers to be on the side of the students – maybe a bit too much so.' Fran's lips tightened for such a brief moment Owen wondered if he'd imagined it.

'Do we have time for a coffee before he arrives?'

'Just about. Would you like me to pop over to Banjo's?'

'Would you? I don't want you to think I'm treating you like the tea lady.'

Fran smiled, her eyes crinkling. 'I'd never think that, and you bring me one every morning. Let's just say it's my turn.'

After a coffee to sustain him, Owen was ready for his next meeting. It proved to be much easier than the first. As Fran had intimated, Joshua Martin was a more laidback prospect with hair almost as long as Owen's. He was younger, too, and relished the thought of being part of an innovative team, even suggesting he was keen to join the new school on a permanent basis if that was possible.

'I've set up a meet with Nick this afternoon,' Fran said when Joshua left. 'I thought they'd go this way and it's best to get these things formalised as soon as possible.'

'Thanks. What time? I said I'd go out to see the acreage around four – and I'll need directions. The ones Bernadette gave me are a bit hazy.'

'Two. You should be finished in time.' There was a pause before she added hesitatingly, 'I could take you out. It's a dirt road. I'm not sure…' her voice trailed off as if unsure if she'd overstepped the mark.

'You must have seen my old Mazda,' he said, ruefully. 'That would be good.'

*

'This is beautiful – and so close to town,' Owen exclaimed, as Fran drove them out through the state forest and into open farmland. He gazed at sheep grazing on one side and wheat growing on the other. There were a few stray pine trees struggling to grow on the verge and a flock of galahs flew past, their pink and grey plumage flashing in the sun. Owen opened the window to breathe in the scent of the country.

'Isn't it?' Fran turned to give him a quick glance. 'We're almost there.'

'This Jo – a friend of yours?'

'I don't know her very well, really. I only met her recently. She's Kay's friend. You met her. Nick's PA and partner.'

'Right. How does that work?'

Owen was curious how the pair could manage to work *and* live together.

'They don't seem to have any problems,' Fran replied after a moment's consideration. 'And I haven't heard any adverse comments. You'd expect to, in our hothouse environment,' she laughed.

The car bumped as Fran veered left to turn off the tarmac onto a narrow dirt road, the gravel surface throwing up tiny stones against the car's paintwork. Fran's little VW wasn't much more robust than his old Mazda would have been, but it seemed to hold the road well. As they headed away from the main road, Owen could see a couple of houses almost hidden by trees, then they reached a rusting white-painted metal gate.

'Would you?' Fran asked.

Owen hopped out to open the gate, a breeze swirling the dust at his feet. There were several goats in the paddock, one of which stopped long enough to stare at him, before continuing to stretch up to pull down the lower branches of a nearby gum tree.

Once back in the car, he stared around him as the house, a long, ranch-style building, appeared before them. There was a fence around the house and, as they stopped, two cats rose from the veranda to stroll cautiously towards the gate. A large motorhome was parked beside a metal shed.

'Okay if I leave you here?' Fran asked. 'Jo and Col live over there.' She pointed towards the adjoining paddock where another house sat in the hollow. 'Jo said I should drop by. You can walk over when you're done here and meet your new neighbours.'

'Thanks.' Owen waved her off, then turned to walk through the gate. His eyes scanned the wide expanse of paddock stretching out beyond the house and what looked like a dam in the distance with several goats standing on its raised edge. He took a deep breath. This would be perfect. It was exactly the sort of place he had in mind. Surely in the six months he was here, he'd manage to find an acreage of his own.

'Hello, you must be Owen.' A tall woman wearing jeans and a sweater bearing the logo of an almost forgotten rock band, her grey hair tied back at the nape of her neck, emerged from an open door. 'Come in. I have the coffee on.'

Owen followed her into the farmhouse kitchen, his eyes lighting up at the sight of an Aga in the corner. An old wood dresser against one wall held a variety of plates, and the cats, who had scurried inside in his wake, were now ensconced in an old rocking chair which sat in a corner. *Was this for real?* It was so close to what he'd imagined, Owen wanted to pinch himself.

Once seated, Bernadette's husband joined them – a tall man with broad shoulders and a grey beard wearing jeans that were torn at the knees and a checked flannel shirt over a navy singlet. 'John,' he said, holding out a hand to shake Owen's.

While they drank coffee and ate some delicious cheese scones, John and Bernadette explained about the house and the animals. 'We just need someone to make sure everything's okay,' she said at last. 'Our neighbour, Col Ford, was going to keep an eye on things, but to have you on site would really set our minds at rest.'

'You're going off travelling?' Owen asked, when there was a lull in the conversation.

'Going to do the grey nomad thing before we get too old,' John laughed. 'You would have seen that monster outside. That'll be our home for the next few months. A bit different to what we're used to. It's all Bernie's idea.' He chuckled, and Owen saw his wife give him a nudge.

'When do you leave?'

The two looked at each other. John cleared his throat and gazed out the window, leaving Bernadette to answer, 'We planned to leave on the weekend. Your coming here today is a godsend. It means we can leave with a clear conscience, knowing the place will be in good hands. If we can get organised, we might even get away tomorrow.'

Owen wondered how they could be so sure he wouldn't wreck the place, let the animals die, and kill the vegetable garden he'd seen through the window, wondering why it was surrounded by a high wire fence and netting.

As if reading his mind, Bernadette said, 'Jo said you were at the university, a professor.'

So that was his endorsement?

'And Col and Jo are just over the fence. He knows what to do with the goats, but it's just a matter of making sure they have food and water and don't get out the gate, through the fence, or into the veggie garden. They can be wily creatures,' John chuckled, 'but I can watch them for hours.'

'I haven't met Col and Jo yet,' Owen said, 'but I'm headed there after this.'

'They're a good pair. Jo's lived there almost as long as we've been here. Col's a recent addition, but he's taken to the land like a duck to water. They'll see you right if there are any problems.'

'Okay.'

As Owen was leaving, John handed him a key and pointed to the green steel shed behind the motorhome. 'By the way, my old Suzuki 4WD is in there, along with the bike. Feel free to make use of them.'

'I couldn't...' Owen began.

'You'll be doing me a favour,' John insisted. 'It's no good for them to be sitting idle while we're away. You can arrange for them to get a tune up before we get back if you're worried.'

'A bike, you say?' Owen couldn't imagine riding a bike on the road they'd driven in on.

'The Honda. We don't have much use for a dirt bike here, but Bernie and I enjoy the odd run on the back of the machine. Reminds us of our youth. Ridden one before, have you?'

The question took Owen by surprise and back to his teenage years when his dream was to own a Harley. He'd never managed to achieve that, but in his student days he'd owned a second-hand Yamaha which he and Brit had used to escape the city at weekends, riding to the Central or South Coasts, where they'd find cheap accommodation before returning to the big smoke.

'Yes, years ago,' he stammered, picturing himself riding like the wind along the country roads. It was all like a dream come true. Was he going to wake up and discover it had been a dream, or was this really happening?

Twelve

Fran smiled to herself as she drove across the cattle grid at Yarran, as Jo and Col's property was called. It was the first time she'd visited Jo's home, and she felt slightly nervous. Although she'd met Jo a few times since the evening with Kay and Nick she'd only met Col that once.

When she parked the car, an old Golden Labrador lumbered out to greet her. 'Hello, old fellow,' she said, ruffling his ears.

'You've met Scout?' Jo called from the doorway. 'He likes to check out our visitors. He'll know you next time,' she said, as the dog sniffed at Fran's ankles. 'I was about to have a glass of wine, and Col is pouring himself a beer. Which would you like, or would you prefer something soft?'

'I'm driving,' Fran said, but the sound of a glass of wine was tempting. 'Maybe a small wine.'

'Lovely. I have a nice chardonnay in the fridge. Come in.'

Fran entered the house with interest. Although she'd lived in Granite Springs for years, she'd rarely visited anyone who lived outside the town itself, keeping herself pretty much to herself apart from a few acquaintances. This was a new experience for her.

'You've not been in a house like this before?' Jo asked, clearly seeing her eyeing everything with curiosity. 'Gordon – my first husband – and I built this house soon after we married. I've lived here ever since. I love this place and everything in it.' She stroked the wooden table which looked old and was scarred as if by the years and the hands of many children. 'It would take a bulldozer to get me out.' The set of Jo's mouth as she spoke made Fran think someone had tried to do just that, clearly without success. 'Would you like me to show you round?'

'If it's not too much trouble.'

'Not at all. Col, will you pour a couple of glasses of wine while I take Fran on a tour?'

Fran turned to see Jo's husband walk in, the dog at his heels.

'Hello, Fran. Good to see you again,' he said. 'I'll see Scout fed and watered and do just that,' he said to Jo.

'Hello, Col,' Fran said, before she was whisked off by Jo on what her companion referred to as *the grand tour*.

'Is your neighbour's house like this one?' Fran asked, after she'd admired the high ceilings, the airy rooms and the wrap-around veranda, and they were making their way back to the kitchen. She was trying to imagine living here. It was so different to her own compact townhouse where, if she stretched out her arms, she could almost touch the walls. It seemed equally incongruous for someone like Owen Larsen, but what did she really know about him? Not a lot, she realised.

'Pretty much. They built a few years before we did, and this was a popular design. It suits the climate, and the traditional wrap-around veranda makes it pleasant to sit outside in all seasons. Now, let's get you a glass of wine. Is your professor going to join us when he's finished with John and Bernadette? Col can steer him right with the goats if they haven't had time.'

They were sitting on the wide front veranda enjoying their wine and beer, Scout at their feet. It was peaceful here, the only sounds the cries of the native birds and an occasional snuffling from the dog. Fran was wondering why she'd never ventured into the countryside before now, when she saw a figure walking along the lane. 'Here he is,' she said, surprised at the hint of pleasure she felt at the sight.

'He'll be ready for a beer,' Col said, rising to go into the house, the dog at his heels.

'Scout follows Col everywhere. You wouldn't think I was his only companion for five years,' Jo said, but her smile belied her words.

'Hello there,' Owen said, walking up, his hand outstretched. Fran could see beads of perspiration on his forehead, and his hair was beginning to come loose from his habitual bun. 'Jo Ford, I presume?'

'The same. Welcome to Yarran, Owen. So, are you going to be our new neighbour?'

'It seems so.' His eyes stared into the distance where the Kelly property could be seen through the trees. 'John and Bernadette are a trusting couple. They're happy to turn over their home to me, give me the use of their car and motorbike and space in their garage to store my belongings.'

Jo started to speak, and Fran was vaguely conscious of Col returning with a beer for Owen, but when she heard, *motorbike*, she froze. She was back sitting behind Ben, hearing the roar of the engine, smelling the bike's fuel, then the crash.

'Are you all right, Fran?' Jo's voice seemed to come from a distance.

'Yes. Sorry. I just…'

'Owen was telling us he plans to move in at the weekend,' Jo said. 'It's good to know the place won't be empty for long. Neighbours are so important when you live out here. I've been grateful for Bernadette and John's help many a time, especially before Col moved in.'

'Oh, I don't know about that,' Col said, patting his wife on the arm. 'Seemed to me you managed most things on your own.'

They smiled, clearly remembering a specific occasion.

Fran felt uncomfortable, as if she'd strayed into a private conversation.

Owen seemed to have no such trouble. 'John said you'd give me the information on the goats,' he said. 'I have to admit I haven't a clue when it comes to animal husbandry, but I'm willing to learn. I should be okay with the cats. I had a pet cat as a child and these ones seem friendly enough.'

'As long as you feed them regularly,' Jo chuckled. 'Do you have any pets?' she asked, turning to Fran.

'No.' Fran's mother had disliked both cats and dogs, and it had never occurred to her to get a pet once she was an adult, even though she loved those her friends had. 'But I love cats, and Scout's a nice dog.'

Scout pricked up his ears at the sound of his name, then gave a grunt.

'Why don't you both stay to dinner?' Col asked, when the men were on their second beer. 'Jo has a casserole in the slow cooker, and I'm sure there's enough for another two.' He looked at his wife for confirmation.

'Oh, please do! Or do you need to get back?'

Fran glanced at Owen who was nodding his agreement and looking towards her with a raised eyebrow. 'I don't have anything urgent to get back to. Fran?'

Did she want to stay for dinner? If it had only been with Jo and Col, she would have agreed immediately. She liked what she already knew of Jo and would love the opportunity to get to know her better. But there was Owen. She wasn't sure why, but the thought of socialising with him made her feel uneasy. She wasn't like Kay. She wasn't about to have a relationship with her boss, and he was so... so unlike the way he should be. There was something about him that brought out all her worst fears. Yet she didn't know what she was afraid of.

'Fran?' he asked again.

Fran didn't know why she was hesitating. The thought of going back to her townhouse to spend the evening alone, like she did most other evenings, should have brought comfort. Instead, she was beset with the prospect of a loneliness she'd never been aware of before.

'That sounds lovely,' she said, regretting the words almost as soon as they were out of her mouth.

In an attempt to disguise her unease, Fran followed Jo into the kitchen. 'Can I do anything to help?' she asked.

'I've got it pretty much covered,' Jo replied, peering into the slow cooker, then opening the fridge and removing some salad makings. 'But you can sit there and talk to me.' She gestured to a chair at the kitchen table. 'Another wine? You won't be driving for some time yet.'

'Thanks.' Fran held out her glass for a refill.

'Owen seems like a nice fellow. Not quite what I expected. He's a lot different from Nick.'

'He certainly is.' Fran twisted the glass by its stem. Now she had more wine, she didn't feel like drinking it.

'How is he to work for?' Jo was too busy chopping tomatoes and cucumber, to be looking at Fran.

Fran didn't reply immediately, unsure of the words to describe how she felt about working with him. 'He's... unpredictable,' she said at last. 'Sometimes I feel I'm on a roller coaster, trying to hang on while he's making it move faster and faster.' *Where had that come from?* Fran had never before put into words exactly what she felt her life was like these days.

Jo stopped what she was doing and glanced up. 'And do you ever feel you want to get off?'

'No,' Fran replied honestly. 'It's scary at times but exhilarating. Though I do worry what will happen when we finally move to the new building. At the moment, I tend to think his most outrageous ideas are being kept in check.'

'And when will that be?'

'The projected finish date is in a couple of weeks. It'll be good to be in the new offices, though I expect we'll rattle around a bit till the other staff are appointed. One of the education staff is coming over on a full-time basis, but I suspect the other will want to retain his office in the education building. His nose was put out of joint when he didn't get the top job.'

'Ron Harris. Kay told me.'

'You know him?'

'He grew up here in Granite Springs, too. We all knew little Ronnie Harris who thought he was going to set the world on fire with his musical ability. I blame his mother for that. She treated him as if he was a child prodigy, instead of a talented young boy. Some parents have a lot to answer for.' She gave a sigh.

'Dinner ready yet?' Col came in, followed by Owen. 'Are we going to eat here?'

'In the kitchen?' Jo seemed to make an assessment, then nodded. 'If you can set the table.'

'Let me,' Fran said, keen to make herself useful, and not sure why she suddenly felt awkward again. 'Where will I find cutlery and plates?'

Jo pointed to the drawer and cupboard.

'Another, mate?' Col gestured to Owen with his beer glass.

Owen nodded.

Fran busied herself with the table setting, taking longer than she actually required, aware of the need to calm herself.

The meal was a happy affair, and Fran managed to relax listening to Owen and Col discuss the care of goats and the delights of living outside town.

'It's a great place to raise a family,' Col said, as they were finishing their meal, 'Jo's three grew up here and her grandkids love to visit.'

'Do you have any children, Owen?' Jo asked.

'A daughter.'

'Daughter? Did you say a daughter?' Fran asked in surprise. Owen was the last person she'd have expected to have children. He was more like a child himself sometimes, with his unpredictable behaviour – a fifty-year-old child. But she had a vague recollection of Nick mentioning something about a child before Owen arrived. She'd forgotten or chosen not to remember. He was such an unlikely person to be a father.

'Yes. Pia. She's named after my grandmother – my dad's mother. They came to Australia when Dad was little. You're surprised?' he asked Fran. 'Don't you think I'm father material?'

'No, it's not that.' But it was exactly that. How could someone as disorganised, as carefree, as reckless have brought up a child, unless her mother was Owen's complete opposite.

He must have read her mind.

'She's not like me,' he said, 'or her mother. Neither of us were good role models. I'm afraid we rather let her down in that respect. No, Pia's the epitome of conservative. She works for a recruitment firm in Sydney, lives with an up and coming lawyer…' He frowned.

'Not your choice?' Jo guessed. 'Our children's choices aren't always ours. More's the pity.'

Owen shook his head. 'But he makes her happy. That's the main thing.'

'She'll be coming to visit?'

'I hope so.' Owen rubbed his hands together. 'Once I get settled in, I hope she and Darren will come down for a weekend.'

'Sounds good. You'll have to bring them over for a drink.'

Fran was beginning to feel left out of this conversation. Jo was *her* new friend, so why did she feel as if she was the stranger, and Owen was an old friend of their hosts? It was this knack he had. Fran had noticed it before. He might get into all sorts of chaos where work was concerned but he was good with people. Apart from Ron Harris, who had no people skills at all and had been set against him before they even met, Owen had managed to win over even the most difficult of the academic and administrative staff.

'You must come again too, Fran,' Jo said, as if she'd sensed Fran's feelings. 'We should arrange it when Col's at golf or some other man thing. Maybe with Kay?'

Fran gave Jo a grateful look. 'I'd like that,' she said. 'Now we should leave. I have a few things to do and I'm sure Owen has too, in preparation for his move.' She knew it was a weak excuse. What could Owen do in his tiny student room to make preparation for moving holus bolus to the neighbouring farmhouse. But she had the urge to get away from here, from this conversation, back to her own home where she could hide away again and pretend, just as she'd been doing for the past twenty-eight years.

Driving back to town, there was a loaded silence in the car, then Owen asked, 'Did I do something wrong? That seemed a sudden decision to leave. They're nice people – will be good neighbours.'

'Yes, they are, and no, you didn't do anything wrong. I'm sorry if you feel I hurried you away. I was feeling a bit tired.' She knew it was a lame excuse, but it was the best she could come up with.

'Thanks for driving me out here. Why do I think you're regretting it?'

Fran felt Owen's eyes on her but kept hers focussed on the road ahead. 'Not at all. I'm glad it's going to work out for you. It's a lovely spot. But won't you be lonely out there all by yourself?'

'Lonely? With twenty goats, two cats, and neighbours just across the fence? I'll be in heaven. I'm not sure who you think I am, Fran, but I assure you that at heart I'm really a likable sort of guy who just wants to be happy.'

'And you think living on that acreage will make you happy?'

'I don't think anything *makes* a person happy. It has to come from within. But I know that living out there will contribute to my happiness if I so choose.'

Little more was said as they drove the final few kilometres to the campus where Fran dropped Owen off, before making her way home. The message light was blinking on her phone when she entered the kitchen. Pressing the button to retrieve the message, her heart sank at the sound of Richard's voice.

'Now you've had time to reflect on my proposal, let's meet for dinner on Saturday. It may be best if you come to Canberra. Let me know what time suits.'

Fran stared at the answering machine, covered her mouth with her hand, then squeezed her eyes shut. What the heck was she going to do?

Thirteen

Owen scratched his head as he dressed next morning. Despite having spent time in the car with Fran yesterday, even having dinner with her and the Fords, he didn't have any more idea of what made her tick. Just when she'd seemed to be relaxing, she froze up again. What was it with the woman? It was as if she pulled down the shutters to keep everyone out. She was good at her job. He had no quarrel there, but as a person…

He tried to think back over the evening, in an attempt to work out where it had gone awry. He closed his eyes. It had been just after he arrived, he decided. The three of them had been sitting chatting, he'd walked up, Col had gone inside to fetch him a beer and… it had been as if the shutters came down right then. Was it him? Had his arrival upset her so much? But how could that be? They worked together every day without any problem, and she'd known he was coming.

Then, he remembered, during their meal, it had happened again when he mentioned Pia. She'd shown surprise, then… hadn't frozen up exactly, but gone very quiet. Was it to do with him, with Pia, with children in general? He shook his head, but he knew it was going to bother him until he worked it out. He supposed he could ask her, but had the distinct impression it might make things worse. Right now, they had a good working relationship, and he didn't want to do anything to spoil that, so he guessed he'd have to let it go – for now.

He slipped his bare feet into a pair of loafers, grabbed his satchel – which some would call a man-bag – and headed to Banjo's to pick up two coffees, before making his way to Fran's office, his first port of call every morning.

Instead of entering immediately, Owen stood in the open doorway and observed the woman who had been the object of his thoughts. Fran was seated at her computer, her short blonde hair immaculate as usual, her upright posture almost too stiff to be natural. For the first time Owen wondered if she was concealing or protecting some injury. He seemed to recall the time he'd been injured in a hockey game as a teenager and, for weeks, had gone around looking, and feeling, as if he had a stake holding his back together and forcing him upright.

Lyn must have sensed his presence, because she turned, to catch him staring.

'I have coffee,' he said, shrugging off his embarrassment and holding up a cup. 'I'll be glad when we're in our own offices and can make it there. You did order that coffee maker?'

'A Nespresso, the same as the one I got for Nick,' she agreed. 'He swears by it.'

'Good.' Unusually for him, Owen felt awkward in her presence this morning. Maybe it was because she'd been so much in his thoughts. 'The Fords seem to be a nice couple,' he said.

'Jo and Col, yes. I like them. I think you'll enjoy living there. You're moving in tomorrow?'

Owen pulled on a loose strand of his hair. 'Yeah. If I can get myself organised in time.'

Fran gave a brief smile. 'Anything I can do to help? I know it's not university business, but I could arrange the removalist, or…'

Owen spoke without thinking. 'I can do that, but it would be great if you could be on hand when they arrive at the property. As you know, I don't have the tidiest mind and it would be a big help to have someone like you there to help get things in order. There won't be room for much of my stuff in the house, but I will need some of my things to make it more like home.'

He saw her eyes widen – with amusement or alarm, he wasn't sure. 'Tomorrow?'

'If you have something else on, I can manage.' He realised it was a bit of an imposition to ask her to give up part of her weekend to help him move.

Owen saw her eyes flicker as if calculating something, then she said, 'No, I could do that. But I do have to be somewhere in the evening.' Her eyes clouded over, then cleared. 'What time did you have in mind?'

Owen had no idea. He'd just assumed he'd head out there as soon as he wakened, whenever that might be. He scratched his head. 'I don't know, whenever…'

Fran smiled. This time her amusement was evident. 'How about you get back to me when you've spoken to the removalist? We'll need to be there when they arrive.'

'Right. Now, what's on the agenda today?'

The next hour was taken up with the organisation of setting up a recruitment committee for new staff, followed by an update from the building supervisor who reported he'd told the capital works manager they were on target to finish on the projected date.

Back in his own office, Owen experienced a sense of satisfaction. All was going to plan. By this time next week, he'd be settled in his new home, albeit for a six-month period, and two weeks hence, they should be able to move into their new building. Then it would be all systems go.

Feeling a glow of happiness that everything seemed to be going his way, Owen took out his phone and sent a text to Pia telling her of his good fortune, attaching a photo he'd taken at the Kelly property, and inviting her and Darren to visit him in his new abode.

He was surprised to receive a reply almost immediately. First, Pia made a rude comment about him feeling right at home among the other old goats in the photo, then she suggested she and Darren might be able to visit sooner than he'd anticipated. It appeared Darren had some "boring lawyer thing" in Canberra the following weekend, and Pia proposed they arrive on the Friday and leave on the Monday. Owen grinned at this news. It meant he'd have two days with his daughter without her partner's arrogant presence. He'd have to put up with two nights of the boor's company, but he guessed he could survive that, if it meant he could spend quality time with Pia.

He was so full of the thought of seeing Pia again, he almost forgot to call the removalist, only doing so when a terse email from Fran asking about his move, reminded him. Damn the woman! Why did she have to be so efficient? But Owen knew he needed someone like

Fran to keep him on track. He just wished sometimes she'd take time to relax. She was an attractive woman. He wondered if she ever relaxed enough to lose that tight control she kept over her emotions, and what she'd be like if she did.

*

When Saturday arrived, Owen awoke early, filled with anticipation. He rose and showered before any of the students were about, and by eight o'clock was ready to leave. He'd packed his car the night before and was all set to subject his old bomber to the dirt road despite Fran's warnings. He'd already decided to look for something more suitable for his new life, the Suzuki 4WD of John's sparking the desire for one of his own. He could probably find a second-hand one locally and consign the Mazda to the dump where it belonged. It had been okay for driving around in the city but not for here. It had taken all his cajoling and a large chunk of hope to make it this far.

Glad Fran and the removalists wouldn't be arriving till later, Owen set off. He opened the car window to allow the fresh morning air to waft around his face, sniffing in the country odours of gum, wattle, and the dry dust on the side of the road. A few pink and grey galahs rose from the tarmac in front of him, disturbed by the car, and the screeching of a flock of cockatoos filled his ears as they flew overhead. He was in his element.

Before too long he came to the turn off the main road. This was where his car would be tested. He held his breath. There were a few bumps and a lot of red dust, but the tyres and suspension held, and he reached the gate of the property without any mishap.

As Owen closed the gate behind him, one of the goats – a lighter colour than the rest – ventured nearer, but still kept its distance as if wary of the newcomer. When Owen took a step toward it, the animal scampered off to join the others grazing on the sparse dry grass.

As soon as he opened the door of the house, the two cats appeared on the veranda as if by magic and wound themselves around his ankles meowing loudly. At least these creatures were pleased to see him.

The car unloaded, he set up his coffee maker in the kitchen, his toiletries in the ensuite, and his laptop in the room he'd designated as his study. While he was brewing his first cup of coffee, Owen emptied the bag of provisions he'd bought the day before into the fridge and pantry, surprised to see Bernadette and John had left a generous supply of food along with a note instructing him to be sure to eat it all.

Owen ensured the cats had food and water then, carrying a mug of coffee, wandered outside to admire what was, for now, his domain. Close to the house was a large pepper tree which looked much older than the house itself and, beyond that, was a stand of what even Owen's untrained eye recognised as fruit trees. The paddock stretching away from the house was larger than he remembered, and he could see there definitely was a dam, but it looked pretty dry. Then there was the vegetable garden, sitting outside the house paddock. He'd only seen it through the window before, but now he was able to take a good look and could see raised rows of green growth. He didn't know much about growing vegetables but was sure he could learn. As one of the goats edged nearer to its surrounding fence, Owen realised the reason for it. This whole thing was going to be a huge learning experience.

He must have lost track of time. The sound of a car making its way along the driveway came as a shock, and he turned to see Fran's little red VW coming towards him. Hell, how long had he been standing lost in thought? Owen could see how easy it would be for him to while away the time out here. He was bad enough with time management at the best of times. But, here, away from the city, away from the university, there was a glorious sense of freedom – just him, the animals, the birds, and the magnificent Australian countryside.

Owen turned reluctantly to greet Fran who, by now, was getting out of her car, carrying a large box.

'Morning,' she called. As she came nearer, he saw the box appeared to be filled with grocery items, much the same as the ones he'd already unpacked. Did she think he was so helpless he hadn't thought of provisions? Evidently!

'What do you have there?' he asked with a grin.

'I thought… Oh!' she said, blushing as she saw his expression, 'You did, too?'

'I'm not quite as disorganised as you imagine,' he said, then, seeing her redden, added, 'but it was a kind thought. Come in. There's time for coffee before my stuff arrives. I'll just open up the shed first.'

Fran put the box down on a table on the veranda and waited while he slid open the wide metal door to reveal the Suzuki, the bike and the large empty space that was to house his belongings.

When Owen joined her, he thought her face appeared white, but put it down to the fact her blush had subsided. 'What do you think?' he asked, opening his arms to encompass the house and the stretch of paddock which surrounded them.

'It looks good, a lot like Jo and Col's place,' she said, gazing towards the fence line, where the neighbouring house could be seen in the distance.

This morning she was dressed in what Owen presumed was her casual weekend gear – pressed blue jeans teamed with a pink top and a denim jacket. She looked good in pink with strands of her streaked blonde hair falling over her forehead. Owen wondered if she knew how attractive she was.

'Come in,' he repeated, having difficulty in swallowing. Damn the woman! She was beginning to get under his skin. He hadn't moved to Granite Springs to get involved in a hopeless liaison – and any sort of liaison with his assistant would be hopeless. Regardless of how she looked, Fran gave off vibes that clearly said, "keep off".

Owen restarted the coffee machine, and while it hissed and gurgled and filled the kitchen with the delightful aroma of coffee, Fran unpacked her box, seemingly able to work out exactly where everything should go. When he turned with two mugs of coffee, she was sitting at the table as if she belonged there, two chocolate croissants on a plate.

'I thought you might not have had breakfast,' she said with a demure smile.

One point to her. Breakfast had been the last thing on his mind this morning, and he was feeling peckish. 'Thanks.' Owen joined her, and one of the cats, appearing as if by magic, leapt up onto Fran's lap, startling her.

'Sorry!' Owen said, rising to rescue the unsuspecting cat, before she waved him away.

'It's okay. He's rather sweet.'

'They seem to be very friendly. There's another one somewhere.' His gaze flickered around the room, before spying the other making its way towards them. 'I can't remember their names. I have them written down somewhere. What?' he asked, mystified, as she began to laugh. *Had he said something funny?*

'Sorry. It just seems so...' Fran laughed again. 'You! You're so incongruous here. I can't imagine how you're going to manage for the entire six months.'

Pleased to see Fran more relaxed than he had before, but irked that she held such a poor opinion of his capabilities to manage a couple of cats and a herd of goats, Owen folded his arms across his chest and pretended to be upset. 'Why not? I know I can sometimes seem disorganised – well, be disorganised – but I *am* capable of looking after myself and this place. And Col is only five minutes away if I run into trouble.'

'There is that,' she said, smiling broadly.

The removalist van arrived as they were finishing coffee, and Fran opted to wipe the croissant crumbs from the table and rinse their mugs while Owen went outside to greet the removalists. By the time she joined them, most of his boxes were stacked in the shed. The remaining ones, plus his keyboard and a few favourite items of furniture were standing on the grass.

'Are those to go inside?' she asked, shading her eyes from the glare of the sun. There was no protection from it out here. The heat would be almost unbearable in the summer.

Seeing one of the removalists check his watch while the other was closing the back doors to the van, Owen nodded, and gestured to the man with the watch that he needed the heavier items brought inside before they left.

'No problem,' the man said, lifting the armchair, then the desk as if they were toys and carrying them inside to be placed where Owen directed. He did the same with his office chair, the travertine coffee table, and two bookcases. There only remained boxes of books and clothes.

'I think we can manage these,' Owen said, seeing the men's reluctance to stay any longer. He met Fran's eyes. She nodded.

They spent the next hour or so carrying things inside and unpacking the boxes. With a touch of what he took to be shyness, but could have been something else entirely, Fran left Owen to sort out his clothes. But she seemed happy enough to unpack his books and CDs, only checking with him before stacking them on the shelves of his bookcases.

By the time they'd finished, Owen felt the place looked more like his than it had before. The simple addition of a few of his belongings made him feel at home.

'I think that's it. You've been a big help. Thanks.' He stood, arms on hips, gazing around the living room where his old armchair, with signs of many years wear and tear, sat in pride of place by the wood stove, and the footstool that had been his father's in front of it, ready for his own feet, and the heavy coffee table having ousted Bernadette and John's from its place in front of the sofa. This was his new home.

'Hello! Anyone home?' a familiar voice called from outside, and Jo's smiling face appeared. She was carrying a covered dish and had a basket over one arm. 'I saw the removal van leave earlier and thought you might be ready for something to eat. Oh, hello, Fran,' she said, as she caught sight of her standing by the window, the two cats at her feet, her hair gleaming in a shaft of sunlight. 'I didn't expect to see you here.'

Jo placed her basket on the newly installed coffee table. She appeared uncomfortable, as if she'd caught them out in some secret liaison, which amused Owen, given his earlier thoughts.

'I prevailed on Fran to give me a hand,' he said, to dispel any wrong ideas. 'I know it's not part of her job description to help me move in, but she was kind enough to agree.'

For some reason, Jo looked relieved. 'Well, this is a quiche and there'll be enough for two. And there's salad and fruit in the basket. I think Col added a couple of cans of beer, too. We weren't sure how well provisioned you'd be.'

Owen was amused – and grateful. Everyone seemed to be concerned for his welfare. This must be what people meant when they talked about country hospitality, how people helped each other. It was very different from the city where you often didn't see your neighbours from one year to the next – might even never have met them. It would take a bit of getting used to. Owen loved company, could be quite the social animal when it suited him, but, at heart, he was someone who liked to keep his life private.

He was starting to realise that might not be possible here in Granite

Springs, where everyone seemed to know everyone else's business and gossip was a way of life. He was beginning to understand why Fran was the way she was. If you kept yourself to yourself, there was nothing for others to talk about.

'You'll help me eat this?' he asked Fran, when Jo had left after reminding Owen to drop over any time. 'There's far too much for me. I'd be eating it for a week.'

'All right,' she said reluctantly. 'But then, I'll have to be going. I have…' She frowned, then shook her head as if to dismiss an unpleasant thought.

'You said.' Owen wondered what it was about her evening engagement that made Fran appear so apprehensive.

He had an urge to smooth away the frown, to take her in his arms and tell her he'd make everything better.

Fourteen

All the way back to town, Fran regretted agreeing to Richard's dinner invitation. What was there to say that hadn't already been said? She'd refused his proposal of marriage – made, she was sure, in haste, in an unguarded moment as a result of her six-month absence. Maybe he now regretted it too, wanted to return to their previous footing, to the uncomplicated relationship they'd enjoyed for years.

But was enjoyed the right word? It had been comfortable, convenient, but enjoyable? The word conjured up a sense of joy, of delight in each other's company. And there had been none of that. Neither of them had looked for or wanted the degree of commitment that would have meant. At least, not until… Fran bit her lip, remembering Richard's seemingly impassioned plea, the champagne, the ring!

That bottle of Moët was still sitting in her fridge, accusing her every time she opened the door, making it impossible for her to forget Richard's face when the word "No" exploded from her lips like the bullet from a gun.

She sighed as she drove into her garage and went into the house to shower and change into an outfit Richard would approve of. It was tempting to choose something different, something that would shock him. But when she raked through her wardrobe, it was to discover that almost every one of the garments there would win his seal of approval. What had happened to her? How had she allowed herself to become so eager for his endorsement?

Or had it already happened long before she met Richard? Was

he merely the result of the woman she'd become, the woman who'd been so determined to forget the bright, lively girl, the girl who loved adventure, the girl who'd died on the back of Ben's bike, as surely as if she'd really lost her life? Part of her had died that day; her youth had died. She'd thought what she wanted was to build a barrier around her heart to prevent it being broken ever again. But she didn't want that any longer.

Suddenly, unbidden, the image of Owen Larsen appeared in her mind's eye as he'd been when she left. He'd been standing on the edge of the veranda, the two cats winding themselves around his ankles, his bare feet thrust into a worn pair of Nikes, one knee peeking through a tear in his jeans – not in a fashionable way. He was wearing an old checked flannel shirt, as if attempting to look like a genuine farmer, and his faded blond hair had been escaping from its tidy bun. He'd looked carefree and happy!

With no idea why she was thinking of him, Fran dismissed Owen from her mind as she dressed in the long-sleeved blue woollen dress and threw a grey pashmina across her shoulders to counteract the coolness of a Canberra evening. Taking time to style her streaked blonde hair just as Richard liked it, she made a face at herself in the mirror, before picking up her bag and leaving.

As she started the car, Fran tried to find a radio station to suit her mood, finally deciding on the quiz show on ABC. Trying to guess the answers would help take her mind off the evening ahead. Fran was glad she'd insisted on meeting Richard in the restaurant. She'd surprised herself, and Richard, by rejecting his suggestion they meet at his flat as usual for pre-dinner drinks. This time, she was determined to be in control. That was why she also refused when he said he'd make a booking at the Rubicon, instead saying she'd prefer somewhere smaller, less ostentatious. What she really meant was somewhere less romantic with fewer memories.

Reluctantly he'd agreed, and she was on her way to a little Italian place in the city she'd heard Nick mention when she worked for him. It was somewhere she hoped to be able to keep the conversation neutral and make Richard understand what they'd had together was really over.

Fran found a place to park and made her way into the small

restaurant where Richard was already seated at a secluded corner table. She bit her lip, wishing she'd been first to arrive. She'd have chosen a more public spot.

'Fran!' Richard rose to give her a peck on the cheek.

Grateful for his habitual reticence to make a public display of any affection, Fran merely smiled and took a seat opposite. Tonight, she noticed to her relief, there was no bottle of champagne. Instead he appeared to be drinking gin and tonic.

'What'll you have?'

'An aperro spritzer,' she said without hesitation. It was a drink Fran had discovered she enjoyed in England, on the few occasions she'd left her mother to meet old friends in the evening. There hadn't been many of those – friends or free evenings. But she'd enjoyed the respite when it was possible.

Richard raised one eyebrow but said nothing to her, merely placing the order. 'You've been well?' he asked.

'Yes, thank you. You?'

'Yes.' He took a sip of his drink and pursed his lips.

Fran wondered why she'd never noticed before how lacking in interesting conversation Richard was, compared to... *Owen.* She gasped.

'Something wrong?'

'No. Sorry. I must have swallowed the wrong way.' Fran took a quick sip of her drink to hide her confusion. She sneaked a glance at her companion. He and Owen Larsen were complete opposites. How could she even think of them together?

The waiter came with the menus, and Fran was able to avoid any further questions while she decided what to order. Richard, as always, studied his menu as carefully as he did everything, finally looking over it to meet Fran's eyes.

'I believe the pappardelle is particularly fine here,' he said.

She should have known. Rather than take her word for it, Richard had checked the place out. Suddenly, Fran lost her appetite. 'The risotto,' she said, closing her menu and placing it carefully on the table. Now she wished she hadn't come. What was she doing here with a man whose proposal of marriage she'd refused, who she no longer had any feelings for, if she ever had?

'A shiraz, I think,' Richard said, seemingly unaware of her discomfort.

'Not for me. I have to drive back.'

His lips tightened – just slightly, but Fran knew that expression. Richard was displeased. He couldn't have imagined…? But he probably had. He was so insensitive to others, lacking in sensitivity himself. He did most likely think she'd be willing, happy even, to carry on as before and go home with him – to his bed.

As the meal progressed, Fran became more and more uncomfortable as, much to her dismay, Richard continued to behave as if nothing in their relationship had changed. He talked of challenges at work, his successes on the stock market, upcoming theatre and a dinner dance he proposed they attend. *Had he completely misunderstood or was he being deliberately obtuse?*

Finally, the rice dish sticking in her throat, Fran laid down her cutlery. 'Richard,' she said as gently as possible, despite seething inside, 'have you heard nothing I've said? When I said "no" to you last time we met, that's exactly what I meant. I didn't need time to think about it. I had six months to think about it. I'm sorry. We had some good times together, but it's over.'

'But…' Richard's mouth fell open. He rubbed his forehead.

'I'm sorry,' Fran repeated. 'I shouldn't have come, shouldn't have raised your hopes.' Because, she realised that's exactly what she had done when she accepted this invitation.

Richard gazed at her, his eyes dull. He was sitting completely still. It was several moments before he spoke. 'I thought that's what you wanted – marriage,' he said at last.

He looked so pathetic, sitting there, blinking slowly. Fran felt tempted to tell him it had all been a mistake, that of course it was what she wanted. But the thought of spending the rest of her life with him, in this city, left her cold. She shook her head sadly, her eyes filling with tears for what, for them both, was the end of an era.

Richard made one more attempt. 'You won't find it so easy to meet someone new – at your age,' he said, with a bitterness she'd never heard him use before.

Telling herself it was his disappointment talking, fifty wasn't old, and she had no desire to meet or marry anyone, Fran drew herself together and swallowed before speaking. 'I'm sorry you feel that way,' she said, giving a weak smile. 'It might be better if I left now.'

All the way home, Fran regretted her decision to meet Richard one more time. She hadn't been fair to him. It had raised his hopes. How could she have been so stupid? It would be a long time before she'd allow herself to become involved with a man again. It was always doomed to end in disaster.

Fifteen

Fran had been subdued all week. In spite of Owen's various attempts at levity, describing the antics of the goats, his attempts to mend the broken connection on a water trough in the paddock, and his delight in living in the country, he failed to rouse a smile.

'Any plans for the weekend?' he asked, as they prepared for a meeting with Ron and Joshua on Friday afternoon. Owen couldn't wait for it to finish so he could head home and get ready for Pia and Darren's arrival. He'd offered to pick them up at the airport, but Pia had assured him Darren would prefer to hire a car. *Of course, he would!* But it made sense if he was off to Canberra next morning. Then Owen would have time alone with his daughter. He couldn't wait to show her around town and share his new home with her.

'Not really.' Fran sounded unhappy, as if something had upset her.

'Something wrong?' Owen knew he wasn't the best of people for her to confide in, but he had to try.

'Nothing.' Fran raised her eyes to meet his and smiled. 'I'm fine. Really.'

Not for the first time, Owen noticed her deep grey eyes. They were the colour of the sky on a cloudy day. He wondered what had happened to sadden her. It was only since last weekend, since… he remembered her rushing off to some engagement. That's when something or someone must have upset her.

'You?' she asked belatedly, perhaps recognising he was wound up, ready to burst with elation.

'My daughter's coming to visit.'

'Oh!' Fran's mouth widened into a genuine smile. 'I'm happy for you. You're settled in, then?'

'Pretty much. There wasn't much to do since the place is furnished. But you saw that.' He pulled on a loose strand of hair, deciding there and then to have it cut. 'What do you think?' he asked. 'Short back and sides?'

Fran gave him an incredulous stare. 'You're going to cut your…?' She gestured to the bun which sat on the back of his head, had done for years.

'I'm thinking maybe it's time. Now I'm a full professor,' he chuckled.

Fran cocked her head on one side and seemed to be assessing him. At least his suggestion appeared to have changed her mood. 'How long has it been?'

'Too long. I started to grow it when I was a student and that was…' he thought back. 'Hell, that was way over thirty years ago. It must be time for a new look.'

There was a silence in the room punctuated only by footsteps in the corridor and the sound of voices coming closer.

Owen regretted starting this conversation. *What had possessed him? Had it been a feeble attempt to get Fran to offer an opinion which wasn't related to work?* 'Forget it. I shouldn't have said anything,' Owen said, as Ron appeared at the door followed by Joshua.

'We're not meeting here, are we?' Ron asked, his eyes taking in the tiny office which was clearly too small for four of them to sit in comfortably.

'Shut up, Ron,' Joshua said. 'If we bring in another couple of chairs…'

'No.' Fran was herself again. 'Owen has a better idea.' She looked at him for support.

Thinking quickly, Owen came up with a solution. He reached into a pocket. 'It so happens I have the security code.' He held up a card. 'The contractors finished early and this was handed to me today. It should get us in. I thought it might be appropriate to meet there. It'll have to be in one of the lecture theatres as the office furniture hasn't been delivered yet, but…'

He heard Joshua give a whistle of approval, followed by a grunt from Ron. There was no pleasing the man who regularly appeared in Owen's office with one complaint after another. If there had been any other option, Owen would have handed him back to Nick with thanks. But, until the new staff were appointed, he was stuck with these two to help set up course materials and timetables for next year.

'When are you interviewing for new staff?' Joshua asked, as if reading his mind.

It was Fran who answered. 'Next week,' she said. 'There's a good selection. It seems word has got around about our new building and Professor Larsen.'

'Our *Professor* Larsen,' Ron said, sarcastically, his face taking on a sullen expression.

Owen felt his temperature rise. He clenched his fists.

'Let's go,' Fran said, before the two came to blows.

Once inside the new building, Owen was in his element. He'd pored over the plans when he first arrived but, apart from a few forays inside when the workmen were elsewhere, he hadn't really seen it. The other three followed while he led them through meeting rooms, offices, rehearsal room with carefully designed acoustics, and finally, into one of the smaller lecture theatres. Even grumpy Ron seemed impressed, though Owen could tell he still thought *he* should be the one in charge.

'Now,' Owen said, when they were settled in the theatre. He was perched on the edge of the podium while the others were seated in the front row. He looked up towards the back of the tiered seating, imagining it filled with students – his students – and a shiver ran up his spine. This is why he was here. This is what it was all about.

'Owen?'

Fran's voice brought him back down to earth.

'I have the agenda.'

'Surely we don't need an agenda? It's only us. We know what we're about,' Ron objected, his earlier appreciative comments seemingly forgotten.

'We need to make sure we document all our decisions.' It was Fran at her most precise. The softer woman he'd caught a glimpse of out at the property on Saturday had disappeared. Something had happened to her. Owen was sure of that. But now wasn't the time to find out what it was.

'Fran's right,' he said. 'Annoying as it may be. The university has spent a lot of money of this school and…' he heard Ron mutter something under his breath, but decided to ignore it, '…we're going to be held accountable for every decision.'

'I'm good with that.' Joshua stretched out his legs and crossed them at the ankles. 'Let's have it, Fran. And stop being such a sourpuss, Ron. Just admit you missed out. Owen's in charge, and you have to accept it. We have to work together. How are the students going to react if they think we're fighting among ourselves?'

Owen was surprised, but grateful for Joshua's support, more so when Ron calmed down and accepted the agenda Fran handed him without any further complaint. 'Thanks, Josh,' he said, only to receive a glare from Ron. He sighed. 'Item one,' he began.

The meeting went well. By the end of it, they'd come to an agreement on which of the university's core courses could be included in the new degrees and decided on the most immediate tasks to be completed.

Walking back to the education building, Owen tried again to get Fran to open up to him without success. He wasn't sure why it irked him that he was finding her so difficult to read. She was only his assistant, after all, and although she was good at her job, she could always be replaced. But he felt a pang of something he couldn't identify at the thought she might not be there to share coffee with each morning, realising she'd inadvertently become an important part of his life.

*

Owen's heart began to beat faster when he saw the car drive through the gate, then a slim figure with long blonde hair standing by, ready to close it again. The car itself looked incongruous in this setting. He should have been able to predict Darren would choose a model more suited to city streets than the country roads he was driving on.

'Hi, Dad!' Pia stepped out of the sleek Mercedes and shook out her hair, before running over to give Owen a hug. Darren followed more slowly, bending down first to examine the paintwork for damage. 'Your hair!' she said, staring at him in amazement

'Lovely to see you, sweetheart,' Owen said, returning her hug. He was glad he'd taken time on his way home to visit a hairdresser to have his long locks shorn, though the new style made him feel lightheaded. 'Like it? I thought it was time your old man moved forward.' Then he turned to Darren who was frowning. 'Darren.' He held out his hand.

'Damned country roads,' Darren said, glaring back at the dirt access road. 'You didn't tell me we'd be in the sticks, Pia. If I have to pay for any damage to the car, I will not be happy.'

'I didn't know…' Pia began, but Owen interrupted.

'Don't know why you had to hire such an expensive model,' he said, though he knew very well. It was so like Darren to want to impress in any way he could – demonstrate his importance to the simple uni lecturer. Owen was just surprised Granite Springs airport could provide him with a car like this.

Darren didn't reply but focussed on taking their cases out of the car.

Leading Pia into the house, Owen tried to subdue his dislike for her companion. It was only for tonight. He'd be gone in the morning, and Owen would have Pia to himself for two whole days. Though Darren would be back again on Sunday.

'This is nice, Dad,' Pia said, as they walked into the large family kitchen where the two cats were warming themselves in a basket by the Aga. 'You didn't tell me it would be like this.'

'I didn't?' Owen scratched his head. He couldn't remember exactly what he'd told her about the place. 'You'll be able to get a better look in the morning. When does Darren have to leave?'

'Early.' She sighed. 'I wish…' she said, her pretty mouth turning down, then she took Owen by the arm and said in a more cheerful voice, 'Now, show me the whole house. I can't believe you're really living in such an isolated spot.'

By the time they returned to the kitchen, Darren was standing in the middle of the room beside the two weekend cases. He looked distinctly ill-at-ease in his city suit and tie. The cats had barely moved, clearly deciding he wasn't a friend.

While the two young people were settling in and freshening up, Owen checked the lamb casserole he'd prepared earlier, thanks to his neighbour's suggestion. Jo and Col Ford had proved to be the perfect neighbours – helpful, but not overly so. The three of them had enjoyed a drink together in the week he'd been here, and Jo had been generous with her advice on country cooking, sharing family recipes with him, especially when she heard of Pia's visit. He only hoped, when he found an acreage of his own, his neighbours there would be equally friendly.

'That was lovely, Dad,' Pia said, putting down her cutlery and pushing away the empty plate. 'I didn't know you could cook like that. Have you been taking lessons?'

Darren gave a mocking laugh. 'Quite the hausfrau, eh, Owen,' he sneered.

Owen clenched his teeth, reminding himself this was his daughter's choice.

'Though I don't know how you can bear to hide yourself away in this hick place after Sydney,' Darren said. 'I wouldn't be able to stand it.'

'No, I don't expect you would,' Owen replied, 'but I like it here. And Granite Springs is a nice town.'

Darren snorted

'*I'm* looking forward to looking around, Dad,' Pia said, glaring at Darren.

Owen sent his daughter a warm smile. She was a good kid, even if her taste in men left a lot to be desired.

'We'll go into town tomorrow,' he promised. 'And Jo and Col – my neighbours – have invited us to dinner tomorrow evening, unless you'd rather do something else?'

'No, that sounds good. I'd like to meet some locals.'

Owen nodded, ignoring Darren's veiled comment of, "country yokels". 'More wine?' he asked, checking the bottle of shiraz which was still half-full.

'Not for me.' Pia yawned. 'I'm for bed. Darren?'

Darren made a show of yawning too, though Owen had the impression he'd have been happy to finish the bottle if it didn't mean having to suffer Owen's company to do so. 'I'll join you,' he said. 'I need to get off early, Owen,' he said, 'so…'

'I rise early out here,' Owen replied. 'Breakfast at six-thirty do?'

A surprised Darren agreed.

'Not for me, Dad. I'm looking forward to a relaxing weekend and I plan to sleep late. 'Night.' She blew her father a kiss and disappeared, Darren following with barely an acknowledgement.

Owen cleared the table and turned off the lights before heading to bed himself. It was a good feeling to have Pia under his roof again. He was looking forward to sharing his new life with her. He just hoped she'd see Darren for what he was – an ambitious, arrogant prick who cared more for himself than anyone else, her included.

Sixteen

Another Saturday! Fran had managed to get through the week without thinking too much about her dinner with Richard the previous weekend. But there had been the odd occasion when she'd felt bad about the hurt she'd caused him.

This morning, she planned to visit the library, then see if Kay and Jo were in Mouthfuls. They'd told her to join them anytime, but she'd been hesitant about it till now. After her visit to Jo's home, however, she was more comfortable with her and, for the first time ever, Fran felt the need for women friends.

Was this part of the new Fran, she wondered, as she checked out the latest book by Ann Cleeves, before heading to the café.

'Fran, lovely to see you!' Jo greeted her, Kay giving her a big smile.

'You don't mind?'

'Of course not. We meant it when we said to join us anytime. Owen seems to be settling in well,' Jo said.

Fran smiled cagily. She hadn't come here to talk about her boss, though why had she come?

'Nick and I haven't seen much of either of you this week,' Kay said. 'But I heard the building's finished, so you'll be moving in soon.'

'Yes.' Fran was on comfortable ground talking about work, but, once her coffee arrived, the conversation changed.

'Is everything all right, Fran?' Jo asked, concern in her voice. 'I don't mean to pry but when you walked in, you seemed troubled.'

'No, I'm...' To her embarrassment, Fran found her eyes fill with tears. She brushed them away. 'Sorry. I don't know what came over me.'

'Is it Owen? Is he being difficult?' Kay asked. 'I can speak to Nick…'

'No! Owen's been great.' Fran thought of how her new boss had gone overboard to make her feel indispensable. She managed a small laugh. 'It's me. I…' She looked across the table at the two women whose faces now both radiated sympathy. This was something new for her. Before now, she'd always kept herself very much to herself, unwilling to share anything about her personal life. But maybe it was time to change that.

'There's this man I've been seeing…' she began.

By the time she'd finished explaining about Richard and blaming herself, Fran's coffee was cold.

While Kay went up to order three more coffees, Jo put a hand on Fran's on the table. 'You did the right thing,' she said. 'You have nothing to blame yourself for. In my opinion you let the guy down lightly. Though I can't talk from experience. I have only Gordon and Col to compare him to, and Kay's not in a much better position.'

'What position is that?' Kay asked, returning in time to hear Jo's last words.

'I'm just telling Fran neither of us have much experience with men,' Jo said.

'Jo's right,' Kay said, 'but what else could you have done? It would have been even more unkind to have continued in a relationship that wasn't going anywhere.'

'Thanks.' Fran felt as if a load had been lifted from her shoulders. She respected these women who were several years older than she was. They might dismiss their lack of experience with men, but they'd seen a lot of life. If Fran had learnt anything in her years in Granite Springs, it was that this town was a microcosm of towns everywhere.

'Oh, this is a neat place, Dad.'

All three looked round as the young woman's clear voice carried over the sound of the café's espresso-maker.

'Owen Larsen!' Jo was first to recover. 'This must be your daughter.'

'Pia. Yes.' Owen walked over to their table, followed by the young woman. 'Pia, these are friends of mine – Jo, Kay and Fran. Fran's my PA.'

Fran experienced a flutter of pleasure. *What triggered that?* She saw Pia inspect them carefully before smiling her greeting.

'Dad's showing me around the town,' she said. 'We've already been to the university campus and the botanic gardens.' Then she stopped and gave Jo a closer look. 'Jo – are you the neighbour who's invited us to dinner?'

'That's me.' Jo smiled. 'Col and I are looking forward to seeing you and your dad at Yarran.'

'Yarran?'

'That's the name of our property. It's called after an acacia tree.'

'Really? I'm looking forward to visiting it.' Then she turned to Owen. 'Do they do chai latte here, Dad?'

'I'm sure they do. Sorry, ladies,' he apologised. 'See you tonight, Jo.'

'Looking forward to it,' Jo said as the pair left to sit at another table.

'So that's his daughter,' Kay whispered. 'She's a lovely girl. Doesn't take after her father.'

'He's not so bad,' Fran objected. She was reeling from the surprise of seeing his new haircut. He'd threatened to do it, but Fran hadn't taken him seriously. She couldn't get over how different he looked – less like a hippie, more… sexy! She gulped.

The two others give her an appraising glance.

'No, I don't mean…' she said, embarrassed.

'We didn't think you did,' Jo said in a comforting tone. 'But he does have a certain something – especially with the new hair. He's brushed up pretty well, today. And I guess he smartens himself up at the university?' She looked enquiringly at Fran and Kay.

'Don't ask me. I don't see much of him. Fran?' Kay asked.

Fran reddened. 'Sometimes,' she said. 'I'm sure he will when he has classes. The school doesn't open till next year.'

'Would you like to come to dinner tonight, too?' Jo asked, as if it had suddenly occurred to her. 'It would take your mind off that Richard guy. We'd love to have you.'

'No. Thanks very much, Jo. But I'll be fine. It was good to get it off my chest this morning. I'm used to my own company.'

Owen and his daughter were engrossed in conversation when the three women left. Fran debated interrupting to say goodbye, but chose not to, instead managing a wave and Owen waved back. She farewelled Jo and Kay and walked home, thinking how much she'd enjoyed the company of the two women – women she'd only come to know in the past few weeks, but whom she now counted as friends. Maybe that's what had been missing in her life. She'd been so intent on keeping herself locked up, maintaining that calm exterior, she'd all but forgotten how to make friends.

She had no need for a man in her life. She'd stick to her new friends for company and maybe get herself a pet. She remembered Jo's old dog, Owen's cats. Which would she prefer?

Seventeen

The two days with Pia passed quickly. The dinner at Jo and Col's was a success, Pia charming them with amusing tales of her recruitment experiences, some of which were familiar to Owen, but many he hadn't heard before. She made hardly any reference to Darren, for which he was grateful. He was dreading his return.

In a vain attempt to instil some sort of celebration into their Sunday evening, Owen booked a table at The Riverside. Surely that would impress even the jaded Darren? Though maybe not. It was difficult to imagine him being impressed with anything about Granite Springs – he seemed to have decided to dislike the town even before the plane touched down. At least Owen and Pia could enjoy the meal in Granite Springs' finest restaurant, which he'd learned last night was co-owned by Jo and her son.

Owen watched from the window as Pia went out to welcome Darren back. She threw her arms around his neck, obviously delighted to see him. But, Owen noted, the man only kissed her perfunctorily on the lips, before removing her arms and bending into the back of the car to remove his bag. He pursed his lips. Was this merely the desire to avoid overt affection in front of Owen, or a sign of a fracture in their relationship. While he hoped it was the latter for his own sake, he knew Pia would be devastated.

All seemed well between them when they entered the house, Pia flourishing a gaily coloured scarf. 'Look what Darren brought me from Canberra, Dad. Isn't it lovely?'

Owen nodded and forced a smile onto his face.

Over a beer to welcome the traveller back, Owen mentioned the dinner booking. 'It's the best Granite Springs has to offer,' he said. 'I haven't dined there myself as yet, but I hear good things about it.'

'Dad's neighbour – the one we had dinner with last night – they live over there,' Pia pointed across the paddock where the goats were lazily grazing, 'she and her son own it.'

'A family business?'

Did Owen detect a sneer in Darren's voice, or was he being oversensitive? 'I guess you could call it that,' he said easily. 'Would you like another beer before you freshen up? The table's booked for half-seven.'

'Thanks, but it was quite a drive. Think I may take a few minutes to lie down. Pia?'

Pia dutifully followed Darren out of the room with an apologetic glance at her father.

Owen sighed. She'd made her bed and now it seemed she was going to lie on it, because he was in no doubt what Darren had in mind when he nodded towards the bedroom. Pouring another beer for himself, Owen went outside. He had no desire to be party to the lovemaking that would be going on inside the house.

It had been some time since he'd been involved in any relationship, sexual or otherwise. He hadn't met anyone he liked well enough to spend time with. That's what he liked so much about this place, he thought, watching the goats wander around, breathing in the fresh country air. There was no one and nothing to disturb his thoughts – or to be disturbed by his music. He thought longingly of his keyboard sitting idle in the study which he now called his music room, being much more at home with his music than a computer – and the new one to be delivered to his office on campus. At her insistence, he'd played a bit for Pia earlier in the day, but he knew it would bore Darren to hear him.

He finished his beer and went back inside to feed the cats. He'd become quite attached to them. They were good company, didn't require conversation, and seemed to enjoy his playing. What more could a man ask for?

'We're ready, Dad!' Pia wafted into the living room in shades of pink and white, her long blonde hair falling on her shoulders in a cloud of golden curls.

She was so like Brit it took his breath away. But Brit didn't look like that anymore. She'd aged in the years they'd been apart; the alcohol and cigarettes she continued to enjoy had taken their toll. 'You look lovely, darling,' he said, his gaze moving past her to Darren who was still dressed in the suit he'd worn to his Canberra meeting. While very smart, Owen thought he was a tad overdressed for their dinner. He saw Darren give his own pressed jeans teamed with a blue shirt and denim jacket a disgusted scowl. *Snap*, he thought.

When they walked into the restaurant, Owen was surprised to see it was almost full. He was glad he'd thought to book ahead. A tall, broad shouldered man showed them to their table and handed them menus.

'This is lovely, Dad,' Pia said, looking out through the large window at the river below, shimmering in the moonlight. 'What do you think?' she nudged Darren.

'I suppose it's not bad for a country town,' he said, his usual sneer curling on his lips. He studied the menu. 'At least they seem to have some decent steak.'

'Thanks for this, Dad.' Pia laid a hand on Owen's arm in an attempt to mitigate her partner's disdain.

Owen smiled at his daughter, determined to ignore the negativity of her companion. He was pleased with his choice of restaurant. From what he could see, it rivalled anywhere he'd eaten in Sydney.

'Dad's been showing me around, Darren,' she said, taking his arm. 'Granite Springs is a nice town. It's bigger than I thought it would be, and the university campus is really something. You should see the new building where Dad will be working.'

'Hmm,' was Darren's reply.

Owen ignored him. 'What'll you have, Pia?' he asked. 'I'm thinking of the salmon dish.'

'I'll have that, too,' she said.

'Steak for me,' Darren said. 'I wouldn't trust fish in a country town. You can't be sure how fresh it'll be.' He seemed determined to put a damper on the evening.

Owen pressed his lips together tightly. 'Right.' He checked the wine menu and, without asking the others' preference, decided to order a pinot noir from the Adelaide Hills. He didn't care what Darren thought of his choice. He wanted to celebrate this visit, his arrival in town, and his new home.

Pia chatted gaily for most of the meal, seemingly unaware – or unconcerned – with Darren's determination to maintain a superior attitude.

Why couldn't the guy just relax and enjoy himself? But he seemed intent on proving how much he despised this town where Owen had decided to settle. By the time the meal was over, Owen was having trouble containing his rage. Normally placid and laidback, only Pia's presence prevented him from telling Darren exactly what he thought of him. But Pia was obviously smitten and blind to his faults. This guy could become his son-in-law. Owen shuddered at the thought.

Eighteen

'Good weekend?' Fran asked, when Owen arrived on Monday morning, carrying the usual two coffees, and settled into a chair in her office. It amused her he treated it as if it was an extension of his – or the one he was currently using – which was one of the more spacious offices on the upper level of the building. Today he was casually dressed in three-quarter canvas pants and a white tee-shirt, his feet in brown leather sandals – more suitable attire for the beach than a university campus – unless you were a student. As usual, Fran was wearing a pair of tailored pants, teamed this morning with a smart white shirt.

'Good to see my daughter,' he said, taking a gulp of coffee. 'God, that's good!' He licked his lips. 'But that partner of hers. Give me strength!'

Fran chuckled, but it sounded as if his weekend had been more eventful than hers.

'Went to that restaurant on the river,' he continued. 'The Riverside. Pretty good place. Know it?'

'I've been there a few times,' Fran admitted, remembering how Richard had barely acknowledged Granite Springs could possibly have a top-class restaurant and tried, unsuccessfully, to find fault with the service, the meal and the surroundings.

'We had a first-class meal there, but that damned Darren did his best to disparage it at every turn.'

'Like Richard.'

'Who?'

Fran didn't realise she'd spoken aloud. 'Richard,' she said more slowly. 'Someone I used to know.' It was good to refer to him in the past tense, though she wasn't altogether sure she'd heard the last of him.

'That the guy you were meeting last weekend – the one who upset you?'

How did he know?

'Sorry?'

'Oh, did I put my big foot in it? I tend to do that. Brit always told me I don't know when to keep my mouth shut. But…' he gestured with his coffee, '…when you helped me move in, you were in a rush to go off somewhere, then last week, you were out of sorts. I just put two and two together…' he peered at Fran. '…and made five. Sorry! None of my business. But if you want to talk about it, I'm all ears.'

Fran didn't know what to say. Owen was right. Of course he was. But she wasn't going to discuss her personal life with him, even if he was sitting there in her office, had brought her coffee, and looked to all intents and purposes like an older brother. Or? He looked as she could imagine Ben might look if he'd survived into his fifties, despite the difference in hair colour, though Ben might have gone grey by now, too.

Shocked by this revelation, Fran drained her coffee and stood up.

'Okay. You want me to get out of your hair.' Owen crushed the cardboard cup and dropped it in the bin, gave Fran a grin, and left.

Alone again, Fran covered her face with her hands. What was she thinking? Owen had hit a hot button, making her mention Richard. But what had taken her back to a place she didn't want to go? Ben! He'd have been Owen's age now if he'd lived. And there was something about Owen that reminded her of the carefree youth. Would they have stayed together? How different would her life have been? What would he have made of the woman she'd become?

Deciding to dismiss such fanciful thoughts, because that's what they were – fanciful – Fran turned back to her computer to check the minutes of Friday's meeting. It was two hours later when she raised her head again to hear her phone vibrating and to see she had a text. It was from Jo.

Good to chat on Sat. I have to be in town today. Can we have coffee – just us? I can come to the campus. Jo.

Fran sat looking at it for a little time. She liked Jo, would enjoy getting to know her better. But Jo was Kay's friend. Would Kay feel she was going behind her back to meet her on her own? Fran gave herself a shake. They were grown women. They could make up their own minds who they met or didn't meet. And she knew Kay was tied up in faculty meetings all day. Fran remembered how it had been when she was Nick's PA. How different her days were now. Whereas before, she'd been Nick's secretary, now, she sometimes felt she was Owen's mother!

She chuckled to herself at the realisation. Owen was intelligent, good at his job, quite possibly a master musician, but when it came to everyday matters, he could be completely useless. As if thinking of him made him appear, Owen walked in carrying a bundle of papers which he tossed onto her desk.

'Here's what you wanted me to check out,' he said. 'The core course outlines,' he added, seeing her look of surprise. 'And, yes, I did them without being reminded. Now I'm going to take an early mark. It's been so dry the paddocks are parched and I'm worried about the goats. Col suggested I supplement their feed with goat pellets. I can get them at the Co-op in town. So, if it's all right with you, that's what I'll be doing for the rest of the day. If anyone is looking for me, can you tell them I'm…'

'I'll tell them you have a dentist appointment,' Fran said, stifling a laugh, and picturing Owen wandering around the paddock, sprinkling pellets and being followed by his herd of goats. Life certainly wasn't dull with him around. But it left her free to meet Jo. She dashed off a quick reply.

*

Three o'clock saw Fran closing her computer and heading to Banjo's. She felt slightly guilty at taking time off in the afternoon and had to remind herself she was virtually her own boss these days, especially with her actual boss looking after his goats. Goats! She shook her head in amazement. Who'd have thought the musician from Sydney would end up caring for a herd of goats?

As Fran neared the café, she saw Jo strolling there from the other direction, looking as elegant as usual, but in a casual way. Maybe she could give Fran some hints. In her attempt to always keep up her professional appearance, Fran knew she sometimes went too far. She looked down at her present attire with a grimace. Then she gave herself a shake. This look had been good enough for her for years; what had changed?

But Fran knew *she* had changed. Since her mother had died, since her fiftieth birthday, it was as if something had moved inside her, something that made her want to come alive.

'Fran, lovely to see you!' Jo greeted her with a peck on the cheek, making Fran immediately glad she'd agreed to have coffee.

'You, too,' she replied. 'Thanks for the invitation. I'm afraid I don't often take time out in the afternoon,' she said, realising how silly that sounded.

'Well, I'm glad you decided to meet me today. Is Owen such a hard taskmaster? He didn't strike me that way.'

By this time, they were inside the café, and Fran laughed. 'Hardly! He went off early today to see to his goats. I swear he's become besotted with them.'

'Farming gets some people that way,' Jo grinned. 'Col too, even though we don't have any animals, if you discount old Scout. He lived in town all his life till we got together and now he's reading up on all sorts of stuff. I think he might be to blame for today's goat interest. They were talking about it over dinner on Saturday, and I believe Col offered to help. Now, what'll you have? My shout.'

'You don't need to…'

But Jo was already on her way to the counter, saying, 'You're a latte, aren't you?'

Fran nodded and took a seat at a nearby table. She wasn't in the habit of having coffee in the afternoon either, lest it keep her awake at night. But today, she decided not to let it worry her. Which was all the more surprising when, once seated, Jo asked, 'Is there something worrying you?'

'Me? Nothing,' Fran said, but avoided Jo's eyes, sensing her own cloud over.

'Here you are, ladies, one latte and one cappuccino.' The waitress set down the coffees and Fran lifted her eyes to thank her, meeting Jo's in the process. They were filled with concern, so much that Fran almost broke down.

'Sorry. It's been a bit of a strange day,' she said. 'Something happened to make me think of the past, of what my life might have been like if...' She rubbed her eyes.

'Do you want to talk about it?'

Fran shook her head to clear it. Maybe she did, and Jo would be the ideal person.

Seeming to understand Fran wasn't shaking her head to refuse, Jo said, 'I know a little about when you first came to Granite Springs.'

'How?' Fran's eyes widened.

'It was in all the papers. You were quite a celebrity – no, that's the wrong word. But it made quite a splash – the unknown young woman who'd survived a dreadful accident. You were still in hospital at the time.'

'No one ever said.'

'People in this community can be sensitive when it suits them. I suspect they felt you had enough to cope with, then as time went on, it disappeared from their minds as other more immediate things took over. He was your partner?'

Fran nodded, the words taking her back. She pictured the impersonal hospital room. 'I remember waking up,' she said. 'I didn't know where I was. Then they told me – about Ben...'

'That was his name?'

'Ben Holland. He was so full of life. I couldn't believe he was gone, gone forever. Then,' Fran heaved a sigh. 'I was pregnant. I discovered I'd lost the baby.'

'Oh, my dear! I had no idea.'

'I was a mess. I couldn't imagine going back to Sydney without Ben. That's why I stayed in Granite Springs. The town seemed to enfold me. I felt safe here.'

'You've never formed another serious relationship, wanted children? The man you mentioned you'd been seeing?' Jo's voice was tentative, as if realising she was touching on something that was difficult for Fran.

'Richard? No – he wasn't who I wanted in my future. And as regards children – the accident put paid to that.' She wiped the corners of her eyes which were gathering moisture.

'I'm so sorry. I can't imagine how you must have felt.'

It was a relief to Fran to have told someone the truth she'd bottled up inside for all those years, but, looking at Jo's concerned face, she saw what she'd dreaded – pity! 'So, there you have it,' she said. 'That's my story. I thought I'd put it all behind me, then… this morning, it all came back in a rush.'

Jo didn't say anything. She picked up her cup and drank some coffee.

'It was Owen,' Fran said. 'For some reason, this morning, he reminded me of Ben – of how Ben was. It made me wonder what he'd be like now if we'd have stayed together. I'm sorry, it was stupid of me. You don't want to hear all this.'

'No, it's not stupid at all. Was it something Owen said?'

'No. He was just being himself, and it suddenly occurred to me that Ben might have turned out like him. They're alike in some ways – both very spontaneous, with a disregard for convention or what people think. The exact opposite of Richard.'

'The man you were seeing?'

'Yes.'

'And very different from you these days, too, I'd guess.'

'Mmm. I used to be like that, without a care in the world. Then I came to understand that life is fleeting – it can be taken from you in an instant. I became more cautious.'

'And you're thinking maybe it's time to let go a bit?'

'No! At least I don't think so.' Fran frowned. She picked up her cup in both hands, cradling it while she considered Jo's comment. 'I hadn't thought of it that way.' She caught sight of her reflection in the café window, noticing the short streaked blonde hair almost sculpted to her head, the neatly starched white shirt. Did she seem as unapproachable as she looked? Was this how she appeared to Owen?

'How do I seem to you?' she asked Jo. 'Am I… unapproachable?'

'I wouldn't say that, exactly,' Jo replied. 'More… self-contained. You give the impression you're sufficient in yourself, that you don't need anyone else in your life. There's nothing wrong with being like that. In fact, many would envy your self-sufficiency. But am I right in thinking you suddenly feel it's not enough?'

'You're very perceptive. But enough about me. What's happening in your life?'

After giving Fran a wary glance as if to ensure she was really happy to change the subject, Jo related the latest news about her family. She prefaced it by saying, 'You don't mind hearing about the grandchildren, do you?' and, taking Fran's shake of the head as consent, continued. Finally, she said, 'Remember it's the Granite Springs Show in a couple of weeks – on the October long weekend. You'll be there?'

'I don't think so.' Fran had never attended the show in all the years she'd lived here. She hated crowds of people, and there were sure to be them in spades at the annual agricultural show. 'I suppose you'll be part of the Country Women's Association stall?'

'No fear. Not my scene. I just enjoy wandering around, seeing everything, and I love to watch the dog trials. Your new boss will be there,' Jo added, as if counting that as an incentive for Fran to attend. 'Do come! We'll be there, too, with Nick and Kay. We can make a day of it.'

Fran was tempted. It would be a first step, but a first step to what? And did she really want to appear to be paired up with Owen at such a popular community event?

Nineteen

Driving home, Owen puzzled over Fran's reaction this morning. He thought he'd only been behaving like a concerned friend. Richard! That's the name she mentioned. Was he her boyfriend, her significant other? If so, he didn't seem to be making her very happy. Owen was willing to bet he was a pompous ass. Fran was too uptight herself. She needed someone to draw her out, to help her see life was meant to be lived, enjoyed. It was too short to spend being safe and circumspect. She needed someone like – him!

Owen pictured Fran as she'd been this morning – and every morning – not a hair out of place, makeup immaculate, neatly dressed, bandbox pretty, controlled. He had a strong urge to see her lose that tight control, become dishevelled, do something outrageous. The closest she'd come to that was when she helped him move, but even then, in casual clothes, she'd managed to retain her innate sense of correctness. Yet he sensed there was a warm, vulnerable woman underneath the façade she presented to the world, and he'd dearly like to uncover her.

Once home, he unloaded the bags of pellets he'd bought and stored them in the shed, only opening one. He carried this one into the paddock and began sprinkling the small green cylinder-shaped pellets made from compressed lucerne on the ground, amused how the goats immediately headed towards him and began to follow the trail of pellets. This was easy.

'Hi there! You're becoming quite the farmer.'

Owen looked up to see Col leaning on the fence, his eyes twinkling in amusement. 'Just following instructions,' he said. 'Have you heard from John and Bernadette?' he asked, emptying the last of the feed, going over to the fence, and leaning one elbow on the fencepost.

'Had an email yesterday,' Col replied. 'They've made it to Queensland and decided to stay put for a bit before moving farther north. Seem to be enjoying life on the road, though I wouldn't fancy it myself.'

'It would have its advantages,' Owen said, thinking of the freedom it would offer, 'but a pity to leave all this.' He gestured to the open paddocks and the goats, who were now happily grazing on their new feed and biting and butting each other.

'I was about to have a beer,' Col said. 'Care to join me? Jo's in town.'

'I'll just clean up and be with you. Won't be long.'

Owen disposed of the empty sack, then went inside to freshen up and rid himself of the smell. A glance in the mirror also had him change into a clean tee-shirt, noticing as he did so that the laundry basket was full again. There was so much to do here, and he enjoyed just sitting around doing nothing. He also wanted to find time to try out the bike which was sitting in the shed waiting for him. Maybe he could find a student who was looking for some part-time work to help him out.

'Just in time. I'd almost given you up,' Col joked, when Owen knocked on the back door of the farmhouse. 'Kept your beer cold for you.' He handed Owen a bottle of Crown Lager dripping with moisture.

'Thanks, mate.' Owen took the bottle and settled in a chair next to Col on the veranda. Scout settled at their feet and Col dropped a hand to lazily scratch the dog's head.

'Your daughter seems a nice girl,' Col said. 'She and her fellow gone back to Sydney now?'

'Yeah. Left on the early plane this morning. She's a good kid, but I don't know about him.' He shook his head. 'Arrogant bastard,' he muttered.

'One of those?' Col chuckled. 'There are a few around. Helped get rid of one earlier in the year. It's harder if the girl's still enamoured with him which I guess she is?'

Owen nodded and took a slug of beer. He didn't want to discuss Pia's love life or his disappointment in her choice. 'You and Jo have a great place here,' he said instead. 'It's about the same size as John and Bernadette's, isn't it?'

'Twenty acres,' Col said. 'It's Jo's really. She and Gordon – her first husband – had the house built on what was a soldier's settlement. They gave these blocks of land to returned soldiers after the First World War, presumably as a thank-you for serving their country. Though, how they expected anyone to make a living from a parcel of land like this is anyone's guess.'

'Are there many of them around – blocks like this, I mean? It's exactly the sort of thing I'm looking for myself. Ideally, I'd like to find one before John and Bernadette get back, so I don't have to endure student housing again. I'm a bit long in the tooth for that lark.' He grimaced.

'They don't often come onto the market, but I'll keep my ear to the ground. Might be worth having a chat with a mate of mine – Ken Thompson, he owns the real estate business close to my old office. He and I were at school together. He's a stock and station agent too. He might know of something. Tell him I sent you. Or...' Col seemed to be considering carefully before adding, '...there's Jo's son, Danny. But he seems to specialise in development blocks. I don't expect you want to start from scratch?'

'Thanks. I would prefer a property with an existing house on it. I checked out a few realters when I first hit town. Can't remember the names offhand.'

The two men sat in silence for a time, enjoying the peaceful scene and their thoughts. Finally, Owen rose to go.

'Don't forget the show,' Col called after Owen as he was leaving. 'It's the highlight of the year for folks like us – and those with much larger properties. It's been a difficult year for the farmers with the lack of rain – makes the chance to get together and let their hair down even more important.'

'Right.' Owen ambled off. He'd all but forgotten about the Granite Springs Show. It was to be held on the Saturday of the October long weekend, the annual public holiday otherwise known as Labour Day – celebrating the eight-hour working day. Owen doubted any of the farmers around here – or anywhere else in the country – knew what an eight-hour working day looked like.

He wondered if Fran would be there. She seemed to be friends with this group of people. It could provide the opportunity he was looking for to get to know her better – away from the university campus.

Owen whistled as he made his way home along the lane, surprised to meet an elderly woman walking with two greyhounds.

'You'll be the new man at John and Bernie's,' she said, stopping to allow the dogs to sniff at his heels. 'I'm Magda. I live up there.' She pointed to a small cottage in the distance.

'Owen,' he said, shaking her hand, which she held for a tad longer than was necessary.

'The woman in your thoughts has been troubled,' she said. 'You need to be patient. It will all work out in the end.'

She continued on her way, and he gazed after her scratching his head in amazement. What the hell was she talking about? Was she a witch or just some crazy woman?

Twenty

It was show day! Fran looked out at the sky as she ate her customary breakfast of muesli and sliced banana with yoghurt. She was a creature of habit and had been eating the same breakfast for over twenty years. The sky was clear and blue, but she'd seen on the television last night that storms were forecast. It would be good to have some rain. The country was parched – tinder dry and ready to flare up at any moment. She just hoped any rain would hold off till evening.

Although she wasn't sure she really wanted to go to the event, Fran had given her word to Jo, and didn't want to break it. But she had misgivings about being in the same party as her new boss. Strangely, she had no such qualms about Nick, even though he'd been her boss for ten years. Somehow, her friendship with Kay, and her move away from his office, had changed how she regarded him. Or was it just that Owen was Owen, and nothing to do with the fact he was her boss?

Fran dressed in a summery dress in keeping with the heat of the day, determined to keep her reservations to herself and try to enjoy the outing.

The showground was swarming with people when Fran arrived. She wondered how on earth she'd find Jo and the others and was on the point of returning to her car, when her phone vibrated with a text.

Are you here yet? We're all in the tea enclosure. Can you make your way here? Kay

With a sigh Fran returned her phone to her pocket. She wasn't going to be able to change her mind. Following the signs, she pushed her way through the crowds to the large marquee set up as the tea area.

'Here she is!' a voice called, and Fran saw her friends, along with Owen, seated on white plastic chairs around a makeshift table. Weaving her way between other similar tables filled with cheerful strangers, Fran finally reached the group.

'You must try these scones,' Jo said, when Fran was settled at the table between her and Kay and had managed to snag a cup of tea so strong the spoon could almost stand up in it. 'They're so light.'

Fran eyed the plate of scones, sitting alongside dishes of strawberry jam and whipped cream, and reached for one. She normally watched what she ate, and scones with jam and cream were certainly not on any diet she'd ever heard of, but they did look delicious. Owen handed her the plate, and Fran took one. As she did, she noticed a smear of jam on the side of his mouth and, for a brief moment, she was tempted to wipe it off, wondering what it would feel like to touch his lips. A sudden and unexpected tremor swept through her.

Fran tried to hide the blush she was sure must be spreading over her cheeks by concentrating on taking a knife to split the scone and spread it liberally with jam and cream, sparking the well-worn debate about which to spread first. The ensuing conversation provided her with a respite, giving time for her emotions to return to normal.

When tea was over, Col and Nick determined it was time to explore, and they all made their way through what seemed to Fran to be a never-ending row of tents containing cages of hens, rabbits and other creatures, tables groaning with cakes and all sorts of baked goods, and pots of a wide variety of plants and vegetables, all seeking the prized blue ribbon. Fran felt claustrophobic with the crowds and the unfamiliar odours and was relieved when they were out in the open again, though she'd been pleased to see Melody's pavlova had won an award.

'Where to now?' she asked Jo, wishing she'd worn more comfortable shoes. She should have realised the ground would be uneven and heels – even the low ones she was wearing – were not the best choice.

'The sheepdog trials. They're held in the arena.' Jo pointed to where a large crowd was already congregating in front of a grassy area in which a ramp and a pen had been set up. The next hour passed slowly for Fran as one dog after another – with unlikely names like Pink and Brown – expertly corralled a small mob of sheep in the desired direction, controlled only by the voice of their master. It was quite a sight, if not monotonous.

The event was drawing to a close when the sky darkened and there was a flash of lightning followed by a loud clap of thunder. Fran looked up, expecting rain to follow, but the air was still dry.

'Let's get inside,' Col said. 'They'll be awarding the ribbons in the main marquee. It's always a good turn.'

Fran had had enough. Unused to being in such large crowds of people, she felt exhausted. All she wanted to do was lie down in the peace of her own home. But she felt it would be rude to leave now, and surely the prize giving wouldn't take too long. She followed the others into the marquee where they managed to annex a row of chairs close to the back.

Fran yawned. It was all taking longer than she'd anticipated and, while the others seemed to be enjoying the occasion, she was bored.

Suddenly there was a commotion in the audience. It was like a wave of movement. Instead of focussing on the platform where the local mayor was about to make his closing speech, people were turning to each other and getting to their feet. There was a swell of confused voices.

'What's happening?' Fran asked, looking around, her heart racing. This was one of the reasons she hated crowds. What if everyone tried to leave at once? She saw Owen and Col simultaneously reach for their phones and realised almost everyone else had been doing the same.

'Col?' Jo was peering over Col's shoulder at the screen. 'Oh, no!'

'What is it?' Kay asked, trying to see over Jo's shoulder.

But just then, there was a crackling from the speakers perched precariously on either side of the platform, and the mayor began to speak.

'It appears there is a bushfire in the state forest on the outskirts of town,' he said. 'There's no need to panic, but those of you who want to check on their homes should leave now. Please do so in an orderly fashion. We don't want anyone hurt in the process. We'll be setting up evacuation points in local halls and schools for those who require them. The rural fire brigade is in attendance, and…'

But he didn't finish. His voice was drowned out in the noise of an immediate charge for the exit. Glad they were close to the back, Fran and her group were able to get out before they were mown down in the rush. From where they stood, Fran could see the horizon had turned red and orange with the glare of flames and an enormous plume of dark smoke was rising up into the sky.

'A bushfire?' Owen seemed mesmerised.

'Dry lightning,' Col said grimly. 'There's been no rain for months. Everything's so dry, it'll spread in no time. That's what the text message was,' he explained to the others. 'It was advice to prepare to evacuate if necessary.'

Jo wrinkled her brow and grasped Col's arm tightly. 'It must be on our side of town,' she said. 'I wonder…'

'You're not going anywhere,' Nick said, taking charge. 'You can spend the night with us. We'll fit you in somehow. You, too, Owen,' he added, almost as an afterthought.

Without thinking, Fran said, 'No. You have the two children too. Owen can come with me.' As soon as she said it, Fran regretted the impulse which led her to make the offer, but it was too late to take it back.

'Thanks, Fran,' Nick said.

Owen appeared bewildered. 'A bushfire?' he said again. 'Can't we get home?'

Jo took him by the arm. 'It's in the state forest between here and home, so the wisest thing to do is to remain in town for the night. With luck it will be out by tomorrow, and we can check out any damage. But there's nothing we can do tonight. Let the firies handle it. You'll be all right with Fran?'

'I guess so.' Owen glanced at Fran for confirmation.

'I have plenty of space,' she said. 'You're most welcome to use my spare room.'

'Though I doubt any of us will be getting much sleep tonight,' Col said. 'I remember the last one – it was less than a year ago. This is early for a fire, but everything's been so dry.'

'You'd better follow me,' Fran said to Owen in the car park as they all prepared to leave. 'You'll need to park outside. I only have a single garage.'

'No worries.'

What a difference from Richard who'd always given Fran the impression she should park her VW in the street to allow his precious BMW garage space.

What had possessed her? Fran drove home in a daze. She didn't even have the excuse she'd been drunk. Nothing but tea had passed her lips. Hopefully the fire wasn't too bad, and Owen could return home tomorrow. But the glow in the sky didn't bode well. She could hear the sirens from the emergency vehicles over the noise of her car engine. It was going to be a hard night for all concerned.

Once home, Fran turned on the lights and closed the windows she'd left open earlier in the day. It had turned dark, and the air was filled with the smell of smoke – that awful burning smell that signified a bushfire.

Owen couldn't settle. He sat, stood, walked around, till Fran thought she was going to have to tie him down. She knew it must be difficult for him. The place he called home, no matter how temporary it might be, could be burning while they were safe in town; all his belongings were out there, too.

'I'm sorry,' he said, finally seeming to realise he was driving her mad. 'I've never been so close to a fire before. It makes one feel so helpless. The goats… the cats…What if…?'

'We're quite safe here,' Fran said, hoping she was right. 'Col said it was on the other side of town, between here and…'

'My place and Yarran.'

'Yes.' Fran knew any attempt to calm him was useless.

Her phone buzzed. She grabbed for it gratefully, glad to have a means of escape from his incessant activity.

'Hi, Jo,' she said, recognising Jo's number and waving Owen away as he started up when he heard Jo's name.

'You got home all right?' Jo asked, only to continue without waiting for a reply. 'We've all got to eat, and Rob's opening The Riverside for everyone who's stranded in town. But he says he can find a corner for us if we don't mind a squeeze. What do you say?'

Fran glanced at Owen who was watching her in anticipation of news of the fire. 'I think that's a great idea. We'll meet you there.'

'See you in an hour.'

Jo hung up.

'There's no news,' Fran said, 'but Jo's suggested we all meet at The Riverside for dinner – something to eat, at least. I expect it'll be packed out, but she says Rob – her son – will keep a spot for us.'

'Oh!' Owen seemed deflated as if he'd prepared himself for bad news that didn't eventuate.

*

As Fran had expected, The Riverside was filled to capacity, and it was Jo who was managing front of house.

'Back to my old job,' she told Fran with a laugh, showing them to a small table in the back corner where Col, Nick and Kay were already seated. 'Steve – Rob's partner,' she explained to Owen, 'is busy serving tonight, so I stepped in. I'll try to join you later.'

'No kids tonight?' Fran asked Nick as she and Owen slid into their seats.

'They have better things to do than spend an evening with us,' Nick said. 'But the fire has given them a shock too. They won't be venturing far from home. We left Sam off at her friend's place, and Ryan has some mates in.'

Fran shuddered at how close the danger was. Imagine if they'd left the show earlier, had decided to go out to Jo and Col's. They might have been stranded there in the middle of the blaze.

'Are you okay?' Owen seemed to notice her shiver and placed a comforting arm around her shoulder. She wanted to shrug it off, but it felt good to have his strong arm there, as if he'd make sure no harm came to her when he was around. She knew that was foolish. That it didn't mean anything. It might even be that he had nowhere else to put his arm – they were so squashed into this corner. But, regardless, Fran decided to enjoy the moment.

'No menu, tonight,' Steve said, appearing at their table. 'We're serving burgers or pizza and all proceeds are going to the Rural Fire Brigade.'

'Great idea,' Col said. 'What'll it be, guys?'

They settled on pizzas and Steve hurried off.

'Let me see if I can scare up something to drink,' Col said, 'There has to be some advantage to the place being in the family.' He disappeared in the direction of the kitchen and Fran carefully disentangled herself from Owen's arm, using the need to use the ladies' room as an excuse. As she walked away, she could feel his eyes on her.

By the time she returned, Jo had joined them and there was a bottle of wine on the table. 'Finished for the night?' she asked Jo.

'We're full to capacity so there's nothing left for me to do.'

Sure enough, when Fran looked around, every table was filled, most as tightly crowded as theirs, and the entire place radiated a sense of camaraderie. Whether they lived in town or were taking refuge there, they were all in this together.

'A bit different to what you expected, Owen?' Col asked.

'Different from Sydney that's for sure. Though we have had fires there too. A lot of Lane Cove National Park was burned out back in 2008. But I've never come this close. Do you think we'll have any damage?'

'I don't think the fire will reach us,' Jo said, consolingly. 'The biggest danger will be from stray embers. It all depends on the wind – whether it blows them toward us or away.'

'And the wind can change at any time,' Col put in. 'That's life in the country for you, Owen, but everyone pulls together. It's not too long ago we had a flood to contend with and we came through that unscathed. We'll be right this time too, you'll see.'

'But there's nothing you can do,' Nick said. 'And you all have a safe possie for the night. Be grateful.'

'We are,' Jo said.

Owen agreed.

Did Fran imagine it, or had his hand touched hers ever so lightly as he spoke?

Finally, the restaurant began to empty.

'I guess we should make a move,' Nick said.

'Fire's still burning.' Col had been checking his phone all night. 'I've been keeping an eye on the Rural Fire Service Facebook page for updates,' he said. 'They're doing what they can to contain the fire and, so far, no houses are at risk. They'll be able to bring in the helicopters and start water bombing in the morning – as soon as it's light. I guess the main risk at this stage is that the wind could change.'

Outside the restaurant they all parted, Fran and Owen heading back to her place. There was an eerie glimmer to the sky. Fran shivered. How were they to get through the night with that threat hanging over them?

Back home, the house was as empty and silent as when they left. Fran switched on the lights. She didn't feel at all tired, couldn't imagine how they'd be able to sleep. 'Shall I make some hot chocolate?' she asked, unsure why Owen laughed. She soon found out.

'Hot chocolate always makes me think of my grandmother,' he said. 'She was a feisty old bird, and hot chocolate was her cure for everything – that and a wet paper towel.' He laughed again. 'But, yes, that'd be good, maybe with a drop of brandy, if you have any?'

'I think so.' Fran peered into the pantry to hide her embarrassment and reappeared with a half-full bottle of Napoleon brandy she kept there for emergencies, which she supposed this was.

They were sitting amicably together, their mugs of hot chocolate having been laced with brandy, when Owen's forehead creased and he said, 'You know, I just can't help thinking of those poor goats – and Oscar and Lucinda.'

'Oscar and who?'

'Lucinda – the two cats. I think they're called after the characters in the book.'

'By Peter Carey. You've read it?' Fran hadn't taken Owen for a great reader.

'Actually no. But I am familiar with the opera based on the book – a collaboration by Elliot Gynger and Pierce Wilcox. I attended a performance at the Carriageworks before I left Sydney. Not such a cretin, you see.'

'Oh!' Fran had never heard of the operatic adaptation, nor of Carriageworks which she assumed was some contemporary music or arts centre. 'I'm sorry, I stand corrected. And I do understand your concern for the animals you're responsible for.'

Now, why had she put it in those terms? She knew she sounded stiff. Why hadn't she just said "your animals"? But they weren't, were they? They belonged to the people who owned the property Owen was minding. Did that make it more difficult for him? Or was it less of a worry when the place wasn't your own?

Owen didn't seem fazed by her remark. 'You don't have any animals yourself?' he asked, looking around as if expecting a cat to creep out of a corner.

'No, you're the second person to ask me that. It's made me think maybe I should get one – most probably a cat,' she said, deciding a cat would be easier to look after. Weren't they supposed to be independent creatures as well as being good company? And there was no room for a dog here. Her townhouse seemed to have shrunk already with Owen in it. 'When this is over,' she said, burying her face in her mug.

The rest of the evening passed slowly. Neither of them felt tempted to watch television. Owen searched through Fran's music selection, making no comment. She wondered if that meant it met with his approval or not but wasn't game to ask. Finally, with her permission, he linked a playlist of his own to her Bluetooth speaker and they sat in companionable silence broken only by Owen's frequent trips outside to monitor the unchanging skyline.

Eventually, Fran felt her eyes beginning to close. 'I think I may be able to get some sleep,' she said. 'I'll show you where the spare room is.'

'Thanks.'

Having done that, Fran closed her bedroom door and lay down fully dressed. She didn't feel comfortable undressing with Owen in the next room. Unsure whether she could actually fall asleep, she closed her eyes.

Twenty-one

Owen opened his eyes with a start. Where was he? He gazed around the immaculately tidy room, the modern furniture, the beige Berber carpet and the cream-painted walls, a bookcase against one wall. He stretched out his legs, remembering. There was a bushfire. He'd stayed in town. He was in Fran Reilly's townhouse. He'd spent the night here. He must have fallen asleep in the chair.

Getting stiffly to his feet, Owen was startled to hear the sound of a helicopter overhead. He opened the door and looked up to see the huge machine carrying an enormous bucket of water. He sighed. So, the fire was still burning. But what had he expected? He took out his phone. What was the site Col was checking last night? It was something on Facebook. He thought for a moment – Rural Fire Service, that was it!

Owen read the most recent bulletin with dismay. The Granite Springs State Forest fire was still burning. Emergency Services hadn't managed to contain it overnight, and it had jumped the road – what road? The warning for their area was still to be prepared to evacuate. He sighed. It didn't look as if he'd get home today.

His eyes were still glued to his phone, as if by staring at it, he could change the message, when Fran walked in. She must have been up for some time, because she was as immaculate as usual – hair and makeup in place and dressed in a pair of neat jeans with a short-sleeved floral shirt of some sort. What would it take for her to lose her cool?

'Would you like to freshen up?' she asked.

Owen glanced down at his creased clothes, and ran a hand through his hair, still unused to feeling the short ends in his fingers. He rather liked the sensation, though he missed his man bun. He must look a mess. 'I fell asleep in the chair,' he said by way of explanation. 'And, yes thanks, it would be good to freshen up.'

'You'll find a clean towel in the bathroom,' she said with a smile. 'I'll make some breakfast while you shower.'

'Thanks.'

Another helicopter flew overhead while he was in the shower. At least they were doing their best, he thought, hoping it would be enough to dowse the flames. He'd read about those helicopters that fought the fires, and how much water they could carry, but this was his first real experience of them – an experience he could have done without. Was this what life would be like in the country? Was he a fool to want to live out there?

When he entered the small kitchen, probably no smaller than the one he'd had for so many years in Sydney, but at least half the size of the one he was now used to, the aroma of freshly cooked toast and bacon greeted him.

'I thought you might enjoy a cooked breakfast,' Fran said. 'I don't normally…but…'

'Wonderful.' Owen rubbed his hands together. He rarely cooked breakfast for himself, preferring to eat on the run after an early morning coffee, or to satisfy himself with one of the chocolate croissants from Banjo's. He wondered if Fran had guessed the coffee and croissants he'd been bringing into her office were in fact his breakfast. He wouldn't be surprised if she had. She was no fool.

'This is delicious. You're a good cook.'

'It's only breakfast, but I do enjoy cooking.'

'Me too. I do a mean paella,' he said, remembering his promise to have Nick and Kay to dinner. He hadn't followed through on that, but he would, he promised himself, just as soon as this was over. 'And Jo's been introducing me to country cooking. I cooked up a lamb casserole when my daughter was here.'

'I'm impressed.' Fran laughed.

'If… when,' he corrected himself – there was no sense in being pessimistic – 'this is over I intend to invite Nick and Kay to dinner with Jo and Col. You must come, too,' he added, suddenly picturing her at his dining table. 'You must try my paella.'

'Oh, I don't know.' Fran busied herself putting another couple of slices of bread into the toaster. She avoided his eyes. 'That may not be such a good idea.'

Deciding not to pursue it right now, Owen said no more on the subject, instead pointing out the window where they could see the helicopter returning for more water. Then the noise changed.

'That's a plane this time,' he said, getting up to peer at the sky and seeing a trail of red. 'I've read about this. It must be the 737 that's been modified for firebombing. It deposits a red gel. They should get on top of it now.'

'I hope so.' Fran came up beside him to watch the plane. It was like a huge white and red bird.

Owen felt her shiver. He placed an arm around her shoulders. He'd done that last night, too, but she'd found an excuse to pull away. This time, he gripped her shoulder with his hand, his fingers sensing the feel of her skin under the soft material of her top. She let it sit there while they watched. Then, reluctantly it seemed to him, she turned back to the table where their breakfast was congealing.

Seeing Fran's dismay, Owen quickly said, 'It's okay, I've eaten enough, but another coffee would go down well.'

They were enjoying their coffee as much as they could, the fire never out of their minds, when Owen's phone buzzed.

''Scuse me,' he said to Fran, seeing Col's number.

'How are you this morning – get any sleep?' Col asked.

'I must have dozed off for a bit. I woke up in the armchair. I think Fran slept.' He saw her nod. 'You?'

'A bit. It was a bad night. Look, I've just been on to a mate who's with the Rural Fire Brigade and he says they're making progress. The water bombers are doing their job. The fire's burning within containment lines. The warning has been downgraded to Watch and Act. If we head out that way, there's a possibility we can get through. The main danger is flying embers. Want to risk it? I've told Jo to stay here.'

'You're on.'

'I'll pick you up. Jo knows where Fran lives. Can you be ready in an hour?'

'Sure thing.'

*

Fran watched Owen drive off, wondering what he and Col were going to find. She hoped all would be well, but things didn't look good. There had been fires close to town before now, but this was the first time she'd felt personally involved. She touched her shoulder where Owen's fingers had gripped. They'd felt… good, strong. But, as she had last night, she'd moved away, even though, both times, she'd enjoyed the contact.

Was there something wrong with her? Ever since Ben died, she knew she'd shied away from any sort of relationship that engaged her innermost feelings. It was as if they were in a box. Had she shut her hope for the future up in a box, fearful of what it might contain?

Fran wondered if she should prepare lunch or if that would be too presumptuous. Owen might have other things to take care of today. If his home was damaged, she'd be the last thing on his mind. Strangely, that upset her, almost as much as the possibility his house could be destroyed.

*

As they drove out of Granite Springs, Owen noticed the carpark for the supermarket on the edge of town had been turned into a rest stop and was filled with fire and emergency vehicles and personnel. The Country Women's Association had set up a stall to provide tea, coffee and sandwiches, and Rotary had set up their barbecue, the aroma of sausages and onions competing with the acrid smell of smoke.

When they reached the main road, the smoke was still intense, and a line of traffic forced them to slow down.

'Doesn't look good,' Col said.

They drove on a few kilometres at a snail's pace, then came to a halt. Both Owen and Col stuck their heads out the windows in an attempt to see what was happening.

'Looks like we can't get through,' Col said.

They sat for a few moments then one of the emergency workers in his distinctive yellow and red gear came along and bent down to the level of the car window. 'Should get going in a bit, mate. But take care. Still a few spot fires. There's been a lot of damage, but only one house gone.'

Owen felt his stomach lurch and could see the blood drain from Col's face. One house, which one? And what was happening to his cats and goats and Col's old Labrador?

'I'll call Jo,' Col said, taking out his phone.

Owen wondered if he should contact Fran. There probably was no need, but she'd offered him a safe place to stay. It would be polite. He compromised by sending a text.

Hold up on the road. Fingers crossed all is well. Owen.

The reply came immediately, as if she'd been sitting with the phone in her hand.

Hope your place and Col's have been spared. Fran.

He sent back an emoji of crossed fingers and smiled to himself.

*

Fran had just replied to his text when her phone buzzed again – a call this time. Expecting it to be from Owen, she immediately pressed to accept the call. It was Jo.

'Hi, Fran. It's like a madhouse here with Nick's two teenagers rampaging about. I can't do anything till Col gets back and I'm going out of my mind with worry. He's just called to say they're stuck in a line of cars waiting to get through and they've heard one house has gone. Would you take pity on me and join me for coffee? Kay says I can borrow her car.'

Fran could hear the stress in Jo's voice. She didn't have to think twice.

'You poor soul! No wonder you're on edge. Why don't you come here? Tea might be better than coffee. I have some very healthy fig and banana bread that needs to be eaten and we can console each other.'

Jo agreed, but immediately she got off the phone, Fran cursed herself. Console each other? What a stupid thing to say! It wasn't *her* husband who was waiting in traffic to determine if their house was still standing. It wasn't *her* house that might have been destroyed in the fire. So why did she feel wound up, too?

Shrugging, Fran took her selection of herbal teas from the pantry, filled the electric jug and cut several slices of the loaf she'd baked earlier in the week. Maybe Jo wouldn't feel like eating, but Fran was feeling a little peckish after having to throw out most of her breakfast uneaten.

Jo arrived within minutes. 'You're a godsend,' she said, accepting Fran's warm hug, designed to comfort her more than Jo. Fran was glad to have company. She'd been a bundle of nerves since Owen left.

'Have you heard anything?' she asked, turning on the jug to boil.

Jo shook her head. 'I know it's silly to worry,' she said. 'If it's gone, it's gone, and there's nothing I can do, nothing anyone can do. But Scout's still there, and my whole life's tied up in that house. I can't imagine living anywhere else. You know my son, Danny, wanted me to let him have it more than a year ago?'

Fran didn't. She shook her head.

'They have their own acreage now, and a nice modern house on it. But I love my old place. It's where the children all grew up, where we all get together. You must think I'm silly, getting sentimental over a house.' Her eyes misted up.

'Not at all. I'd hate it if anything happened to this place and it doesn't hold the memories Yarran does for you.' She gave Jo a minute or two to recover, then said, 'I have a variety of teas, but maybe camomile?'

'Magda's cure for all ills,' Jo smiled. 'I hope she's okay. I think I saw her at the show yesterday.'

'You go to her, too? I don't know what I'd have done without her healing hands over the years, but you don't want to hear about that now.'

'Tell me. Anything to keep my mind off what Col's doing.'

'My accident left me with ongoing problems in my back and neck. I need constant treatment. I attend my physio regularly, but Magda's ministrations provide that extra something.'

'I know what you mean. And the ambiance she manages to effect in that little cottage of hers is so peaceful. But I'm sorry to hear about your challenges. I didn't know.'

'No. I don't talk about it as a rule. I don't want anyone's pity.'

'So that's why you have such great posture,' Jo said, pensively. 'I've admired your upright back, the way you hold your head – almost as if you have a ruler in your clothes.'

'I wish that was the reason,' Fran said ruefully. 'But enough about me. Tea.'

She dropped the camomile teabags into two china cups and carefully filled them with water before handing one to Jo and passing the plate of loaf slices. 'Have one of these. I bet you haven't eaten much today.'

'Thanks. You're right. Food has been the furthest thing from my mind.' She nibbled on the corner of a slice before putting it down again. 'I'm sorry. It's lovely, but I can't do justice to it. I'll be right once I've heard more from Col.'

'Tell me,' Jo said, when they were on their second cup of tea and had all but exhausted any talk of the show, the bushfire and Magda, 'You and Owen Larsen…' She raised one eyebrow.

Fran felt herself redden. 'There is no me and Owen Larsen, not in the sense I think you mean. He's my boss. I'm his PA. That's it.' But even as she spoke, Fran knew she wasn't being completely honest with Jo. There was something, something she couldn't quite pinpoint. She'd felt it last night in the restaurant and again this morning.

But Jo wasn't so easily deterred. 'Nick is Kay's boss, too,' she said. 'It didn't stop them.'

'That's different,' Fran protested.

'Is it?'

*

Owen didn't know how long they sat there with Col drumming his fingers on the steering wheel, but eventually the line of cars began to move forward slowly.

The devastation from the fire was terrible to see. Great swathes of the forest had been destroyed, the trees burnt almost beyond recognition, their black trunks standing like skeletons, and the undergrowth completely gone. It was almost the same story when they moved to open country, but here, the fire seemed to have been selective, with some paddocks razed to the ground, while others were barely touched. Owen shook his head in dismay. He'd never seen anything like this. And the smell! It permeated the car, filling it with the stench of burning.

By the time they turned onto the dirt road, Owen was expecting the worst. How could anything have survived unharmed?

As soon as they turned into their lane, Owen searched for signs of the damage inflicted here. He didn't have long to wait. A line of scorched fenceposts greeted them on both sides of the road. In the distance he could see the now familiar emergency personnel and vehicles. His pulse raced.

'It's Magda's,' Col said.

'Magda?'

'She lives farther up the lane, with her two greyhounds. Jo knows her, goes to her for massage. The poor woman. I hope she's all right.'

Owen remembered the elderly woman he'd met walking her dogs, the one who'd made such a strange comment to him. It must be her house that had burned.

Col turned the car in the direction of the vehicles. 'I need to see what's happened. You don't mind, do you?'

They had to stop some distance from the house around which the emergency workers were now erecting a barricade. 'You can't go any nearer, mate,' one said.

'I'm a neighbour. The owner?' Col asked.

'Lucky she wasn't home. Looks like the show saved her.'

'Her dogs?'

'Don't know anything about them. Now, I must ask you to leave.'

The two men walked slowly back to the car.

'What'll she do now?' Col spoke to himself. 'She's older than Jo and I by about ten years. It'd be hard for her to start again. And her dogs. She was devoted to them.'

'Do these horses belong to her, too?' Owen pointed to three horses which had taken shelter under a clump of trees at the far end of the paddock from the house.

'Yes. The poor creatures, they must have been terrified.'

They were about to get into the car again, when a dirty white ute came roaring up the lane, stopping just short of them. The door flew open and the tiny woman Owen remembered jumped out. She started to run then stopped, her hands going up to cover her face. She emitted a loud wail.

Col rushed over to hug her and, after a few moments, she pulled away. 'I'll be all right, now,' she sniffed. 'I knew it would happen. It's just… seeing it… But I'm okay. The dogs are okay. We were all in town.

I just need to see to the horses.' She moved over to the fence, made a clicking sound with her tongue, and the three horses came galloping towards her, only slowing when they reached the fence line. 'I'll be all right now,' she repeated to Col. 'It's only stuff. It can be replaced. You should go check your own place.'

'Come with us, Magda, you shouldn't stay here.'

She hesitated for a moment, then shook her head as another car drew up and an elderly man hopped out. Magda turned to him with what appeared to be a sigh of relief. 'George,' she said.

'Come here,' he said, stretching out his arms.

But Magda was more intent on the horses.

'I'll see her and the beasts right,' George said. 'You guys need to check your own places.'

'Come on. There's nothing we can do here,' Col said to Owen, getting back into the car.

Both men were silent on the drive down the lane, till they were able to see their homes still standing, although the charring to some fenceposts showed how close the fire had come.

Col let Owen off at his gate and continued on home, promising to pick him up again when he'd checked everything out.

As soon as Owen set foot on the veranda, the two cats raced up to greet him, meowing and purring. Owen dropped to his knees on the bricked veranda and hugged them, overcome with emotion. He'd seen what the fire had done to Magda's house, only a short distance away. It could have been this one.

The cats suffered his hugs for only a few seconds before slipping away and slinking off around the corner, as if satisfied all was well. Owen stood up and dusted off his pants, then went inside to change and fill their bowls.

In a clean shirt and pants, he took out his phone again and sent another text to Fran.

All good here. One house destroyed up the lane. Back soon to pick up car.
O

Expecting another text reply, he was surprised when instead, the phone rang.

'Was it Magda's house that was destroyed?' Fran asked, without any preliminaries, her voice shaking.

'I think that's who Col said she was – a small elderly lady. She has two dogs…'

'Oh, no!' Fran wailed. 'The poor dear.'

'You know her, too?'

'For years. I go to see her regularly. She's the best masseuse. Oh, dear. She'll be devastated. Her animals?'

'They're fine. She arrived when we were there. She'd been in town with the dogs and the horses are okay, too. She was at the show like us.'

'I'm so glad. But I wonder what she'll do now. How did she seem?'

Fran sounded just like Col. Owen considered for a moment before replying, 'She appeared quite philosophical about it. Said it was just stuff.' Then he remembered. 'She said something odd, too. It was as if she expected it to happen.'

'That's like her. She's a bit of a witch, reads tealeaves and such. I've never got involved in that side of things, just the massage.'

No, Owen couldn't imagine Fran having her tealeaves read, or tarot cards or any of those other things that Brit and Rosemary seemed to thrive on.

'Where is she now?' Fran asked. 'You didn't leave her there?'

'No, a friend of hers turned up – an elderly guy. I think she called him George?'

'George Turnbull. He's been around forever. She'll be right with him.' Fran paused. 'Will you be back for lunch?'

Owen didn't know what to say. He had no idea how long Col would take and he was reliant on him for his ride back. 'I'm not sure what Col intends,' he said, 'but don't plan anything around me. It was good enough of you to offer me somewhere to stay for the night. I don't want to put you to any more trouble. I'll just come around and pick up my car when we get back.'

Owen would have loved to spend the rest of the weekend with her, to put his arm around her shoulder again, maybe even to steal a kiss. But he was ever conscious of what seemed to be her inbuilt resistance to any attempt at closeness.

'It's no trouble.' The change in Fran's tone stopped him in his tracks. What had she expected?

He shook his head. Women!

Twenty-two

'Magda!' Jo only needed to say her name. Fran knew exactly what she meant.

'Col told you?'

Jo nodded. 'She's such a lovely lady. I wonder what she'll do now. She may feel she's too old to start again.'

'Would you?'

'No, absolutely not. But she's older than me. I never discovered exactly how much.'

'She has children?'

Jo nodded again. 'But they don't live here. Kenny's interstate and I'm not sure about her other son. He was older than my three. Oh, it's such a dreadful thing to happen. I wonder what we can do to help.'

'Owen told me they left her with old George Turnbull.'

'That sounds good. But if she doesn't have anywhere else to go, she could stay with us until she decides.' Jo gazed into space. 'I can imagine how I would feel if it was me. I'd be devastated. But Magda's a different breed. They don't make them like her anymore.'

'Do you think she knew? You know, with her second sight. I don't go for any of that stuff, but she believed in it. And Owen told me she said she'd known it would happen.' Fran shivered. 'I'd like to do something, too. She's lost everything. Could we get some sort of whip around going, do you think?'

'I'm sure we can. Leave it with me.' Jo's forehead creased. 'Firstly, I need to find out where she is. Col should be back soon with Owen. He might know more by then.'

'Mmm.'

'Something wrong?'

'Owen. You know what you implied – whether there was anything between us? Well, not on his side, anyway.'

'What do you mean?'

'When I suggested lunch, he put me off. The man's a boor. After…'

'After?'

'It's nothing, but you were right, I thought there was. There's something about him that reminds me of Ben.'

'Your old boyfriend, Ben?'

'Yes. But, seems I was wrong – on both counts. Oh, you've more than enough to worry about right now than me.'

'I wouldn't dismiss him quite so quickly, Fran,' Jo said. 'Could it have been something you've done or said? If I'm being honest, you're not the easiest person to get to know.'

Fran wilted. She knew it was true. She did tend to keep herself aloof. But had she done that to Owen? She tried to remember. Both times he'd tried to comfort her, put his arm around her shoulder, how had she reacted? She suddenly felt cold. She'd pushed him away. At least, that's probably how he'd interpreted her behaviour.

'You're right,' she said. 'I'm a fool. I've forgotten how to behave with people. That's most likely why I put up with Richard for so long. We were alike. He was unfeeling, too.'

'Oh, Fran, I wouldn't say you were unfeeling. It may be that you need to learn to give a little more. You've made friends with Kay and me recently and have begun to open up to us. It may be that you need to take that into the rest of your life – to be willing to share more, even if it means you risk being hurt.'

'I'll try.' Fran knew it wouldn't be easy for her to change the habits of a lifetime. But that's what she wanted, wasn't it? That's what she'd decided. If she wanted her life to be different, then she had to change, and that meant being willing to take risks.

Twenty-three

After calling the Kellys and Pia to assure them all was well and he and the property – and animals – were safe, Owen was out checking on the goats when Col's car drew up. 'All good?' he yelled across the paddock. 'Ready to leave?'

'Coming!' Owen made his way back to the house. The goats seemed none the worse from the fire that had surrounded them, except perhaps being a bit more skittish than usual. It was difficult to tell. The cats were a different matter. They'd stayed close to him in the house, seemingly afraid to venture out. He'd left them lying on the sofa, curled up together.

'Back to Fran's,' Col said. 'Seems Jo's there. She got sick of the racket at Nick's. Don't blame her. I imagine two teenagers can create quite a ruckus.'

'Umm. Maybe I'll just pick up my car and head back.'

'Why on earth would you do that?' Col appeared puzzled. 'The woman was good enough to put you up for the night and I thought… correct me if I'm speaking out of turn, but I thought there was something going on between you two. Was I wrong?'

'You were.' Owen sighed. He didn't know Col well, but the older man seemed to be a willing ear, and Owen sure as hell needed that. 'She's a good woman, perhaps too good for me, Col. I haven't been the greatest… Well, suffice to say, I'm not proud of a lot of the things I've done in the past. But I can't seem to get through to Fran. At work, she's efficient but distant. Hell, sometimes I think she treats me like she's my mother or big sister. Maybe that's my fault.' He dragged a hand through his hair, still surprised there was no man bun to disturb.

'Look, Owen. I don't know you well. But, going through this together, I'm pretty sure you're a decent guy. My advice, for what it's worth, is that, if you think you want to pursue some sort of relationship with this woman, go for it. You're probably more experienced with women than I am. There have only been two in my life, and I've been lucky with both of them. But Jo and I hit a few bumps along the road. There was a time when I almost gave up, I can tell you. But the end is worth the means. Give her a chance – give yourself a chance. You may be exactly what she needs – what she wants, even if she doesn't realise it. But one of you has to take the bull by the horns as it were.' He chuckled. 'Sorry if I've gone on a bit.'

'No, you're right, mate. So, you think I should make the first move? I did try, but…' Owen remembered how Fran had shrugged off his arm – although not immediately. There'd been a moment when it seemed she welcomed it – or was it only the fear of the fire. He shook his head. 'Oh, I don't know.'

'At least give it a try. We're almost there. We can go in together.'

The two women were seated at the table when Col and Owen walked in. They looked up, and Fran seemed surprised to see Owen.

'You came back,' she said.

Col replied, 'We thought we'd take you two ladies out to lunch.'

We did? This was news to Owen, but he decided to go along with it.

'The golf club does a good Sunday roast,' Col said. 'I think we all need something to take our minds off what's been happening.'

'Good idea,' Jo said.

Owen intercepted an odd glance between her and Fran. What had the two women been discussing before they walked in? He'd never understand women, not if he lived to be a hundred. But right now, he didn't need to understand all women. It'd be enough to have some insight into Fran's thinking.

'How's Scout?' Jo asked as they were preparing to leave. 'He doesn't cope well with thunderstorms. I remember the last one. I had to entice him out from under the bed – and he spent the rest of the night in mine,' she added ruefully.

'That's where I found him,' Col chuckled, 'But he's settled down, now. Nothing a good hug and a feed couldn't fix. I gave him one of those bones you save for special treats. He liked that.'

'He would.' Jo seemed satisfied.

'They're very fond of their old dog,' Owen said, following Fran outside. 'I'd never understood the lure of animals till now. D'you know, I swear those cats were pleased to see me. Didn't you say you were thinking of getting a pet – a cat was it?'

'Yes. I think I could cope with a cat. A dog might be too demanding and this place is so small.'

Owen could see Fran with a cat. There was something feline about her. Maybe it was her independence, the way she didn't seem to need people the way other women he'd known had. She was a strange one, but one who intrigued him. Maybe Col was right. Maybe it was up to him, But what if he'd read her wrong? What if he lost her as his PA too?

Jo had decided they'd all drive to the club together, so there was no chance of furthering the conversation with Fran. Owen was glad. He'd probably have made a fool of himself.

The car park at the club was almost full, an indication they weren't the only people wanting to try to forget the evening before.

'That's Nick's car,' Fran said, pointing to a black SUV. 'They must have had the same idea.'

'Good, we can join them,' Jo said, leading the way inside where they immediately spied Nick and Kay.

'Isn't this nice,' Kay said, when after a bit of jostling, they were seated and had placed their orders, all of them choosing the roast lamb.

'No children again today?' Jo asked.

'No. They cleared off to the showground to *help* clean up. Not too sure what help a group of teenagers will be, but it gets them out of our hair and involved in a supposedly useful occupation.'

'Don't you remember?' Jo said to Kay with a nudge. 'We used to do that after show day. It was an excuse to get together with the boys we'd been trying to interest.'

'And for us to get together with the girls,' Col laughed.

Nick looked astounded. 'Sam, maybe,' he said. 'But I don't think Ryan…'

'How old is he?' Fran asked.

'Fourteen, going on fifteen.'

The others roared with laughter.

'That's about the age I started noticing Alice,' Col said, referring to his late wife. 'You must have been a late starter. What about you, Owen? You're being very quiet.'

Owen was startled. He'd been content to let the conversation flow over him. 'Oh, I definitely started young,' he said, seeing Fran give him a wary smile.

Despite their intention for lunch at the club to take their mind off the bushfire, it was the main topic of discussion during the meal.

'Did you see Magda again?' Jo asked, during a lull in the conversation. 'We – Fran and I – want to do something for her, maybe have a whip around for clothes, toiletries and suchlike.'

'She said she was staying with friends in town,' Col said, 'I don't know much more.'

'And I think you'll find Rotary and some of the other service clubs are already on the case,' Nick said. 'Although hers was the only house that burned down completely, a lot of others were badly damaged. I heard some of the tradies are already offering their services for free to help repair the damage.'

'I'd still like to do something,' Jo said with a worried look. 'I wonder...'

'I have her mobile number,' Fran said, as if suddenly remembering. 'I can call her – maybe tomorrow – and see how she is.'

That seemed to satisfy them, and Owen marvelled how the community seemed to be coming together to support those who had suffered loss. Another difference from the city, though he supposed there were some good Samaritans there, too.

'A bit of a trial by fire for you, Owen,' Nick said. 'Things are not always this dramatic. Rough for this to strike so soon after your arrival.'

'Not so soon, really,' Owen replied. 'I'm beginning to feel I belong here. Though, I admit I didn't expect to be facing the threat of losing my home. Or should I say my borrowed home. It's a good place, and the Kellys have been generous to entrust me with the care of it.'

'They're the lucky ones,' Col said. 'You're taking much better care of the place than I could have from across the paddock.'

'Speaking of that,' Owen said, deciding now was the time to issue the invitation he'd been holding back on. 'I want to invite all of you to dinner. I've enjoyed enough of your hospitality since I got here, and I'd like to repay it. What about next Saturday? With a bit of luck all this will be over by then.'

He could see from her face Fran was about to refuse. 'You, too, Fran,' he said. 'You were good enough to put me up last night. Having you to dinner is the least I can do.'

Fran appeared undecided for a moment then said, 'Well, if you put it like that, I can't refuse.'

'Of course, you can't,' Kay said. 'We'd be delighted. And I'm sure I speak for Jo and Col, too.' She glanced across at Jo, who nodded.

'Right then, Saturday at seven. And I'll treat you to a sample of my cooking.'

'Let me bring a pavlova,' said Jo, 'or do you do desserts, too?'

'Sadly, no. That would be good, thanks.'

Not long after, their meal over, they rose to leave, Jo and Col dropping Fran and Owen off outside Fran's townhouse before driving off again.

The pair stood awkwardly on the paved driveway, alone again after being protected by the company of the others.

'Well,' Owen said, his hands in his pockets, 'thanks again. I guess I'll see you in the office tomorrow.'

'You will.' It was as if Fran suddenly morphed from friend back into her PA persona. Her barrier was up again, making Owen wonder if he'd imagined it was ever down.

Twenty-four

The week passed in a blur for Fran. Now the new building was finished, she was up to her eyes in arranging the delivery of furniture and connecting with the newly appointed staff. Most of them wouldn't be taking up their positions till January, but HR had suggested Fran touch base with them to keep them informed of the progress.

She was glad to be so busy, as it prevented her from dwelling on what had happened between her and Owen on the weekend. Nothing had happened, really. But she couldn't dismiss how she'd felt when Owen put his arm around her shoulder. At the time, she'd assumed the trembling she experienced had been fear of the fire, but she'd been in no danger – no danger whatsoever. And she knew, deep down, that it had more to do with Owen's nearness than anything else. She'd felt it in the restaurant, too. And it scared her.

After Ben, she'd vowed never to allow herself to care about a man again. And she'd managed that very well – too well, as she'd discovered with Richard. But, she reminded herself – usually when she was in her lonely bed – she'd decided Richard wasn't what she wanted. She'd made up her mind she wanted something different, something more. She remembered Magda's prediction that she had changes ahead, a prediction she'd put down to her change of job. But what if Magda had meant something else?

She remembered, too, her conversation with Jo. Jo was a wise lady, but what could she know of the terror Fran had experienced? Jo was safely married to a man she'd known almost all her life – even if it was second time around for them both.

Thinking of Jo and Magda made Fran realise she'd been so busy she'd forgotten to contact Magda as promised. That was easily remedied. She picked up her mobile and dialled Magda's number. She got through immediately to discover Magda was still staying with a friend in town, and she arranged to meet her, along with Kay and Jo, on Saturday morning. She knew the two others wouldn't mind her muscling in on their weekly get-together, but she texted them just the same, pleased to receive a thumbs-up emoji from Jo and a smiley one from Kay.

*

By the time Saturday came around, the thought of dinner at Owen's loomed large in Fran's mind. He hadn't mentioned it all week, apart from a brief, 'See you tomorrow evening,' accompanied by a smile, before he left the previous afternoon.

Fran was glad she had the meeting with Magda to look forward to, and to fill part of the morning. Otherwise, she was sure she'd have been a nervous wreck.

She was last to arrive at the café, and the others rose to greet her with a peck on the cheek – all except Magda whom she hugged warmly. 'How are you?' she asked the older woman who was looking much brighter than Fran had expected.

'I'm okay,' Magda said. 'The important thing is I'm alive and so are all my animals. I couldn't bear it if I'd lost the dogs and the horses.'

'What will you do now?' Jo asked what all three were thinking. It wasn't everyone who'd take in Magda and her two rescue greyhounds, and there were her horses, too.

'I'll rebuild,' she said without hesitation. 'It'll be a good chance to put something modern on the old block, something that'll last me out. There's always an opportunity to build something out of the ashes of a disaster.' She gave a faint chuckle. 'And the amazing thing is that many of my plants survived the blaze. It's uncanny, as if there was an unseen hand guiding it and protecting them. I'll still have my garden.'

Fran remembered Magda's beautiful garden, the fragrance of the lavender, mint and thyme that greeted her each time she visited. She was glad something had been spared. But rebuilding would take time. What would Magda do in the meantime?

'I was glad you got in touch, Fran,' she said. 'I need to contact all my old friends and clients. I won't be around for a few months. It'll take some time to get the insurance all sorted out and my son Kenny – Jo knows him – is coming up from Adelaide. He's going to drive me and the dogs down there, and I'll stay with him for a bit. He did suggest I move down there permanently, but what would I do away from everything I know and love? We'd soon get on each other's nerves, too, if I was a permanent fixture. So, I'll be back. But I'm afraid you'll have to find another masseuse in the meantime, Fran. You, too, Jo.'

'That's the least of our worries,' Jo said. 'The important thing is that you're well and as happy as you can be in the circumstances. Is there anything we can do to help – anything you need?'

'Rotary and the Country Women's Association have provided me with all I need in the meantime. I don't need much. But you can do something for me.'

'Anything.' Fran and Jo spoke together.

'It's Jo I'll be asking,' Magda said. 'She's closest, though you might not be too far away either, Fran,' she added, giving Fran a look that sent shivers up her spine. 'It's my horses and my garden. Can you and that lovely man of yours make sure they're looked after?'

'We certainly can,' Jo said. 'I'm sure Col would love that. And maybe Owen can help him – he's the man who's looking after the Kellys' place.'

'I know who he is,' she said, giving Fran another of her looks.

Fran shivered again. What was it about this woman that could make her shiver like this on such a warm day?

The talk then became more general, and Fran blanked out when it turned to children and grandchildren. She felt, rather than saw, Magda's eyes on her from time to time, as if she knew how difficult Fran found such conversations.

When they finally parted, it was to assurances they'd keep in touch and have a grand reunion when Magda returned.

Fran gazed after Magda's retreating figure as she stood outside the café with Jo and Kay. 'She's amazing!' she said. 'I'm not sure how I'd cope with the loss of everything I own, everything I've built up here in Granite Springs. And Magda's a lot older than I am. She had more to lose.'

'I think it's what she says. To her, it's all stuff, stuff that can be replaced. She has an inner strength that sees her through. We don't all have that. Though you've managed to come through a lot, yourself, Fran,' Jo said.

'I suppose.' Fran thought back to the physical and emotional wreck she'd been when she first came to Granite Springs. She had come a long way from that, but felt she still had a long way to go. She thought of what Magda had whispered to her as they hugged goodbye.

"There's a light at the end of the tunnel. Be patient. Accept what is given to you. Be willing to give in return." What did she mean?

*

Fran dressed carefully for dinner at Owen's, telling herself it was nothing special, but pleased with the result as she admired the effect of the turquoise calf-length dress matched with a pair of white wedge-heeled sandals. But when she picked up the wine she'd bought and slung her bag over her shoulder, she had butterflies in her stomach.

All the way out to the property she tried to tell herself it was no big deal. It was simply dinner with a few friends – one of whom happened to be her new boss. Passing through the State Forest, she was shocked by the devastation caused by the fire. This was the first time she'd seen it first-hand, and the television shots had failed to do justice to the starkness of the landscape with the blackened trees and brown scorched leaves. The amazing thing to Fran was that, already, there was new growth – a scattering of green shoots popping up everywhere below the scarred branches. It was true what the pundits said about the Australian undergrowth being able to adapt to fire and regenerate.

Hopping out of the car to close the gate, Fran gave a sigh of relief to see two cars already parked beside the shed. She was last to arrive. The thing she'd been dreading most was that she might be first. She wasn't quite sure why that would have bothered her. She and Owen worked together; they were alone together in her office every morning and several times during each day. But this felt different. This wasn't work.

'Welcome, Fran. A bit different from last time, eh?' Owen greeted her at the door. At least he didn't make any attempt at the pecks on the cheek or hugs she received from his other guests, merely touching her gently on the arm as he thanked her for the bottle of wine. Before long they were all seated on the veranda with glasses of wine or beer, the cats prowling around their feet trying to decide where to settle.

There was an air of reprieve among the group in recognition of how close this and the neighbouring property had come to being destroyed. The women reported on their conversation with Magda, and they all fell silent for a moment. Then Col looked up at the sky.

'It's looking a bit dark up there,' he said. 'I wouldn't be surprised if we got some rain. Pity it didn't come last weekend when we needed it.'

'We still need it,' Jo said. 'The land's bone dry.' Then she turned to Owen. 'See what you've subjected yourself to,' she said with a chuckle. 'We're obsessed with the weather. But it can mean life or death in the country. We only have small acreages, here. What the big farmers are suffering doesn't bear thinking about.'

Owen disappeared into the house to finish cooking, the cats following him, having decided on their loyalty.

'So, Fran, are you liking The Mad House?' Nick asked. That's what the students are calling our new school,' he explained to a puzzled Jo and Col.

Fran laughed. 'I sometimes think they've chosen a most apt term. There are many days when I think that's exactly where I am – in a mad house. But, on the whole, I'm enjoying the challenge. Owen's very different from you to work with, but I enjoy the challenge of setting up something from scratch. You've heard we're moving in on Monday?'

'I heard something of the sort. Young Joshua is very excited at the prospect. I'll be sad to lose him from education, but it was a foregone conclusion at least one of my guys would go.'

'Pity it wasn't one of the others,' Kay said, pursing her lips. 'Talking of which, I haven't seen you at choir since you got back, Fran.'

'What's that got to do with your choir?' Jo wondered.

'Nothing, really,' Fran said. 'It's the connection. The person we were referring to lectures in music education. He's keen to take over as director of the choir Kay and I belong to when our current director retires. And the reason I haven't been, Kay, is that I've had a few run-ins with that person at work. For that reason, I decided to give choir a miss for a bit.'

'Did someone mention a choir?' Owen asked, joining them. 'I didn't know there was one in Granite Springs.'

'There are probably a few,' Jo said, 'but Fran and Kay belong to the most popular one. The Granite Springs Choristers have been going for years, led by one of the town's prominent musicians. Old George Turnbull founded the choir when he was a young man. He must be close to eighty now and still going strong. I always wondered about him and Magda,' she said, a twinkle in her eye. 'They must be about an age.'

'You women,' Col said, 'always trying to match people up.'

There was a deathly hush, during which Fran blushed, and Owen looked awkward.

'What have I said?' Col asked, seemingly bewildered at the effect of his words on the group.

'Nothing, darling.' Jo patted him on the leg. 'Drink your beer.'

'Tell me more about this choir,' Owen demanded. 'I'm interested.'

'It's quite a large group,' Kay said, 'Men and women. We meet weekly out at the campus in the old music room. Then we put on a couple of recitals each year and, of course, the Messiah at Christmas.'

'Why haven't I heard about this before?' he asked, directing his question to Fran.

She shrugged. 'I guess it never came up. I haven't renewed my membership since I got back and… it's something Ron Harris sees as his.'

'How so?'

'He's been a member since he was a teenager and has always assumed – I guess we've all assumed – he'll take over from old George one day. Oh, no!' she said, seeing a wicked glint in Owen's eye. 'But, yes, he saw that as being part of his new role if he was named the new Head of School.'

'I'd love to come along. Can anyone attend – join?'

'I think anyone can come along to practices to listen. No one ever does. But George has a stringent test for anyone wanting to join.' She gave Owen a wry glance. 'You're not thinking… Oh, hell. I can imagine Ron's face if you turn up.' She started to laugh, suddenly feeling relaxed.

'We meet on Tuesdays at seven,' Kay said.

'Would it be all right if I came along this week?' he asked, then, turning to Fran, said, 'Why don't you come, too? You must be missing it.'

'Yes, do!' Kay said.

Fran wished the ground would open up and swallow her. But wasn't this what she wanted – to see Owen outside work? And this way there wouldn't just be the two of them. Kay would be there, too – and the rest of the choir. She stifled her previous objection – that she wanted to keep out of Ron's way – and found herself saying, 'Okay. Sounds good.'

'Great. Now, dinner's ready.' Owen rubbed his hands together. 'I haven't done one of your wonderful country recipes, Jo,' he said. 'It's my old standby.'

As they trooped through the kitchen to the dining room, a delightful fragrant and spicy aroma assaulted their nostrils.

'Mmm, smells good,' Nick said, as Owen ushered them through.

He waited till they were all seated before disappearing again, only to reappear with a large dish of paella, followed by a bowl of salad and a platter of crusty bread.

'Feels like we're in Spain,' Nick said. 'Didn't you…?'

'Take a sabbatical there back when? Yes. Brit and I spent several months in northern Spain at the University of Salamanca. Some wonderful music around there. And I discovered Spanish cooking.'

'You speak Spanish?' Fran asked in surprise.

'*Ciertamete, mi señora,*' he replied with a grin. '*Te ves muy bonita esta noche.*'

Fran felt herself redden. She didn't know what he said but it sounded like a compliment.

'*Hablas español?*'

That much she thought she understood. She shook her head then looked around to see the reaction of the others. She needn't have worried. Nick had started to pour wine, and the others were equally distracted. It was as if she and Owen were caught up in a little bubble of their own. Fran wasn't sure how she felt about that.

'I see you discovered Granite Springs' best kept secret,' Kay said, helping herself to a serving of paella which included a selection of squid, prawns, mussels and white fish fillets.

'If you mean Lennie, the fishman who brings his van up from

the coast, then yes, I have. I was wrong when I imagined it would be difficult to find fresh fish here.'

'Mmm, delicious,' Fran said, taking her first taste. There was more to this man than she'd given him credit for. It was easy to dismiss his casual appearance and lackadaisical manner. She threw a discrete glance in his direction. He was engaged in some apparently serious debate with Col. She heard the words "goats" and "horses" and assumed they were discussing animal care. Who'd have thought the disreputable figure who'd appeared in her doorway those weeks ago would turn into this?

By the end of the meal, Fran was feeling very mellow – the wine had helped – and was glad she'd come. They were a nice group of people and, even though Kay and Jo must be around ten years older than her, she felt drawn to them. They'd become friends. The only other real friend she'd made in Granite Springs was Marie from The Bean Sprout. She'd neglected her shamelessly since she started in her new position, and Marie hadn't been in the café when Fran had hoped to have the chance to chat with her. She planned to rectify that in the coming week.

Suddenly, it was all over, and they were standing outside in the moonlight, saying their farewells. The property looked like a ghost town, the tall silhouettes of the trees reaching up into the darkness, into a sky which was filled with more stars than Fran ever remembered seeing before.

'Beautiful, isn't it?'

Fran was startled out of her dreaming by the sound of Owen's voice. Looking around, she realised that, while she was stargazing, the other two couples had left. There was only her and Owen left. Her stomach did a flip and she drew in a breath. It was as if they were alone in the world.

And it seemed the most natural thing in the world when Owen reached an arm around her and drew her towards him.

'I've been wanting to do this all night,' he said, his breath on her face, his lips so close to hers that...

Fran's heart raced madly, her breath coming in gasps. Was this what she was afraid of? Or was it what she wanted, what she'd been waiting for, too?

Their lips met, and her world stood still.

Twenty-five

Owen stood on the veranda with his morning coffee and breathed in the fresh morning air. The storm which had blown through overnight had been fierce and brought a much-needed deluge. But now, the sun shone brightly and, apart from a few puddles and drops of water still hanging to the leaves of the trees, you could be forgiven for thinking it had never happened.

Like last night with Fran. It had happened so suddenly, felt so right, and been so wonderful, that Owen wondered if he'd imagined that, too.

He'd just waved off the two cars when he turned to see her gazing at the heavens looking so tempting in the moonlight that, against his best intentions, he hadn't been able to resist taking her in his arms. The sensation of her soft, pliable body so close to his had been all he'd dreamed it would be and their lips had met in a searing kiss. At first, Fran had clung to him in a moment of shared passion, then, seeming to remember where she was, who he was, she'd pulled away, lifting a hand to her mouth, her eyes wide in astonishment.

They'd stared at each other for what seemed an eternity then Fran said, 'I… I think I'd better go,' and made a dash for her car.

Owen remembered how he'd stood watching her leave, too stunned to speak by the combination of his own actions, her response, and the feelings she'd aroused in him.

Now he wondered if, in giving into his instincts, by pulling her into an embrace, he'd ruined everything. He was still trying to work out if it had been the best thing that had ever happened to him or a dreadful mistake, when he became aware of a small black object sitting on one of the fenceposts close to the front gate.

He blinked then decided to stroll over to see what it was. Putting down his half-drunk mug of coffee he made his way to the fence line where a small black cat was curled up on top of the corner post. Owen reached out a hand, only to have the creature spit and stretch out its claws. He smiled. It was only a kitten. But what was it doing here? Where had it come from? And how long had it been sitting on the post?

Carefully, Owen reached over the animal's shoulder and, pinching his fingers, he picked it up by the loose skin on its neck. It relaxed and curled up into a ball, allowing him to carry it back to the house.

Once there, he wreaked the ire of Oscar and Lucinda who, rather than welcoming the kitten as a new addition to the household, seemed to see his intrusion into their territory as a personal affront. They prowled around, growled, and ignored all of Owen's attempts to cajole them into meeting the new arrival, hissing every time he came close.

The kitten, too, began to hiss as soon as Owen released him and deposited him in an empty box in the laundry. He provided him with food and water and closed the door. What was he to do? Obviously, the kitten couldn't stay here, but equally, Owen wasn't about to turn him out.

Then he remembered the conversation about pets with Fran. Hadn't she said she was thinking of getting a cat? Had she been serious? The arrival of this tiny creature might be the very thing he needed; an excuse to get in touch with her. After last night, any overture by him might be seen as suspect, and he'd been dreading Monday morning in case she considered he'd overstepped the mark.

But he knew he couldn't just let it go. After that kiss, he had to say something, do something. Owen scratched his chin. Fran was different from the women he'd known in Sydney. And, after Brit, there'd been a few – quite a few. But none in recent years, and none who'd got under his skin the way Fran had in the few short months they'd been working together.

Impetuous, as always, he picked up the phone and called her number.

*

Being Sunday, the road into town was almost deserted, so it didn't take long for Owen to drive to Fran's. It was just as well. Driving with an angry cat shut inside a box on the passenger seat was no fun.

The phone conversation with Fran had been odd. He should have taken time to consider what he was going to say, but that was in hindsight. In his usual fashion, he'd blundered in, telling her about the cat and making no reference to the previous evening. Maybe he should have – but what was there to say? Should he apologise? For what? Or should he pretend it had never happened? No, he couldn't do that. He was still wondering how he should have handled the conversation when he drew up outside her townhouse.

Lifting the box containing a now very agitated cat out of the car, along with a bag of cat food, Owen took a deep breath before heading to the door and ringing the bell.

'Hello. Is this the cat?' Fran's greeting was as impersonal as ever. The night before might never have happened.

'It might be best if we take it into your laundry or somewhere small. He's not very happy. I'm not sure what he'll do when we open the box,' Owen said.

'Through here.' Fran led the way into a tiny laundry and closed the door behind them. The size of the room forced them so close together Owen could smell Fran's perfume – that same fragrance of lemon and jasmine he remembered. He inhaled, his body remembering how hers had felt pressed against him.

'Can I let him out now?' Fran's question jerked him back to the present.

'Do it carefully. I'm not sure how he'll react. And watch out for his claws. He may be little but they're sharp.' Owen had cause to remember; his fingers bore the scars where they'd pierced his skin.

Slowly and carefully, Fran opened the box. To Owen's surprise, the kitten was now still and looked up at Fran, his eyes like saucers of blue ink.

'Oh, he's beautiful!' she exclaimed. 'And you found him on your fencepost? How could anyone put him out into the storm? I'm going to call him Stormy. You like that, don't you?' she said to the cat, picking him up and cuddling him.

Owen waited for the spitting, hissing and scratching. It didn't happen. The kitten, who had been so angry, so full of fire and fury, was as docile as… a kitten. Owen grinned at the analogy. Stormy was behaving just as a kitten should. Somehow, in a matter of seconds, the creature had taken to Fran, had sensed her love for him and had calmed down completely. 'Well, I'll be…' he said, lost for words to describe the transformation he'd just witnessed. 'He seems to like you.'

'Of course he does.'

'I brought some food, too.' Owen said, pointing to the bag of cat food. 'But you may need cat litter and some other stuff.'

'I can get that later today. Now you're here,' she said, putting down the cat who immediately began to explore his new surroundings, 'would you like a cup of tea or coffee?'

'Coffee would be good.' Owen followed Fran into the kitchen and stood feeling helpless as she busied herself with filling the electric jug and the coffee maker.

'I prefer tea at this time of day,' she said by way of explanation, her back to Owen.

He took a deep breath. 'About last night…'

Fran turned, her face reddening, the electric jug in one hand. She carefully placed it on the kitchen bench and met his eyes. Hers were full of what he took to be… fear.

'I hope… I… Hell, Fran, I'm not going to apologise. I know I'm your boss. I know I acted without thinking – like I often do. But you looked so damned good, standing there in the moonlight, the soft light glinting on your hair, I couldn't help myself. And I don't regret it, not for an instant. So, if you…'

To his surprise, Fran stepped up to him and placed a finger gently on his lips. 'I don't either,' she said with a smile. 'But don't think that means I'm ready to hop into bed with you.'

Owen gasped. He hadn't thought… Well, he supposed it had crossed his mind. But that it had occurred to her too meant… What did it mean?

'I thought for a moment you were going to tell me you were too drunk to know what you were doing,' Fran admitted later, when they'd finished their tea and coffee and were seated together on the sofa. Stormy, now released from the laundry, was playing with a ball of wool at their feet. 'But it won't make any difference at work, will it? I mean we still have to keep up the appearance of being…'

'Like Nick and Kay?'

'No! I mean I don't want any gossip about us.'

'Well, no one will hear it from me.'

'Nor me. Now,' she said, 'I do have something planned for this afternoon, and I need to get a few more things for this little one.'

As if aware he was the subject of their conversation, Stormy rubbed himself around Fran's ankles. It was difficult to believe this was the same cat who'd hissed, spat and scratched at Owen that morning. 'He's certainly made himself at home,' he said. 'It's as if he's been here forever.'

'Isn't it?' Fran said smugly. 'I think he knew exactly what he was doing when he arrived on your fencepost.'

'Hmm.' Owen thought that was taking the idea of predestination a bit far, but said nothing, unwilling to spoil the intimacy they'd built up in such a short time. And it was all due to this cat, so maybe there was something in what she said, after all. 'There are more things in heaven and earth, Horatio,' he muttered to himself, then in a louder voice, 'Okay, I'd best be off.'

At the door, they stood apart. Owen scuffed the concrete path with one foot. I don't suppose you'd have dinner with me again. At The Riverside?'

Fran blushed – she was pretty when she blushed, more approachable. It was as if the blush broke through the barrier she'd erected around herself – or was it last night's kiss that had done that?

'Are you sure?'

'I'm sure.' Owen realised he'd never been more sure of anything in his life, not even when he and Brit were young and in love. Was that what this was about? Was he falling in love with Fran Reilly? Or was he only intent on breaking through to find the woman who was hiding underneath the mask she showed the world?

'Then okay.'

Twenty-six

Fran couldn't believe it. She'd just made a date with Owen Larsen, Professor Owen Larsen. Her heart was singing as she drove into town. She didn't want to get carried away. Owen was her boss, after all – they'd have to meet in the office on Monday – and what did she really know about him?

Nick's rundown on his background had been brief, but that had been before she'd met him, before she'd experienced his personality – and before she likened him to Ben, she reminded herself. But it was more than that, she was sure, immediately doubting her judgement. And that kiss! The memory of it had kept her awake, though she'd never let him know. It had touched a part of her she'd thought dead forever.

Fran knew one of the supermarkets would be open, so she'd be able to buy what she needed for her new house guest. Before leaving home, she'd made a list – cat litter, a litter tray, something to use as a cat bed – the box would have to go – and some toys for Stormy to play with.

And she'd promised herself to call in on Marie this morning, a phone call prior to Owen's to her, confirming she'd be home and be pleased to see her. She could tell Marie about Owen. It would be good to talk with someone completely unconnected with the university scene. Kay and Jo were all very well, but they were too involved. They knew Owen, and they were older and happily married. They probably wanted to match up everyone they met – just as Col had said. How much could she trust their opinions?

Then Fran saw things in a new light. It was as if she had an epiphany. She'd relied on her own counsel for too long; she was beginning to suspect everyone's motives. Jo and Kay were good friends who only had Fran's happiness at heart. She remembered her conversation with Jo when the other woman had suggested it might be time for her to let go a bit. Well, she'd certainly done that last night. She hugged herself at the memory of Owen's arms around her, his lips on hers. It had been as if… No, she wouldn't go there. Ben was dead. Owen was very much alive.

Fran was glad she'd decided to drive to town this morning. By the time she'd finished her shopping, she'd managed to collect a heap of stuff. Who'd have thought a tiny kitten would need so much? By the time she reached Marie's home, she was feeling exhausted.

'Hello, stranger,' Marie greeted her with a hug. 'It's good to see you.'

'Good to see you, too. I've allowed myself to get caught up in this new position at the uni. I need to manage my time better.'

'Well, you're here now. I hope we're going to see you back at choir soon, too.'

'Oh!' Fran remembered her promise to Kay – and Owen – that she'd be there on Tuesday. It could be even more awkward now she and Owen were – what?

Her consternation must have shown on her face.

'What's wrong?'

'Oh, Marie! Let's have a cuppa and I'll tell you everything.'

Once Fran was clutching a steaming cup of peppermint tea, she began to speak. Marie was one of the few people to whom she'd confided the story of her and Ben – the only one until Jo. They'd met soon after Fran was released from hospital. She'd found the little café on Main Street and had ventured in, to be welcomed by the lively dark-haired woman. Marie had proven to be exactly what Fran needed to help her through her pain. It had been Marie who suggested she stay in Granite Springs while she recovered. And she was still here.

'So, you see,' she said at last. 'It's brought it all back – Ben, the accident. And I don't know if it's Owen I like, or if I'm seeing Ben in him and trying to relive the past. It's all such a mess!' She took a sip of tea, inhaling its distinctive aroma.

'I can see how you might think that,' Marie said gently, 'but it was years ago, Fran. In your heart you know that. You know Ben's dead. Sorry to put it so bluntly, but it's true. The lovely young man you were in love with didn't have the chance to grow up. Owen did. He's a grown man in his fifties, from what you've told me – a far cry from the young man in his twenties you loved back then. And you're a different person, too. You've grown, changed, matured. I remember that young woman very well. She was scared of her own shadow. You're a strong, independent woman – who sometimes gets herself tied in knots.' She grinned to take the sting out of her words.

'You think?'

'I do. I think what you and Owen have may be something special. It may not. But only time will tell. You need to give it a chance. And I do know a thing or two about relationships – what makes them work and what doesn't,' she said ruefully.

Fran peered at Marie, recalling the woman's own story. She and her former husband still worked together in the café – the café which had been in his family for generations. They'd remained friends when he moved out of the house to live in the little flat above the café. It seemed to work for them.

'You don't think I'm being stupid?'

'I'm the last person to call anyone stupid, after the mess I made of my life. But no. Not stupid. I think you're just being cautious, and that's not a bad thing. This Owen of yours sounds like an interesting guy.'

'He's not mine,' Fran objected, but she felt a thrill of pleasure at Marie's words. And she felt vindicated in her decision. Decision? Had she really made the decision to have dinner with Owen, or had she just given in to her animal instincts?

It was as if Marie read her mind. 'So, tell me, he's hot, isn't he?'

Fran pictured Owen with his new haircut, the thick fading blond hair falling over his face, his penetrating blue eyes, his… 'I suppose,' she said. 'But you'll see for yourself on Tuesday night.'

'Tuesday night? You mean?'

'He's coming to choir. And that's another thing.' Fran sighed. 'He and Ron haven't hit it off. Well, I guess they couldn't be expected to since Owen got the job Ron wanted.'

'You'd have hated working for him.'

'Yes,' Fran acknowledged. 'I might not have accepted the position. But it's meant Ron has it in for Owen and tries to aggravate him every chance he gets. What he'll do when Owen turns up at choir, I can't imagine.'

'Should be fun to watch.'

'Oh, you!' One of the things Fran admired about Marie was her ability to find amusement or a positive slant to almost everything. 'You still running those classes and birthday parties in the back room?'

'I sure am. But it's beginning to wear thin. It's been almost every weekend these past few months. I barely have any time to myself. It may be time for a change for me, too.'

Fran looked at her friend more closely. It hadn't occurred to her Marie was anything less than happy with her life. She seemed to have it all – a nice house, an amicable relationship with her ex, a plum job in the café…

'Oh, don't listen to me,' Marie said in a rush. 'It's just been an exceptionally busy time. Maybe I only need a few days respite. Now, when are you moving into this magnificent new building of yours?'

'The Mad House?'

'The what?'

'It's what the students call the School of Music and Drama. But tomorrow's the big day. Then things should slow down a bit till the staff and students arrive next semester.

After catching up on some local gossip and Marie's tales of putting people up during the bushfire, Fran took her leave.

On the way home, she pondered on Marie's advice, coming to the conclusion nothing in this life was certain, but that, unless you were willing to take a risk, nothing would change. Was she willing to take that risk – and was the possibility of a relationship with Owen worth the risk of her being hurt again? Marie's own experience was an example there were many ways for a good relationship to end.

Twenty-seven

Today was the big day! They were finally going to move into the new building. And not a day too soon. Owen had become tired of making do in someone else's office space and he was sure Fran must feel the same way.

He rose early, wakened by the birds and, as had become his habit, took his coffee outside to survey what he now thought of as his domain. He'd be sad to leave this place when the owners returned. To his surprise, he'd be sad to leave the cats, too. He'd come to welcome their sporadic forays into the house and to feel flattered by their indiscriminate spells of attention. Maybe he'd have to get himself one when he found a more permanent home.

His thoughts turned to Fran and the kitten he'd taken over to her the day before. It had been a good move, allowed him to see her again, to dispel any wrong impressions. And, to set up a dinner date. Although he knew he'd see her away from the office at this choir thing tomorrow, it would be with other people again. He wanted her to himself and had been unsure how to arrange it. The words had flown out of his mouth in his usual thoughtless fashion. But she'd agreed. That was the important thing.

This morning he could smell spring in the air. The jasmine covering one end of the veranda was beginning to bloom and its sweet cloying scent was almost overpowering. Out in the home paddock, the fruit trees were a riot of colour, and farther away the blooms of the dreaded Patterson's Curse formed a pretty purple carpet. He was glad they'd escaped the scourges of the fire. He'd seen the goats grazing on it and wasn't sure if it was poisonous to them. He made a mental note to check.

After a quick breakfast of toast and vegemite, Owen was on his way. He'd taken John at his word and was now driving the Suzuki. It handled the dirt road so much better than his old bomber, that he'd determined to trade his old friend in for something similar. He still hadn't tried out the bike, though he'd looked at it longingly several times, imagining himself hurtling along the back lanes, or even the highway – maybe with Fran on the pillion.

The car park was empty when he arrived, and he walked briskly to his new workplace. He used his card, entered the security code, then pushed open the door.

He sniffed in the unfamiliar smells – new carpet, polish, and that indefinable odour new buildings seemed to release. It would all disappear in a few short weeks to be replaced by the more familiar smell of young bodies, the silence replaced with chatter. Heading to his office on the second level of the building, Owen stroked the smooth surface of his new desk, then turned to where an electronic keyboard had now been set up. His fingers itched to touch the keys, but that was an indulgence that would have to wait.

Glad he'd arrived before Fran, Owen made his usual trip to Banjo's to pick up two coffees and his now regular order of croissants. He could see no reason to change his habits now they were in their own space.

'Hi, Prof,' greeted the long-haired student serving there this morning. 'Big day, huh?'

Owen agreed, paid for his order and headed back, whistling as he went. Life was good and about to get better. This move to Granite Springs had been a good decision.

Fran was already in her office when he returned. The offices were designed much the same as in the Education building, with Fran's office an adjunct to his. This meant he had to pass through hers to access his own. He'd get to see more of her this way, without having to make his way down a flight of stairs and along a corridor of other offices.

'Good morning and welcome!'

She turned.

'Coffee?'

'You went to Banjo's? I've been setting up your Nespresso machine.'

'Old habits die hard. What's a morning without croissants? And we have to keep Banjo's in business. We can try out the new machine later.'

'I know who to blame when I can no longer fit into my clothes,' Fran said with a laugh, looking down at her slim figure. They'd polished off the coffee and croissants in no time and Fran was brushing the pastry flakes from her new desk into her equally new wastepaper bin.

'You look pretty much all right to me,' Owen said, immediately looking round to ensure there was no one within hearing distance. But it seemed they were the only ones in the building. He didn't want to be accused of impropriety. You never knew these days with all the talk of sexual harassment. Someone might take it the wrong way.

'We'll be having a deputation from the vice chancellor down, later this morning,' she said, reverting to her professional persona without blinking an eye.

Owen wondered how she did it. One minute she appeared to be the woman he'd been with yesterday, the one who'd agreed to have dinner with him, the one whose finger he could still feel on his lips. The next she was back to being his very correct PA.

'Right. Guess I should get organised, then.' Owen went into his own office which was at least twice the size of the one he'd occupied in Sydney. The boxes of books he'd brought with him were stacked on one side, close to a wall of empty bookcases.

'Do you need any help? I can't do much till the deputation's over. I've organised morning tea for the masses.'

'Masses?'

'Well, I expect all the faculty heads will want a look, and the library manager. Then there will be those staff who're curious, maybe the odd student. And don't forget your nemesis.' She chuckled.

'How could I? Will he want to be assigned an office?'

'I expect so. Joshua will have one since he'll be on permanent staff. I suppose we could get away with suggesting Ron stick with his current one in Education, but…'

'I know, I know. Let's give the guy an office if it'll make him happy

– at least till we have the full complement of staff, which won't be for another year, at least.' But the thought of seeing Ron Harris's unhappy face every day did nothing to cheer him. 'Anyway,' he recalled Fran's question, 'I could do with some help in unpacking these boxes and shelving the books in some sort of order.'

'Alphabetical?' asked Fran with an amused smile.

Owen nodded, returning the smile. This was a bit like playing house. Just him and Fran unpacking and setting things up.

They worked easily together for a while, then there was a knocking from downstairs.

'That'll be the catering,' Fran said, rising from her knees where she'd been emptying one more box. 'I'll help them set up. The foyer okay?'

'Go for your life. I can finish up here so it's all neat and tidy for the grand tour.' It was an odd feeling – being in charge. Owen hadn't felt it till now. Until today, he'd had the title of professor, but had barely been aware of his change in status. Today it was finally sinking in. He was glad he'd had his hair cut, and he'd made an effort to dress more smartly this morning – though it had been more in an attempt to impress Fran than any visitors.

Owen continued to order his books on the shelves, though without Fran to keep him on task, he would pause to study a favourite tome, the voices and rattle of dishes from down below only barely audible.

It was a shock when he heard footsteps, a gentle knock on his door, and a discrete cough. Turning from a favourite collection of essays by Alfred Brendell, which he'd picked up a few years earlier, he saw Aaron Peters standing in the open doorway.

'Vice Chancellor! I didn't realise you'd arrived. I'm sorry I wasn't downstairs to greet you. Fran didn't…'

'Don't blame your PA. She wanted to fetch you, but I told her I could find my way up here. It's looking good, isn't it? Are you pleased with what I understand they're calling The Mad House?' he chuckled.

'I'm thrilled to be here and delighted with this building. I hope your faith in me is justified. I know there were others who…'

'You were the outstanding candidate, Owen. Don't let anyone tell you otherwise. I know there may be a few noses out of joint – one in particular – but it's up to us – to you – to make sure you demonstrate we made the correct choice.'

*

'Well, I'm glad that's over.' Owen gave a heartfelt sigh of relief when the crowd eventually left and the catering staff had removed all the dishes and debris. 'I didn't expect so many of them to turn up.'

'I did,' Fran said as they walked upstairs together, her perfume distracting him.

Now he knew how it felt to have her in his arms, Owen found her very nearness tempting. He forced himself to concentrate on what she was saying.

'Do you want to keep going with the unpacking?' she asked.

'No, you can get on with what you need to do. If it won't disturb you, I need to check the keyboard hasn't sustained any damage in transit. I'll close my door.' It was an excuse. Although he was eager to check out the keyboard, he had to get out of Fran's way lest he disgrace himself by acting unprofessionally and ruining his chances for good. He was very conscious they were alone in this huge building. It would be better tomorrow when Joshua – maybe even Ron – had moved in.

Thinking of Ron reminded Owen of the choir he was going to visit tomorrow. That should prove interesting.

*

The music room was in a building Owen hadn't been in before. It sat at the edge of the campus as if it had been an afterthought, but had the look and feel of a much older building. As he walked towards it, he could hear the sound of voices raised in the familiar bars of *For unto us a Child is born*. He stopped to listen. They were good, very good. Much better than he'd have expected from a small-town choir. He berated himself. He was being just as bad as Darren – denigrating Granite Springs and assuming things here wouldn't match up to those in the city. He switched his mobile to silent, pushed open the door and walked in.

Once inside, the sound swelled to a crescendo, then stopped, the silence deafening. Unable to control himself, Owen applauded.

Everyone turned to stare at him. He flinched. He hadn't intended to signal his presence, not so soon, anyway. Confronted by a mass of faces, most noticeably the angry red face of Ron Harris, he moved forward.

'Sorry, I didn't mean to interrupt,' he said to the conductor – the same elderly grey-haired man who'd been with Magda after the fire. 'That was a superb rendition, I couldn't help myself. You're all to be congratulated.' His eyes swept over the group. He saw Kay, but there was no sign of Fran. A wave of disappointment swept over him. 'Owen Larsen,' he added, realising he should introduce himself.

'Owen Larsen! We meet again! I've heard about you, young man.' George left his place to come forward and shake Owen by the hand. 'A worthy addition to our community. I believe I heard you play in Sydney – when was it?'

'It would be quite a few years ago, now. I haven't played in public for a long time. But don't let me interrupt your session. I only came to observe.'

'You're most welcome to do that, but do consider joining us. I'm sure you'd add to our humble group, and maybe… But more of that later.' George turned back to the choir and they continued.

Owen took a seat and leant back, prepared to be entertained.

He sensed someone slip into the seat beside him, felt a gentle hand on his arm and smelt a now familiar fragrance.

'George likes you,' Fran whispered. 'But look at Ron's face.'

Owen glanced at the choir whose members were silently waiting for George's next directions. Sure enough, from his place in the bass section, Ron was glaring at Owen as if he'd usurped the other's domain. 'Too bad! I think I may take George up on his invitation,' he whispered back with a grin. 'You'll be re-joining, too?'

'Wouldn't miss it. But you do know what George was implying, don't you?'

'Implying?' Owen was puzzled.

'He's been wanting to retire for some time, but Ron has always been his natural successor. I think the poor man has only kept going till another potential contender appears.'

'You don't think? The man doesn't even know me.'

'But he obviously knows of your reputation. Just wait. Shh.' She put a hand to her lips as the choir began again, this time with *Glory to God in the Highest.* This was followed by the bass rendering of *The people that walked.* Owen had to admit Ron had a good voice. He was a talented musician. It was just such a pity he had trouble communicating and seemed to harbour such a grudge against Owen.

As the last piece was drawing to a close, Owen took Fran's hand and led her outside. 'I don't want to face the bastard,' he said. 'Time enough next week. They meet every Tuesday?'

Fran nodded and tried to pull her hand away. Owen had been enjoying the feel of her fingers in his, but released them, unwilling to risk her annoyance.

'So,' he said, wondering if he dare invite her for a drink. But his hopes were dashed when Kay rushed out of the hall.

'I'm so glad you came, Fran,' she said. 'We could do with your input. The contralto section is a bit weak. Good to see you, too, Owen,' she added. 'Can we expect you to join the choir, too? George seemed pleased to see you.'

'I might just do that,' Owen replied, smiling at her enthusiasm.

'Good. Coffee, Fran?' she asked.

Owen saw Fran nod, and the two women strolled away, much to his disappointment. But he'd see Fran in the office tomorrow and there was dinner on Friday to look forward to. As he made his way to his car, Owen automatically checked his phone. There was a missed call and three texts from Pia. He frowned. That was unusual. He was normally the one to initiate contact. He pressed her number to call her back, but there was no reply. He left a message, then headed for home.

Twenty-eight

It had proved to be a busy week. After moving in on Monday, Fran found herself faced with a number of unexpected tasks, not least of which was to attempt to satisfy Ron Harris, who'd taken umbrage at Owen's appearance at what he thought of as *his* choir and demanded one of the better offices with a view over the lake.

That done, she'd been able to focus on setting up timetables for the following year and providing Owen with a list of potential attendees for the grand opening, which was to take place early December. The vice chancellor wanted it to be a big affair with not only all the local dignitaries, but some national figures to act as a drawcard and symbolise the university's standing in the Arts arena.

Now it was Friday, and Fran was in two minds about the dinner date she'd agreed to. But it was too late to pull out now. And she'd still have to face Owen next week.

'What do you think, Stormy?' she asked the cat, who'd become the recipient of her confidences since his appearance in her life only a week earlier. And she had Owen to thank for him, too. But, as usual, the creature ignored her, preferring to curl up on her bed and close his eyes.

Checking her outfit in the mirror, Fran wondered if she looked as if she was trying too hard. She'd ignored the dresses favoured by Richard, choosing instead a pair of wide-legged black pants – supposed to be fashionable – and a fuchsia shirt she'd been told suited her. She wasn't sure why she was going to so much trouble. It wasn't as if she fancied the man and *his* sense of fashion was non-existent. Then she remembered how his kiss had made her feel, remembered Marie's advice, remembered her friend's phone call the morning after Owen's appearance at choir.

'Go for it, girl,' Marie had said. 'He's seriously hot. Exactly what you need after that cold fish, Richard.'

Marie had never met Richard, but Fran had told her about him, though not about his proposal. She smoothed her hair across her brow, picked up her bag and, with a, 'See you later. Be good,' to Stormy, who lazily opened one eye before closing it again, went to her car.

The Riverside car park was almost full, but Fran spied an empty space next to the Suzuki Owen was driving. She slid her car in, checked her hair in the mirror, wondering as she did so, if that was something else she should change.

When the long blonde tresses Ben had loved were relentlessly shorn by the medics after her accident, she'd made the decision to keep it short, and had done so ever since. It was easy to care for, and she thought the highlights she'd added as the grey began to peek through, gave it an extra something and kept her looking smart. It had been a look Richard appreciated. All the more reason to change it now. *What did Owen's ex-wife look like?* The thought came from nowhere, to be immediately dismissed.

Fran smelled the familiar aroma of garlic, spices and herbs as she entered the restaurant. It was one of her favourite spots to dine in Granite Springs, and she didn't get here nearly often enough. Owen had chosen well, though it wasn't somewhere to go if you wanted to keep your liaison secret. Gossip was clearly something that didn't bother him. Deciding to take a leaf out of his book, she walked to the desk, head held high. 'I'm meeting...' she began, only to have Steve give her a welcoming smile.

'Prof Larsen's at the table by the window in the far corner,' he said. 'Can I show you...'

'No, it's fine.' Fran saw Owen give her a not-so-subtle wave from one of the restaurant's best tables. She'd forgotten Steve knew both of them.

'You came!' Owen rose to greet her, and for a moment, she thought he was going to kiss her on the cheek, but he took her hand instead.

Fran grinned to herself. How did he know she'd almost had second thoughts and cancelled, only the thought of having to face him again in the office on Monday morning forcing her to keep her promise?

'I ordered wine,' he said. 'Pinot noir. I think you'll like it. All the more for me if you don't,' he chuckled, 'and we can order you something else.'

Another difference from Richard who'd have asked for her preference, or just assumed she'd enjoy what he ordered. To her surprise, Fran found this careless disregard for her preference refreshing. 'That'll be fine,' she said.

'Isn't this a great restaurant?' Owen enthused. 'I brought my daughter and her fellow here when they came down to visit. It didn't impress Darren – don't think anything would. But I was thrilled to find the quality of food you'd be hard-pressed to find in the city.'

'We don't do so badly here,' she said. 'And we were all here the night of the bushfire – remember?'

'Shit, so we were! You must think I'm a prize idiot.' Owen ran a hand through his hair. 'Can't get used to this,' he said ruefully.

'Wine, sir, madam?' A waiter appeared with a bottle of wine and proceeded to pour a glass for Owen to taste.

He waved him away. 'No need to fuss with that. Pour the lady a glass, too.'

Fran smiled again. This was going to be an interesting evening. She picked up her menu.

After they'd ordered – Fran choosing a pumpkin risotto and Owen a steak – he sat back regarding her with an enquiring look. 'Tell me more about yourself,' he said. 'Who is Fran Reilly when she's not organising me out of existence? Don't get me wrong, I'd be lost without your skills in the office. But there must be more to you than the woman who keeps me on the right side of the policy makers. I've already seen a little chink in your armour.' He gave her a wicked smile.

Fran felt her stomach lurch. Was he referring to the evening he'd kissed her, or what she now privately called *the episode* in her townhouse when he'd brought Stormy to her?

She played with the stem of her glass, delaying her reply. How much should she reveal? How much could she trust him with her story?

He looked encouragingly across the table at her. 'I don't bite,' he said, as if sensing her reluctance. 'I really want to know. You know my story – disreputable past, married young, divorced, grown daughter with unsuitable boyfriend, no better than I should be, come to the country to veg out.' He spread out his hands.

Fran laughed. He was such a fool. But she knew that, behind the confident, deprecating façade, was a sensitive, vulnerable individual. She'd seen glimpses of it from time to time, and it made him all the more attractive.

'There's not much to tell,' she said at last. 'I discovered Granite Springs by accident,' she began, and proceeded to give Owen a potted version of her story, omitting any mention of Ben, his bike or the lost baby – some things were too personal to share. 'So here I am,' she finished, 'and I've never regretted my decision.'

'I can understand why,' he said. 'It's a beaut spot.' He paused. 'And you… no marriage, no entanglements, no children?'

'No, none of the above.'

'I'm surprised. You're a beautiful woman, Fran. I can't believe there's been no man in your life.'

Fran blushed. 'I haven't been a nun,' she said in embarrassment, 'but no one special, no one currently.'

Was she giving away too much? Would he take that as an invitation?

Their meals arrived, and the conversation turned to the choir and the university, but every so often, Fran caught Owen glancing at her speculatively, as if he knew there was more to her story than she'd shared. Well, let him speculate. She had no intention of revealing any more of herself at this point. Maybe, if they got to know each other better… But that was all in the future. If they had a future together.

'Coffee?' Owen's question made Fran realise she'd allowed her attention to wander.

'Thanks.'

'One black and one latte,' he said to the waiter who was removing their plates. 'How's the cat?' he asked Fran. 'Is he settling in okay?'

'Stormy's just perfect,' she said, her face softening as she remembered how she'd left the new addition to her home. 'I don't know why I didn't get one before. I left him asleep on my bed. It's one of his favourite spots – that and my old rocking chair. It's one I bought at a garage sale soon after I arrived. I love to sit in it and read.'

'Good.'

They seemed to have run out of conversation. Fran was surprised. She'd never seen Owen lost for words before.

He leant his elbows on the table. Propping up his chin with his hands. 'I've enjoyed this evening, Fran, getting together away from the office, away from the campus. I'd like to see more of you.'

Fran felt the now familiar flutter in her gut. She wanted this, too. It was time, she realised, to really accept the changes Magda had foretold. She was tired of thinking "what if" or worrying about tomorrow, about other people. She wanted to take life by the horns and devil the consequences. She smiled across the table at Owen. 'I think I'd like that, too.'

He reached across to cover her hands with his and smiled, his eyes crinkling up in the way she found unbearably attractive.

How could she ever have considered him to be untidy, disreputable, a wastrel? He had more integrity in his little finger than Richard ever had. He was a man who understood emotion, passion. She tingled at his touch and a shiver of what could only be anticipation ran up the back of her neck.

'Your place?'

She nodded, too filled with excitement to speak.

It was too soon!

Fran's head told her this as she drove home, the headlights of Owen's car shining bright in her rearview mirror. But her heart was leaping in a way it hadn't for years. She knew she was throwing caution to the wind, risking losing her job – because there was no way she could stay if this went sour – but she suddenly didn't care. The old Fran was dead. This was a new woman – a woman Fran barely recognised.

To Fran's surprise, there was no awkwardness when they reached her townhouse. As if realising she was in danger of having second thoughts, Owen took charge, drawing her into his arms as soon as the door closed behind them, pressing his lips – and his body – close to hers. She felt herself melt into his embrace, her lips parting to allow his tongue to seek out hers, her whole body flooded with a warmth and strength of desire she'd forgotten.

By the time they reached the bedroom, her limbs were weak; she could barely move. She was lost in a torrent of desire for this man who'd broken down all the barriers she'd taken years to erect.

Twenty-nine

Owen opened his eyes and turned his head to see Fran fast asleep beside him. Gently he traced the contours of her face with one finger and kissed her forehead. Last night had been tremendous. Their passion had reached heights he'd only dreamed of, had never envisioned experiencing at this time of his life. But he had – they had, because he was pretty sure Fran had felt the same. Either that, or she was good at faking it.

No, her outpouring of emotion was real. He knew that. She wasn't like some of the women he'd spent time with in Sydney over the years – women who were only out for what they could get from a man. There had been a few of those after Brit – more than a few. He'd been no saint. But this was different. And Owen was different. He knew his feelings for Fran were real. This was no flash in the pan romance, no fleeting liaison. He wanted this to last. Owen gazed down at her face and smiled.

Fran opened her eyes. She stretched, her legs entwining with Owen's. Her eyes widened as she clearly remembered their night of passion and her lips turned up in a lazy smile. 'Good morning.'

'Good morning. No regrets?' He held his breath. Maybe he'd been wrong.

She shook her head. 'No regrets. You?'

'Absolutely not! Last night was… beyond belief.' He kissed her again – this time on the lips, stroking her neck, loving the feel of her soft skin under his fingers.

'Mmm.' She relaxed against him, her body awakening his again.

Suddenly a ball of fur launched itself onto Owen's shoulder, a sharp claw making contact with his neck.

'Ow!' he yelled and, releasing Fran, sat up quickly in an attempt to free himself.

The ball of fur uncurled itself to turn into the kitten he'd given Fran only a week earlier. He took hold of the cat by the scruff of its neck, seeing Fran pull the bedcovers over herself and hearing her break into a peal of laughter. 'I think Stormy's jealous,' she laughed. 'Maybe we should get up.'

'Hmm.' This would be the first time he'd been ousted from a woman's bed by a tiny kitten, but Owen agreed and laughed, too. It was probably time to start the day, anyway. And he had a plan. It had only come to him in the last few seconds, and he couldn't wait to share it with Fran. But not yet.

Once Fran had fed the cat, the creature seemed to calm down, but Owen still regarded it warily. While it seemed to have accepted Fran as its saviour, in some part of its animal mind, it still appeared to regard Owen as the enemy.

'What do you have planned for today?' Owen asked Fran over breakfast. She'd gone to town and cooked up a delicious scrambled egg dish with spinach, tomatoes, mushrooms and what looked like goat's cheese, all served on rye toast with steaming cups of herbal tea. He'd have preferred coffee but didn't say so. He could rectify that when he got home.

'Oh, just the usual,' Fran replied. She began enumerating her tasks counting them off on her fingers, 'Library, shop, laundry – maybe fit in a relaxing read. A typical Saturday for me.'

'I have a better suggestion.'

'You have?' Fran took a sip of tea, but Owen could tell he'd intrigued her.

'Why don't you come home with me? I have something I'd like to share with you. I think you'll enjoy it.'

'What is it?' She put down her cup.

'Wait and see,' he said, deciding to keep his plan as a surprise. He wanted to see the look on her face.

'O…kay.'

Why did Owen get the impression she didn't like surprises? But she'd like this one. He was sure.

They finished breakfast, and Owen waited patiently while Fran ensured Stormy had food and water and gave him a cuddle. The cat seemed content to be in her arms. Did he reserve his bad temper for Owen?

Finally, they were on their way, the Suzuki speeding out of town and through the countryside. Wanting to avoid conversation, lest he be tempted to spoil the surprise he planned, Owen turned on the radio to the local country station he'd recently discovered, pleased when it appeared it was a favourite with Fran. They drove happily along, singing together to the old eighties melodies.

Owen's cats greeted them as soon as they got out of the car, and Fran bent down to stroke them. Both Oscar and Lucinda rubbed themselves against her ankles in delight while Owen unlocked the house.

'Okay, what's the surprise?' Fran asked, following him inside and gazing around as if he was hiding something.

'All in good time. Coffee first.' He turned on his coffee machine, fed the cats, then poured two mugs of coffee.

Perched on one of the two high stools at the kitchen bench, Owen thought Fran looked good enough to eat. Today she was dressed in a pair of tight white pants, a pink and white striped shirt hanging loosely to her hips. Pink was definitely her colour, he thought, his eyes roaming over the body he now knew so well. It was all he could do to resist the temptation to take her back to bed, but there was something he wanted to do first.

As soon as they'd finished, Owen took Fran by the hand and instructed her to cover her eyes. She did this, giggling with a barely suppressed excitement. He led her outside to the shed, slid open the door, and took her inside. When they reached the Honda bike, he raised his free hand to remove hers from her eyes.

'Here it is!' he said enthusiastically. 'There are two helmets. We're going for a ride!' His eyes feasted on the object about which he'd been thinking ever since he moved in, just waiting for the right moment. The right moment was now.

There was silence – no answering yell of excitement. Nothing.

Owen turned to look at Fran. Was she so overcome she couldn't speak? Was she silently admiring his plan?

Fran stood as if transfixed. She was shaking, her whole body going into spasms. Tears were streaming down her cheeks. What the hell was the matter? Was she having an attack – some sort of fit?

'Fran!' he said, putting both hands on her shoulders. She didn't move. The shaking continued. 'Fran!' he said again, louder this time. 'What's the matter?' Owen felt helpless. He was becoming really worried. Should he call an ambulance?

Fran pushed him away and, still sobbing, her head in her hands, made her way out of the shed and dropped to the ground.

Owen rushed after her and joined her on the grass. The cats, sensing something unusual was going on, circled the pair curiously but kept their distance.

'Fran! Speak to me! Are you ill?' Owen didn't know what to do. The woman he'd spent the night with, whose body he'd made beautiful love to, the independent woman he worked with every day, was a shaking, sobbing mess and he didn't have any idea what was wrong or how to help.

He wrapped his arms around her and rocked her like he remembered doing with Pia when she was a small child. They sat like that for several minutes till, finally, Fran ceased sobbing.

She buried her face in Owen's shoulder. 'I'm sorry,' she sniffed, 'It was just…' She hiccupped.

Owen wiped her cheeks with the tail of his shirt and put one finger under her chin. 'Want to tell me what happened?'

She nodded and tried to rise.

'Let's get you to the house first.' Owen helped her up and they walked slowly inside. He could tell she was still traumatised but didn't know what had set it off.

Once they were inside, Owen helped Fran take a seat at the kitchen table and put a box of tissues in front of her. For a moment, he stood looking at her – wondering again what had caused such a spectacular meltdown – then he said, 'I think you need a glass of brandy.'

'No… Well, maybe.' Her eyes were red, but her face was still as white as a sheet.

'You need some sort of stimulant. Did something scare you? Are you ill?'

With a glass of brandy cradled in both hands, Fran gave Owen a grateful glance. 'Thanks. I'm sorry to have subjected you to that, I don't know what… well, I do, but…'

Owen took a seat beside her, turning his chair to face her side. He felt in need of a strong drink himself, but he wanted to get to the bottom of this. Fran was always too controlled, so contained, but, out there in the shed, she'd completely lost it. Was there something in the shed? But there was only the bike, some garden implements and the furniture from his Sydney house he was storing there.

'I'm sorry,' Fran said again. 'You deserve an explanation.' She took a sip of the brandy and grimaced as it went down.

Owen put a hand over hers. 'Take your time.'

'It was the bike,' she said, 'and the thought of riding on it. It brought it all back. It was a long time ago, but it was as fresh as if it was yesterday. I heard the roar, felt the thud, smelled the fuel.' She went on to explain how she came to Granite Springs – Ben, the bike ride, the accident, his death, the loss of their child and her resulting injuries. 'So, there you have it,' she finished. 'I hated seeing the bike when you moved in, but I could blank it out then. It was the idea of getting on it, of history repeating itself… I guess it stirred something inside me – the memory of that moment, and… Sorry,' she said again, 'you weren't to know.'

'*I'm* sorry.' Owen put his arms around her. He tightened them, his chin on her hair, inhaling her unique fragrance. 'My poor Franny. What a terrible experience. And you've kept it bottled up till now?'

'A couple of people know.' She raised her head, her eyes meeting his. They were wide and their grey hue seemed even deeper than usual. 'I don't see any need to broadcast my story to all and sundry. I suppose I'd have told you in time if we…' She dropped her eyes to the table.

'I'm glad to know now.' Suddenly it all became clear to Owen – why Fran was always so controlled, why she seemed to have erected a barrier around her. No wonder she'd been that way. The poor woman had suffered so much. And yet she'd managed to make a life for herself in this small country town. It must have been hard to start again, to try to put the past behind her, to blot out what had happened. He'd admired her before, but now… he was in awe of what she'd managed to achieve. No one would imagine, from her calm exterior, that she was hiding all this.

'Thanks,' she said. 'I'm feeling better now. Maybe you should take me home?'

'No. I don't think you should be alone just yet. In case you have a relapse,' he said with what he hoped was a light-hearted smile. But Owen was feeling anything but light-hearted. He'd panicked out there, thinking he was going to lose her. He'd felt dizzy, his breath coming in short gasps. He'd thought he might be having a heart attack himself. Only the need to care for Fran had kept him going. It had brought home to him just how much Fran had come to mean to him in the short time they'd known each other.

'I'm okay now.' She smiled.

'Still, I think you should stay here for a bit, then I promise I'll drive you home. Why don't I settle you on the sofa with a cup of tea? I think there's some of that herbal stuff you like in the pantry.'

Owen went to the pantry, to the shelf where he remembered seeing several boxes of herbal teas that must belong to Bernadette. He read the names on the packets, trying to remember what Brit used to drink to *relieve stress*. He'd always thought it just another of her notions. Which one was it? He stood, a box of peppermint in one hand, one of camomile in the other, trying to decide. It probably didn't matter. He chose the camomile, dropped the teabag into a mug of boiling water and took it through to Fran.

'Thanks, I'll be fine, now.' She took a sip, then clasped the mug in both hands and leant her head against the back of the sofa.

'Are you sure?' Owen's forehead creased. But the colour was beginning to come back into Fran's cheeks. 'Well, just stay there for a bit. I should check on the goats. Won't be long.'

Owen headed outside and changed his sandals for the gum boots he kept on the veranda. He normally checked on the animals first thing each morning to make sure they had enough water. They were wily creatures and had the habit of chewing on the hosepipe feeding the water trough, which meant their water supply dried up – they'd chew on anything. He'd already had to replace the hose several times.

He was striding across the paddock, his mind full of Fran, when his mobile vibrated. Stopping, he took it out of his pocket, pleased to see Pia's face on the screen. He knew she'd been trying to reach him, but each time he'd attempted to return her calls, her phone had either been busy or switched off.

'Pia darling,' he said. 'I'm so glad we've connected at last. What's up?'

'Dad,' she wailed, I'm pregnant!'

Thirty

Fran cupped her hands around the mug of fragrant camomile tea, embarrassed about her meltdown. She was glad Owen had left her alone for a bit. It was so unlike her to lose control like that. She never had before. But, she reminded herself, she'd managed to avoid motor bikes. She'd known there was one here in the shed, but it had never occurred to her Owen would want to ride it, would want to actually take her out on it.

She probed the idea, like one would a sore tooth, and felt her head spin. No, best not to think about it. It was over. Owen had been wonderful, much more caring and sensitive than she'd have expected him to be. Though why should she be surprised? After last night when she'd lost control in a different way – a much pleasanter way. She smiled to herself, thinking about how he'd made her feel, how he'd managed to take her to heights of passion she never experienced with Richard, with his cautious ordered lovemaking that had always made her feel like one of his projects. Had it been like that with Ben? She barely remembered. It had been so long ago. They'd been so young, so inexperienced.

She sighed for what might have been, then gave herself a mental shake. There was no guarantee they'd have stayed together if he'd lived. But, because of his untimely death, she recognised she'd put him on a pedestal, measuring every man she met against him, and finding them wanting. That *and* her own determination to keep her emotions locked up.

So, what was different now? What was it about Owen that had managed to break through her self-imposed boundaries? Or was it the decision she'd made on her fiftieth birthday that had made her more receptive to his advances?

There was the sound of footsteps, and the cats, who had been slumbering at her feet, rose in unison to greet Owen as he walked in.

Right away, Fran could tell something had happened to upset him. He was swaying slightly, his forehead creased.

'What's wrong?' she asked, carefully placing the mug on a side table, and sitting upright.

'It's Pia, my daughter,' he said. 'She's pregnant, and the bastard she's been living with doesn't want to know.'

'Oh!' Besides motorbikes, the other things that tended to upset Fran, remind her of her own past – were babies and pregnant women. Even seeing mothers with their small children reminded her of what she could never experience. It had got better as she became older and passed her child-bearing years, yet she still felt a twinge of loss, when her peers chatted about their children and grandchildren. Her daughter – a girl – would have been in her twenties by now, around the same age as Owen's daughter.

Fran took a deep breath. She could do this. 'What will she do?' she asked.

'I've told her she can come here,' Owen said, pushing a hand through his hair. 'I never did like the guy, but I thought he'd stand by her. She doesn't have anywhere else to go. Her mother's no bloody use in a crisis. I'm sorry. I don't know...'

Fran found the strength to get up. 'Is there anything I can do?'

Owen shook his head. 'Sorry,' he said again, 'I can't think straight. I told her to come right away, not to worry about her job. What does that matter at a time like this? She's going to throw everything in the car and drive down. She'll be here tomorrow.'

Fran thought Pia's job might matter very much. It was *Fran's* job that had kept her going all those years. But she decided to say nothing. Owen was so impulsive. That was one of the things she liked about him. Equally, it was one of the things about him that could annoy her if she let it. Was his daughter like him in that regard? She seemed to recall his saying she wasn't, that she was more conventional. Maybe she'd have the sense to only take leave from her job until she sorted herself out.

'You'll have things to do, then. You won't want me hanging about. Can you take me back home?'

'There's no rush. I can check the spare room now, make sure there's a bed ready for her. John and Bernadette left the freezer full of food, so I only need to top up the fresh stuff. I can do that in the morning. I can take you back. We can go out to dinner, then… if you feel like it after the shock you had.' Owen wiggled his eyebrows, making Fran laugh. The hide of the man! He'd bounced back quickly. Was there nothing that would faze him?

But when they were driving back to town, Fran realised Owen's seemingly swift recovery had been a front. He was really worried about his daughter.

'I'm not sure how to play this,' he said. 'I know it's probably a situation you want to avoid at all costs,' he glanced at her out of the corner of his eye, 'but I'd really appreciate your help.'

'What can I do?' Fran asked, now regretting her offer of help. How could she, who'd lost her own child before she drew breath, who'd been unable to bear any others, who froze at the very mention of babies, be of any assistance to his pregnant daughter?

'You're a woman,' he said, as if that explained everything.

'But… wouldn't Jo be better – or Kay? They're both mothers themselves, whereas I…' her voice trailed away, before she called herself a failure, a woman who'd failed to produce the child she'd have loved so dearly.

'You're younger,' he said, 'and I think Pia would relate to you better. You're alike, in a way.'

What way, Fran wondered, but didn't ask. She was gratified Owen wanted her help, but unsure what she had to offer.

By the time they reached town, Fran was feeling better. It was almost as if the incident in the shed had never happened. But it had, and she was wary of a recurrence. In her heart, she knew it was something she had to overcome. She couldn't go through the rest of her life avoiding situations which reminded her of her past. It was how she'd lived up till now. But she'd decided to change. And taking charge of how she dealt with the memory of her accident was one of the things she had to change. It was only a bike, for goodness' sake, an inanimate object.

And, perhaps the accident hadn't only been the result of the bike skidding on the gravel surface, perhaps it had been due to Ben's need for speed, his love of adventure, his desire to take risks – all of which she'd loved and encouraged. For the first time, she wondered if part of the responsibility for the tragedy had been hers.

'Okay there?'

'Fine.' Fran had been silent as she reflected on her past. Now, she brought herself back to the present. 'Are you sure you want to go out tonight? I'm quite happy to stay home.'

'No. I think it would do us both good. This business with Pia hasn't come at the best time. I realise that.' He sighed. 'You're probably lucky, not having children, though I'm sure you don't see it that way. And, don't get me wrong, I love my daughter to bits and wouldn't be without her, but sometimes…' He sighed again.

*

Fran was pleased they'd decided against The Riverside tonight. The Italian restaurant Owen had chosen was much more intimate. Pavarotti's was another favourite of Fran's, one she and Marie had often eaten in. It was owned by a local Italian family and offered genuine Florentine food from the district of Italy from which the family had emigrated many years earlier.

She and Owen had spent the afternoon relaxing at her home to the delight of her new pet. Stormy, while still cagey around Owen, loved to curl up on Fran's lap and had spent most of the afternoon there while Owen, who'd put his guitar into the car, entertained them with what Fran suspected were his own compositions.

Tony, the waiter, greeted Fran like an old friend and showed them to their table, Owen having taken time to book ahead.

'I like this,' Owen said, looking around and clearly appreciating the dim lighting and the soft background music.

'I thought you would.'

'What do you recommend?' he asked, picking up a menu, and peering at the blackboard which listed the evening's specials.

'The Gnocchi Pavarotti's always a favourite,' she said, 'and the garlic bread is rather special, although…'

'As long as we both have some,' he grinned. 'Okay, the gnocchi for me. What about you?'

'I love the spaghetti carbonara,' Fran said. 'The way they do it here is special, too.'

Owen ordered a bottle of prosecco. 'I think despite everything, we should celebrate finding each other, don't you?' he asked, raising his glass. 'Once Pia arrives, it may be more difficult for us to get together, and I'm not sure how long she'll stay.' He dragged a hand through his hair, then smiled. 'So, let's make the most of the time we have, shall we?'

Fran remembered the bottle of Moët still sitting in her fridge. This was a much more welcome celebration. Maybe she and Owen could share that other bottle – when the time was right. The thought gave her a warm glow, though the intense feeling she was experiencing might have had more to do with her present company than anticipation of a bottle of bubbly.

After their toast, Owen reached across the table to take Fran's hands in his. She loved how hers felt tiny in his larger ones. 'I want to thank you for sharing your story with me,' he said. 'It can't have been easy. I'm glad you felt you could trust me with your confidence.'

'Of course.' But Fran knew those two words conveyed a wealth of meaning. A week ago, she'd never have imagined she could be sitting here with Owen having this conversation; never have believed she'd have shared the story of her life with him; never in her wildest dreams thought she'd have gone to bed with him.

But here she was, here they were, and after the meal, they'd go to bed again. Then… Fran knew there would be a "then" but she found she didn't care. For the first time in years, she was prepared to take a risk, to risk being hurt if that's what it took to take the chance of finding the sort of happiness she'd never dreamt could be hers.

Thirty-one

Owen opened his eyes with a start. Where was he? He turned his head to see Fran's spiky blonde hair on the pillow beside him and remembered. Sliding down the bed, he reached for her.

When they emerged sometime later, the sun was already shining through the shutters. It was going to be another beautiful day. Owen knew he should get up, but he was loath to move. It was so comfortable lying beside Fran, their legs entwined, her hair tickling his cheek, her soft body close to his.

'Breakfast?' she asked, extricating herself from his grasp and leaning up on one elbow, a satisfied smile on her face.

'Mmm. Come here!'

She succumbed, falling back into his arms.

The next thing Owen knew they were disturbed by a familiar sound, and Stormy launched himself onto the bed. 'Ow! Does he always do that?' Owen asked, remembering the previous morning.

'Only when you're here.' Fran gave a gurgling laugh. 'But then, when I'm alone, I'm usually up and about by now. The poor thing only wants his breakfast. Speaking of which…' This time he made no attempt to stop her as she rose and shrugged on a long tee-shirt. He laughed at the *Bad Hair Day* logo inscribed on the front of the turquoise-coloured garment along with the picture of a bear with a very wild coat.

'Cute, isn't it?' she asked, seeing his amusement, and pushing a hand through her short hair making it almost stand on end.

Owen grinned again. Like this, Fran was so far removed from the reserved, well-disciplined woman he met every day, it was difficult to believe she was the same person. Would she revert to that other woman in the office tomorrow, he wondered, or had he brought her out of her shell sufficiently for her to retain this new character? He suspected the old Fran would reappear in the office, this new version buried under her professional outward appearance.

'I like you like this,' he said, folding his arms behind his head and making no effort to move.

This time it was Fran's turn to grin. She gave a deft tug to the doona, leaving him lying there naked. 'Time to get up,' she said.

Showered and dressed again, Owen wandered into the kitchen to the aroma of freshly brewed coffee and the smell of bacon. 'Looks great,' he said. 'I could get used to this.' Then he remembered. Pia! His daughter was arriving today, and that would put paid to mornings like this – at least for the time being.

As if sensing his thoughts, Fran said, 'Sit down and enjoy your breakfast. It's going to be a big day for you. Do you want to tell me about your daughter?'

Owen pulled out a chair and took a gulp of coffee. He looked at the toast topped with bacon and poached egg and picked up his knife and fork. Pia. What could he tell Fran about her? 'Well,' he said, between mouthfuls, 'she's the best of both Brit and me. She's amazingly well adjusted considering she had us for parents and spent her teenage years gravitating between our two homes. Did I tell you my ex shacked up with her best friend, Rosemary? I'm not sure if that made it easier or harder for Pia.' He stopped, his fork in the air. 'Anyway, that's the way it was. Most of the time she was with me – it was closer to school for her – but she often joined Brit and Rosemary on weekends. I was out a lot,' he said, 'and it set me free to… well, you can imagine.'

He didn't meet Fran's eyes but heard a sharp intake of breath.

'I've never pretended to be a saint,' he said, cutting into the egg which was cooked to perfection. *How did she do that?* 'Then,' he continued, 'she went to uni and found her own set of friends. They weren't the hippie-types Brit and I had been as students. They were more serious-minded, as if she was rebelling against what she'd known. Of course, by that time, I'd become respectable, too.' He grinned at Fran's sceptical expression. 'Well, practically respectable – more than I had been. Then, a couple of years ago she met this Darren – budding lawyer, Mr Respectability himself, and arrogant beyond belief.'

He took another gulp of coffee. 'This is great stuff, Fran.'

Fran had barely touched her own breakfast. She was seated opposite, her feet curled up under her, her hands cradling a cup of one of her favourite herbal teas –he could smell the peppermint fragrance – apparently totally engrossed in what he was saying.

'And he's the father of her child?'

It was on the tip of Owen's tongue to say it wasn't a child yet, but he saw Fran's expression and nodded. 'He's the one.'

Fran's chin trembled. She stared down into her tea. 'Your poor daughter,' she said. 'How old is she?'

'Twenty-seven.'

'Older than I was,' Fran murmured, her voice still low. 'We were too young. We weren't ready for a child. We were only children ourselves. But we were determined to make it work. How far gone is she?'

'I don't know.' Owen pinched the top of his nose. He hadn't thought to ask. A woman would have. Had Pia told Brit? Probably not. She'd know as well as Owen how useless her mother would be in a situation like this.

'I should go.' Owen pushed back his chair. 'Great breakfast, Fran. You know how to please a man – in more ways than one.' He lifted her out of the chair she was still sitting in and twirled her around, marvelling at how light she felt in his arms. 'I need to get Pia settled, then I'll be in touch.'

Fran pushed against his chest with both hands. 'I'll see you in the office tomorrow. You can fill me in then. What do you think she'll do?' she asked.

'I have no idea.' He let Fran down gently, realising how little he knew of how his daughter thought about her pregnancy. He'd assumed – what had he assumed? That she wouldn't want to let a child interfere with her life? He shook his head. 'Yes, tomorrow.'

*

It was late afternoon, and Owen was sitting on the veranda drinking beer and watching the road when the white Prius stopped at the gate and Pia emerged to open it. He'd spent the day pondering Fran's questions and knew he needed to have a serious talk with his daughter.

Col had wandered over earlier seeking Owen's help in checking out Magda's horses, and he'd been glad of the distraction as they ensured the beasts had sufficient food and water. The horses themselves, former racehorses for which Magda had provided a home, had galloped to the far end of their paddock at the two men's arrival, glaring at them balefully from a distance. But at least Col would be able to report to Magda that they were well.

Owen put down his beer and walked out to greet his daughter.

'Dad!' Pia fell into his arms as she stepped out of the car. Her eyes were red from weeping, his daughter's pretty face swollen and blotchy. Had she wept the entire trip?

'My poor darling! I'm so glad you're here.'

'Me too,' she sobbed. 'I'm sorry. I can't seem to stop crying.'

Owen felt helpless. He wanted to take her in his arms and tell her he'd make it better, just as he had when she was little. But this was something he couldn't fix for her. Was she crying because she was pregnant, or because the bastard had let her down? He'd find out, but now wasn't the time. He remembered the herbal tea he'd plied Fran with – camomile. The box was still sitting on the kitchen bench.

'My bags,' she said, looking back at the car.

'We'll get them later. What you need now is a cup of tea and something to eat. When did you last eat?'

Pia shook her head as if unsure.

Owen made tea and found some biscuits, then fetched Pia's bags from the car and took them to the spare bedroom. He wondered what he should say to her, unusual for him. But he knew how vulnerable his girl was right now.

He needn't have worried. By the time he returned to the kitchen, Pia had finished her tea. She slid out of the chair.

'I think I'll lie down for a bit, Dad, if that's all right with you,' she said, sounding much more subdued than usual. 'I'll maybe have something to eat later.' Without waiting for his reply, she drifted off.

Owen gazed after her, frowning. What had that bastard done to her, to turn his vibrant, independent daughter into this shadow of herself? It couldn't just be the pregnancy. He tried to remember what Brit had been like when she was pregnant. It was so long ago. They'd both been in their early twenties. He understood what Fran had said about not being ready, being too young. That's how he'd felt. But he and Brit had loved each other – or at least what passed for love back then – and, like Fran and her fellow, they'd decided to give it their best shot. And, for a number of years, they had. It had worked, after a fashion, until it hadn't.

Taking another beer out of the fridge, Owen wandered outside to indulge himself in his now favourite pastime of watching the goats. He found it relaxing to observe their antics while mulling over his own problems.

He stood there, leaning on the fence, until the light began to fade, and a light breeze blew up, causing the goats to become even more skittish than usual. With a sigh, he went back inside to make a start on dinner, hoping Pia would appear soon.

He'd just put the tuna pasta casserole dish – another of his stand-bys – into the oven, and fed the cats, when Pia joined him in the kitchen yawning.

'Sorry, Dad. It was a long drive.'

Owen looked at her still pale face, the shadows under her lovely eyes which were normally filled with life, and wondered where his lovely daughter had gone. 'Dinner's almost ready,' he said. 'Wine?' As soon as the word left his mouth, he knew he'd said the wrong thing. Brit had drunk alcohol throughout her pregnancy, but he was aware things were different now. There were all sorts of rules and lists of things pregnant women shouldn't do, eat or drink. It was a minefield.

Pia grimaced. 'I probably shouldn't, but...'

'I'm sure one small glass won't hurt,' he said, being nothing of the sort, but seeing how despondent she was and wanting to do something – anything – to try to bring back the Pia he knew. He opened a bottle of semillon and poured two glasses, a small one for Pia and a larger one for himself.

She sat down at the table, clutching her glass in both hands without drinking, and gazed into space.

Owen took a seat, too. Dinner could wait. He took a sip of wine.

'I'm sorry you're having to go through this on your own,' he said. 'Do you want to talk about it?'

'Oh, Dad!' Pia focussed on her wine without saying any more, then she raised her eyes. 'He said he loved me.' She looked down into her glass again. 'It was lies, all of it. I don't know how I could have been so stupid as to have believed him. He said dreadful things about you, too – and about Mum and Rosemary. I just thought he was feeling insecure.'

Insecure? That idiot? But Owen didn't say anything. He knew this was one time he had to listen without interrupting.

'I didn't realise at first,' Pia continued. 'I just felt sick. I thought it was something I'd eaten. Darren thought I was imagining it. He hates it when anyone's sick. He wants to have fun. Instead, I needed someone to look after me.'

And the arrogant prick would hate that!

'I can look after you, sweetheart.'

'I know, Dad. That's why I thought of you.' She gave a watery smile. 'Does your mum know?'

She shook her head. 'Not yet. I have to decide how to tell her. You know what she's like.'

Owen knew very well. Brit and Rosemary would be all over Pia, being overly-protective, wanting to take over her life, make all her decisions for her – but they would be their decisions, not hers.

'You're here now, and you can stay as long as you want.' Owen knew he sounded more magnanimous than he should. He was only here himself for six months, six weeks of which had already gone.

'Thanks, Dad. I don't have anywhere else to go. Darren…' she said, her voice breaking, '…he told me I could find somewhere else to live. I have all my belongings in the car.' She sniffed. 'It's not much. He said all the things we'd bought together belonged in the flat.'

Owen felt himself tense, his muscles quivering. The hide of him, thinking he could treat Pia like a discarded piece of clothing. 'I'll…' he began, his voice rising.

'No, Dad.' Pia put her hand on his. 'I don't want you to do anything you'll later regret. Let it be. I don't want anything more to do with him. He's toast.'

While Owen knew he'd never regret anything he did or said to the jerk, he also knew Pia was right. Darren wasn't worth his anger.

The oven beeped reminding Owen they had still to eat dinner. 'Hungry?' he asked.

'Yes. What delicacy have you cooked up tonight?' Pia asked, with a hint of her usual manner.

'Surprise pasta,' he replied, his old name for the dishes he created when she was a teenager and he threw together scraps from the pantry to create what did turn out to be a surprise result. The familiar term brought a smile to Pia's lips. That was better. Owen was determined to do whatever it took to help Pia find her old animated and enthusiastic self.

While they ate, Oscar and Lucinda prowled around under the table as if sensing the presence of someone different and an unusual atmosphere in the house.

'That was good, Dad,' Pia said when she'd finished. 'I'd forgotten your old pasta dishes. I should start cooking again myself. Darren liked to eat out.'

'You need to forget about him,' Owen said, tempering his words with a tender smile, and a light touch on her arm.

'I know. It's hard. He's been such a part of my life for so long. I thought...'

I did too, and I'm glad I was wrong, but that doesn't help Pia.

'You're the important person now, you and...' Owen wasn't sure whether to mention the baby. What if Pia had decided she didn't want to go through with it? Of course he'd support her decision, whatever it might be.

'I don't know what I'm going to do, Dad. I need time, time to work it out. This isn't what I planned.' Tears began to run down her cheeks, and she made no effort to brush them away.

'Can I...?'

Pia waved him away. 'I'll see you in the morning, Dad. Thanks for dinner – and for everything.'

Owen sat at the table feeling helpless. He was way out of his comfort zone here. He scratched his head. He was glad Pia had chosen to come to him, but what help could he be to a pregnant twenty-seven-year-old?

Thirty-two

Fran was wakened by Stormy leaping onto her bed and rubbing against her face. 'No, puss,' she said weakly, trying to push the persistent little kitten away. 'I suppose you're hungry and you want me to get up?' The tiny creature seemed to understand, meowing loudly and jumping off the bed, only to stop at the door and look back at her.

'Aren't you the clever one,' Fran said, rising and slipping on the oversized tee-shirt that had amused Owen only the morning before. Once her pet was fed, Fran made her own breakfast, filling a bowl with muesli and topping it with blueberries and yoghurt to accompany the lemon and ginger tea she'd selected from her collection. She knew Owen would arrive in her office with coffee later and would wait till then for her caffeine hit.

An hour later, dressed for work in tailored white pants and a turquoise shirt, and wearing a pair of comfortable flat shoes, Fran threw a kiss at the cat, now lying smugly in a pool of sunlight, and set off. As she drove out to the campus, she wondered how Owen was getting on with his daughter. She'd half-expected a call from him last night and had been disappointed when there was none. But, she reasoned, he had enough to do with Pia's arrival, and Fran had told him she'd see him this morning. It was foolish to have expected anything more.

Exactly on time, there was the now familiar commotion in the doorway, and Owen hurtled in carrying two coffees and a paper bag which Fran knew contained two croissants –almond or chocolate.

'Morning!' He handed one coffee to her, tearing open the bag to reveal two almond croissants which he placed on her desk before perching on it himself.

'Good morning to you, too. Did your daughter arrive safely?'

'Yes.' Owen's expression changed, his normally open face creasing. 'She's feeling pretty low. I'm not sure what to do. If it's okay by you, I might head home again later this morning after the VC's dreaded Monday bash.'

'You're the boss.' Fran knew to what he was referring. The vice chancellor held a faculty heads meeting every Monday morning without fail and woe betide anyone who missed it. But it was unusual for Owen to go home again afterwards. Pia must be seriously upset. 'Is there anything I can do to help?'

'Just be your lovely self.' He downed his coffee in two gulps, crammed half of a croissant into his mouth, then slid off the desk, swallowing quickly. 'Guess I'd better check the agenda before I head over there. Did you...?'

'It's on your desk,' Fran said, following him into his office. 'Is everything all right. You seem tense.'

Owen sighed. 'That bastard Pia's been living with has sapped her confidence – as well as leaving her pregnant and alone. She's not coping too well. I think she needs company. And I'm her dad.'

Fran felt her heart sink. This was a side of Owen she hadn't seen before. She'd known his daughter was important to him – of course she had. But she hadn't expected him to be so... so what? Angry? Hurt?

'Well,' she said helplessly. 'If there is anything...' But what could she offer – a woman who couldn't even save her own child, who'd never experienced childbirth, never been a parent? How could she even attempt to imagine how he must be feeling?

'I'm sorry, Fran. I'm not being fair to you.' He moved closer and held her by the shoulders, then tipped up her chin with one hand. 'I know you want to help, and I appreciate that. But right now, it's all I can do to come to grips with the situation myself. Pia's changed. My little girl has lost her sparkle, and I don't know how to help her get it back.' He touched his lips to Fran's brow. 'I haven't forgotten. But I need to give all my energies to Pia right now. Maybe, in a day or two, if she feels up to company, you could come out to dinner.' He released Fran and began to search through the papers on his desk.

Fran walked back into her own office and stood still for a moment, taking a deep breath to calm herself. She had to try to understand. But, not being a parent, she had no experience to draw on, no idea how she'd react to the sort of situation in which Owen found himself.

The morning passed slowly. Fran checked her emails, completed some outstanding paperwork relating to new staff members, fended off Ron Harris who stomped into the office with a batch of complaints about his teaching load for the following semester and demanding a meeting with Owen. Then a distracted Owen arrived back from his meeting, dismissed Ron's request and left for home.

Fran was sitting, staring into space and wondering if she'd imagined their closeness on the weekend, when her phone rang.

'Fran Reilly, School of Music and Drama, how can I help you?'

'Good morning, Fran Reilly. It's Kay.'

Fran could feel her face brighten at her friend's voice. 'Kay! Good to hear you.'

Her relief must have been evident in her voice.

'Well, I didn't expect that sort of response, I only rang to check on Ron Harris's commitments for next semester. He's been bugging Nick about not being able to do anything in the faculty because he's too tied up with you lot. Can you help?'

Fran was able to fill Kay in, then she had an idea. 'Are you doing anything for lunch, Kay?' she asked. 'I'd love to have a chat.' It should have occurred to Fran before. Kay was in the same position she was. She was in a relationship with her boss, seeing him every day on campus. Fran wondered if they'd had any challenges to overcome with the enforced closeness while their relationship was in its infancy. And she was a mother. She was the ideal person to talk to; she might be able to allay Fran's fears – though she and Owen weren't actually in a relationship yet, were they?

*

'Oh, dear, Fran! I can sympathise.'

The two women had eaten a lunch of toasted sandwiches and were enjoying a second cup of coffee. They were seated in a secluded corner table at Banjo's, surrounded by chattering groups of students, and could barely hear each other speak. But the cacophony of noise provided them with a degree of privacy. No one was interested in what they had to say.

Fran had bared her soul to Kay; told her about her and Owen, the arrival of Owen's daughter and the way her own past had risen up to almost choke her. 'What should I do, Kay? I feel so helpless, but I want to do something – and I'm worried this has happened so soon after Owen and I…' She looked away.

'It wasn't all plain sailing with Nick and me either,' Kay said. 'I was beset with all sorts of doubts, then there were Nick's children, and my daughter appeared on the scene with all her own problems. That's the challenge with meeting someone at our age. There's always baggage.'

While grateful to hear Kay and Nick had had challenges, too. It didn't help Fran's predicament.

'Firstly, it doesn't sound to me like there are any problems between you and Owen. Right?'

'Right, I think.' Fran wanted to believe that, but Owen's behaviour this morning had her worried.

'It's only natural he'll be anxious about his daughter,' Kay said, clearly understanding Fran's worries. 'She'll be his first concern right now. But that doesn't mean he no longer cares about you. I know it's hard and I know, not being a parent yourself, it's difficult for you to understand the bond between a parent and a child.'

Fran froze. She had no need to be reminded of her childlessness. She remembered every day; every time she saw a mother with her children, it was as if a screw turned inside.

'Sorry if it hurts, but it's a fact. What I'm trying to say is that, right now, Owen is trying to get his head around Pia's situation and there's no room for you. Oh, hell, I'm not saying this well. He's a man. He can only focus on one thing at a time, and now it's Pia. But you're still there, in the back of his mind. And my guess is he needs to know you're there for him.'

'He did say something about going to dinner, meeting Pia, when she's had time to settle in,' Fran remembered. 'But I just wish there was something I could do.'

Kay was silent for a few moments, then tapped a finger on the table. 'I wonder…'

'What?'

'Well, we've all been in Pia's situation, one way or another, but we're a different generation. Why would she listen to us? But Jo's daughter, Eve, is close to her in age. She has three of her own. And there's Sally.'

'Sally? Who's she?'

'Of course. You wouldn't know. It was quite a scandal. This young woman appeared in town and turned out to be the illegitimate daughter of Jo's ex-husband. Set a cat among the pigeons, I can tell you. Poor Eve was devastated. But they all worked it out and have become friends. She's a nurse and, if I remember correctly, works in the maternity ward at the Base Hospital.'

'But how can they help?'

'Maybe they can't. But it sounds like Pia could do with a few friends of her own age and Eve and Sally fit the bill. Let me talk to Jo to see what we can arrange.'

'Okay,' Fran agreed. She didn't see how it would help, but she did feel reassured at the mention of Jo. She'd developed a lot of respect for Jo Ford and knew she'd do what she thought best. Owen seemed to value her judgement, too.

'Why don't I get back to you when I've spoken to Jo, and perhaps you could mention it to Owen and his daughter when you go to dinner?'

'Maybe.' Fran wasn't sure. How could she casually bring up the idea of Pia meeting these two other young women without sounding interfering? But the thought of having something to offer did make her feel better.

'I'm glad about you and Owen,' Kay said, as they walked back from lunch. 'He seems like a nice guy, and Nick says there's more to him than meets the eye.'

'Mmm.' Fran may have confided in Kay that she and Owen were seeing each other, but wanted to keep some things private. 'Thanks for today, Kay. For listening.'

'No worries. And I'll be sure to get back to you when I've spoken to Jo. You'll be at choir tomorrow?'

Fran nodded, wondering if Owen would be there, too.

She was kept busy for the rest of the day, so had little time to worry about Owen and his daughter. It was only when she was home again that she began to wonder how they were getting on. Her hand went to her phone a couple of times, only for her to think better of it.

She made dinner, cleared up, fed Stormy, checked out various television programmes, before sitting down and opening her current library book. But she couldn't settle. The wild Cornish landscapes of Liz Fenwick's writing failed to hold her attention. What did she do before she met Owen? Thoughts of Richard had never interfered with her life, threatened to interrupt her regular routine. But Richard had never made such an impact on her in all the years she'd known him as Owen had in a few short weeks.

Thirty-three

'How's your daughter?' Fran asked a couple of days later, when Owen handed her the customary morning coffee and dropped the bag of croissants on her desk – chocolate this morning.

'She's still pretty down but getting there. The cats seem to have adopted her. We never had pets when she was growing up. I think it's doing her good to be away from the city, away from everything that reminds her of him.'

'Oh, the poor girl!'

'Sorry I didn't make it to choir last night. I intended to, but… I'd been gone all day and I didn't want to leave Pia alone again. I know it's stupid. She's not a child.' He thrust a hand through his hair, something he rather enjoyed doing since he had it cut. 'How was it?'

'Pretty much as usual. I think old George is getting close to giving up, and Ron is preening himself ready to take over. He'll be insufferable. I suspect we might lose some of the better voices.' She gave a sigh. 'But it was good to get back into the routine. I hadn't realised how much I'd been missing it.'

'I will come next week. Maybe I can persuade Pia to join me. She needs to get out. It's not good for her to spend all her time on the property with the cats and the goats.'

He sensed Fran was aching to say something. 'What is it? You look as if you have something else to say.'

'I had lunch with Kay on Monday,' she said, haltingly. 'She suggested… she thought Pia might want to meet some people her own age – women.'

Owen scratched his head. 'Who did she have in mind? I think Nick's daughter is a bit young.'

'Jo has a daughter, and there's another girl who's tangentially related.'

'Tangentially related? That sounds complicated.'

'It is, sort of. Anyway, Kay said she'd check with Jo, and last night at choir, she told me she had.'

'And what have this coven of women decided?' Owen liked and respected Kay and Jo, but he wasn't sure he wanted them to interfere in what was his private family business. On the other hand, he didn't want to offend Fran.

'Jo's going to arrange a get together the weekend after next. Oh,' she said, clearly seeing his annoyance, 'it'll be very casual, a family affair where it would be perfectly natural to invite you both as neighbours.'

'Hmm. And what about you?'

'I'm neither family nor a neighbour.'

'But if you were at my place on the weekend, I could take you along?'

'I guess.' Fran smiled, and her whole face lit up.

Owen mentally rebuked himself. He was so out of practice in dealing with women of Fran's calibre – if he ever had been good at it. He'd made love to the woman, spent most of the weekend with her, confided his concern about his daughter. Then, as soon as Pia arrived, he'd all but shut her out. He didn't want to lose her because of his own stupidity. 'Come to dinner tonight,' he said without thinking. 'I want you to meet Pia.'

'What have you told her about me?'

Nothing, Owen realised. His face must have shown what he was thinking.

'I can't just turn up,' she objected. 'You have to…'

'Don't worry, I'll fill her in before you arrive. Tell her I've met this beautiful woman who has blown me away and…'

'No need to get carried away,' Fran laughed. But he could see she'd lost the apprehensive expression she'd had earlier.

Thirty-four

Fran was still wondering if this was a good idea as she drove out of town that evening. While she was pleased Owen had invited her to dinner, wanted her to meet his daughter, she was unsure how the girl would react to meeting her. Even though Owen had been divorced from Pia's mother for most of her life and, by his own admission, had been involved with several women since, Fran sensed this was different.

Or was it that she hoped it was different? Should she turn the car around? No, that would be stupid. Both Owen and Pia were expecting her. He'd promised to surprise her with his cooking and had even sent a text an hour ago, confirming Pia knew she was coming and was looking forward to meeting her. She chewed the inside of her cheek and tapped her fingers on the steering wheel, determined to be pleasant and to avoid any awkward conversations.

Owen was waiting on the veranda when Fran arrived. He came forward to help her out of the car and give her a kiss. Fran looked around warily, fearful Pia might be watching, but there were only the goats who, as usual, were more intent on their own pursuits than the two humans.

'Come in and meet Pia,' he said, leading Fran inside to where a slim girl with long blonde hair was stirring something on the stove. 'Here she is.' He drew Fran forward.

The girl turned, a dripping wooden spoon in her hand. 'I'm Pia,' she said, holding out her free hand. 'You must be Fran. It's good to meet you.'

'You too.' Fran felt as if she was the younger. This young woman was beautiful and much more composed than Fran had expected. 'It's nice for your dad to have you here for a bit.' She wasn't sure how much she was supposed to know about Pia's sudden arrival, so decided not to mention the pregnancy unless she did.

'So, you work with Dad?' Pia chuckled. 'What's he like as a boss? I bet he's useless,' she added, without waiting for a reply.

'Oh, I wouldn't say that.' Fran gave Owen a look. 'But he is a tad disorganised, and he does often need a bit of a prod. He'd be happy sitting at that keyboard of his all day – and,' she said confidingly, 'he hates meetings.'

'Hey, I'm right here,' Owen objected. But Fran could see he was enjoying their banter. She liked Pia already.

'Wine?' Owen asked, nodding at both women.

'Not for me,' Pia said, while Fran nodded.

'You take Fran outside,' Pia said. 'I can handle this now, Dad. He thinks he's the only one who can cook pasta,' she said to Fran, as if they were in league against him.

'Okay. Come on, Fran.'

He and Fran walked back outside to sit at the wooden table which was already set with three places.

'No cats tonight?' Fran asked, looking around.

'They're probably in Pia's room,' he replied. 'They've taken a shine to her, and it's doing her good to have their company. Seems to have cheered her up.'

'Cats can do that.'

*

'So, tell me about Granite Springs,' Pia said, once dinner was over. 'Dad says you've lived here for years.'

'He's right. I came here when I was a few years younger than you, and I've been here ever since.'

'What made you decide on a country town – on this country town? You're English, aren't you?'

Fran nodded, aware she'd never been able to lose her accent. She decided to abbreviate her story. 'I was in an accident,' she said. 'This town helped me recover, and I came to love the community. It's a pretty special place.'

Speaking about it, reaffirmed to Fran just how much she did value the community of Granite Springs. 'I hope your dad likes it here, too.'

'Oh, he does! But then, Dad takes these sudden notions,' Pia said carelessly. 'Right now, it's life in the country, the goats, the whole rural scene. Who knows what it'll be next?'

Fran felt her stomach shrivel. Was that all Granite Springs, the university and Fran herself, meant to Owen – a fleeting fancy?

Owen was quick to refute it. 'Steady on, Pia. That's not quite true. I was at Sydney uni for years, lived in the Glebe house all your life, till I came here. I don't know where you get such ideas.'

Seeming to forget what she'd just said about her father, Pia continued, 'So what's so special about Granite Springs?'

'As country towns go, probably nothing,' Fran replied, trying to work out exactly what it was that had encouraged her to stay. 'All of them are probably much the same. But this was the one I landed in and it does me pretty well. I managed to make a life for myself here, joined a choir, volunteer at the hospital, have a few friends, a good job...' But even as she said it, Fran thought how boring her life must sound to the younger woman, accustomed to the buzz of city life. 'It suits me,' she finished.

'And it suits me, too,' Owen put in. 'Stop interrogating, Fran, Pia. She doesn't have to answer to you.'

Fran threw him a grateful glance. Pia's questions were making her feel uncomfortable, as if she had something to hide. She was glad Owen had evidently not told Pia her whole story, and she wasn't about to share it with her now – maybe later, when they got to know each other better, if the younger woman stayed around long enough. But what she said was, 'I don't mind, Pia. I don't know how long you intend to stay with your dad, but you'll soon get to know Granite Springs and be able to make up your own mind. It's not very big. Why don't you get your dad to bring you out to the campus one day?'

'That's a good idea, Fran. Why didn't I think of that? Pia?'

'I don't think so, Dad. Not my scene. I wouldn't fit in there.'

'You don't want to see where I work?'

Pia wrinkled her nose.

'Well, perhaps not. But you can join me at the choir next Tuesday. I'm to try out to see if I'm good enough to be allowed to join.'

'You've already been in touch with George?' Fran asked. 'Is he really going to make you jump through the hoops?'

'I insisted.' Owen grinned. 'Don't want anyone to say I pulled rank, though I have to say the old man seems keen enough to get me in.'

'I'll bet.'

'You'll come, Pia?' he asked.

This time it was Pia who grinned, the grin brightening up her pretty face. 'I wouldn't miss it. Will everyone be there to watch and listen?'

'No. I've been instructed to turn up early so we can get it all over before practice starts. But you can be there if you like, Fran.'

'I just might.' Fran was curious to hear Owen's singing voice. Given his other musical talents, she was sure it would be pretty spectacular – and provide another reason for Ron Harris to be annoyed.

By the time Fran rose to leave, Pia was already yawning. She headed off to bed before Fran and Owen reached the door. Outside, Owen took Fran's hand and led her to her car where they stopped. He turned her so her back was towards him, wrapped his arms around her waist and looked up to the sky.

'Last time you were here, I caught you stargazing,' he said, 'Now, let me tell you what you were looking at.'

Fran stood still, enjoying the sensation of Owen's strong arms around her while he pointed out Venus and Jupiter, then the Southern Cross, Orion, and the Big Dipper. 'That's just for starters,' he said, whirling her around to face him, his lips meeting hers.

'Is the sky always so clear here?' she asked, when she came up for air.

'You'll have to come more often to find out.' He nuzzled her neck, sending shivers up and down her spine.

'What about Pia?'

'She'll be cool with it. She knows her old dad has a life, and it won't be the first time... Sorry. But I'm no young kid,' he apologised.

'It's okay,' Fran said. But was it? Was she just one in a long line of women his daughter had seen come and go in her dad's life? Why should Fran think she was different?

'This is different,' Owen said, as if reading her mind. 'This time I'm not playing around. I want you to know that, to believe it.' He pulled Fran into his arms again, then pushed her away and gave her a gentle pat on the bottom. 'Now, shoo, or I won't be able to let you go, and you'll still be here in the morning.'

Laughing, Fran opened her car door, and slid in, pressing the starter and pushing the button to roll the window down.

Owen leant in to give Fran one last kiss, before moving back and waving her off.

Driving away, Fran touched her lips with one finger. It would have been good to have stayed, but she knew Owen was right. Best they wait till another time. And there was the barbecue next weekend to look forward to.

She drove home in a warm glow of anticipation.

Thirty-five

'Morning, Dad.' Pia appeared in the kitchen, yawning, her long blonde hair in a tousled cloud on her shoulders. 'Wow! I slept so well. The air here is fantastic. It's so clear.'

'Isn't it? Maybe you should think of moving here.'

'Me? Dad! It's okay for a little while, but…'

Owen poured himself a coffee and leant against the sink. Pia had been here for two weeks now, and he still hadn't been game to ask her what she intended to do – if she intended to have the baby, to keep it. From his rudimentary knowledge of such things, he thought she'd have to make up her mind soon. And while he'd never imagined becoming a grandfather at his age, he rather liked the idea. Maybe he could do a better job in that role than he had as a father. Though he hadn't really done too badly, had he?

'Coffee?'

'No. Couldn't face it. I'll stick with herbal tea. The peppermint works well for me.'

'Right.' Owen brought the box of teas out from the pantry. He must remember to buy replacements before Bernadette and John returned. Fran liked them too. Thinking of Fran brought a smile to his lips. Meeting her had been a bonus, something completely unexpected. She'd brought out qualities in him he hadn't known he possessed. She was such an independent woman, yet vulnerable, too. And Pia liked her.

'It's today we're going to that barbecue, isn't it?' Pia asked, biting into the piece of toast and vegemite that served as her breakfast most mornings.

'It is. You've met Jo and Col. I believe Jo's daughter's going to be there, too, with her children – she has three, twins and another little girl. And there'll be another girl, Jo's…'

'Jo's what?'

'I'm not sure what the relationship is, maybe stepdaughter, though from what I've heard, Jo was already divorced from her father by the time she turned up.'

'Hmm. And I suppose I'm expected to become immediate friends with the two younger ones?' Pia asked with a wry smile.

Owen held up his hands defensively. 'Don't blame me. I didn't set this up, but I do think you'll enjoy it. And it's not far to come home if you feel completely out of your depth.'

'Unlikely. I can usually get on with most people. It's just… I didn't come to Granite Springs to make new friends.'

'Why did you come, sweetheart? I know I'm your dad and you said you needed my help. But, so far, I don't know how much help I've been.'

'You've given me space, you *and* Fran. You've allowed me to live here in these gorgeous surroundings.' She spread her arms to encompass the house and the paddocks in which the goats could be seen getting up to their usual tricks. 'And you've been very patient and haven't asked any questions – till now,' she chuckled.

'Well?' Owen took a long draught of his coffee and met Pia's eyes.

'I don't know anymore, Dad.' Pia ran her fingers around the rim of her cup. 'When I discovered I was pregnant, I thought I did. I was excited. I was in love. It wasn't intentional, but I'd imagined we'd start a family at some stage. It was just happening a bit sooner than we'd planned. I expected Darren to be as excited as I was. I was wrong. He blew a fuse. Blamed me. I realised I didn't know him. I'd never known him. I couldn't bear to stay there, to be in the same room as him. And he didn't want me there anymore. It was as if he was a stranger. That's when I rang you.'

'Your mother?' Owen asked, though he had a good idea why she hadn't gone to Brit.

'Mum? She'd have been useless. She and Rosemary are in a world of their own. You know that better than anyone.' She was silent, cradling her cup in both hands and gazing out the window.

Owen didn't speak either, giving her time to work out what she wanted to say. When she still didn't speak. 'Now?' he prompted.

'Now?' she sighed heavily. 'I really don't know. The initial excitement I felt has gone. It seemed to fizzle away as soon as Darren began to rant and rave. If there was no baby, we'd still be together, so I suppose in a way, I blamed the baby for a bit, but…' her hand dropped to cradle her still flat stomach, 'I know that's not the case. I have to consider what life would be like as a single mother, whether I'm strong enough to handle it.'

'You *are* strong, honey. But it's your decision, and I'll be behind you whatever you do decide. Maybe you need to talk to someone who can give you more advice than I can. Someone your own…'

'Uh-oh. Is this what the barbecue is all about? Providing me with women *my own age* to talk with?'

'Sprung! But you must admit, if you're going to be here much longer, you need friends to talk with, go out with – all the things women like to do together.'

'Oh, Dad! I love you!'

What had Owen done or said to deserve that? He had no real idea but wasn't going to argue with her.

'What about Fran?' she asked. 'What does she think? You can't tell me you two haven't discussed your daughter's *interesting condition*.'

'Fran's… it's different for Fran.'

'Because she's never been pregnant?'

'No. She has.'

'But…'

'She lost the child. So your *condition* as you refer to it, brings back memories for her.'

'Oh, I'm sorry. I didn't know.'

'No reason why you should.'

'And she never had another?'

'She can't.'

'Oh!' Pia said again, and Owen could see her digesting this fact.

'Well,' she said, rising. 'I think I'll shower and dress, then maybe go for a walk before this lunch do. Okay with you?'

'Yes. I need to pop into town. Sure you don't want to come with me? I have some shopping to do and I'm picking up Fran.'

'No, I'm right here. I have some thinking to do.'

Owen gave Pia a penetrating look.

She shrugged. 'You're right,' she said. 'I do have a decision to make.'

*

Owen took a quick trip around the supermarket. He was finding it difficult to adjust to having an extra person to feed. He needed to change his shopping habits. Living here wasn't like being in the city where he could just pop out to the shops when he ran out of something. He had to get into the habit of planning ahead and had been managing pretty well with his once-a-week shop until Pia arrived. It was amazing the difference one more person made.

As he pushed the shopping trolley along the busy aisles – it seemed half of Granite Springs were here this morning – he remembered to select a variety of herbal teas, along with the garibaldi biscuits he knew were favourites of Pia, and the apricot and almond crackers which would go well with the herbal cheese he'd picked up in the deli section.

After stacking his purchases in the boot, Owen headed to Fran's, filled with excitement. Since Pia's arrival, their time together outside work had been severely curtailed. It had been wonderful to see her at choir and he'd enjoyed the audition George had insisted on with Pia and Fran as an admiring audience. But it was agony to have to go home without her. Not that it would have bothered Pia, but Fran had suggested it might be better for father and daughter to have some private time together.

But surely two weeks was enough? And now Pia had opened up to him a bit, Owen intended to continue what he and Fran had begun with so much promise. Today should be the perfect opportunity. When he picked up Fran, he'd tell her to pack an overnight bag. He couldn't wait any longer.

Fran was waiting for him, dressed in white culottes and a blue tee-shirt, and he laughed to see the croissants and coffee ready on the kitchen bench. 'My turn, today,' she said, giving him a kiss on the cheek.

'Is that all I get?' he asked, drawing her into his arms to take her mouth in his, savouring her taste and inhaling her unique fragrance.

'Mmm,' she murmured as they drew apart.

'There's plenty more where that came from,' he said. 'Pack an overnight bag. You're staying with me tonight. I mean, you'll stay overnight, won't you?'

'How could I refuse such an invitation?' Fran asked, chuckling, then her forehead creased. 'You are sure Pia will be okay with it? I don't want to do anything to upset her.'

'I'm sure.' *She damned well better be. I need you. I can't bear being kept apart.*

'Well, sit down and have your coffee first. Then, tell me what brought this on.'

With a mouthful of croissant, coffee in one hand, Owen stroked Fran's hand with the other.

'I've missed you,' he murmured.

'You saw me in the office yesterday,' she said.

'You know what I mean. In the office I can't…'

Fran laughed. 'We should probably leave soon. What time does Jo want us there?'

'Leave?' Owen pretended to be disappointed. 'I was hoping…'

'No time, if you want me to pack.' Fran evaded his arms and slid out of her chair. 'Won't be long. You can keep Stormy company.'

When Fran left, Owen looked over into the corner of the kitchen where the cat, no longer the tiny kitten Owen had rescued, was gazing at him with his customary not-so-veiled hostility. 'What is it with you, Stormy?' he asked. 'What have you got against me? I rescued you, found you a good home, yet you still don't want to be friends.' The cat let out a loud 'Yeow' and scampered off out of the room. 'So much for my charm,' he said to himself.

'What have you done to my poor cat?' Fran walked back in carrying a small bag.

'He doesn't like me,' Owen said ruefully. 'He'll be okay here on his own?'

'I think so. He has plenty of food and water and can go outside. He's learned how to use the cat flap after a few false starts.'

'Okay. Let's go.'

*

'I have something to confess,' Owen said as, after manoeuvring the car around the busy main street traffic, they left town for the quieter country road.

He felt Fran give him a startled look.

'I told Pia about you losing your baby.'

There was silence.

Owen stole a glance at Fran who was staring ahead as if frozen. 'I'm sorry. I know how private it is for you. But you can't keep it a secret forever. Pia's pregnant, trying to decide what to do. She wanted to know if you had… if you'd ever… It just slipped out. Forgive me?' He reached over to touch Fran's thigh.

She pulled away.

Owen drove on, cursing his stupidity. Of course she'd be upset he'd revealed her confidence to Pia. He should have realised. But how could he have done otherwise? Pia was his daughter. It had seemed only natural to tell her about Fran. It might even help if Fran talked to Pia about it – or was he being even more stupid to imagine that could happen?

They were almost halfway to Owen's property when Fran spoke. 'Does Pia intend to keep her baby?' she asked.

'I don't know. I don't think she does either. But I expect she'll have to decide pretty soon. I have to say I rather like the idea of being a grandad.'

By the time they reached the gate, Fran appeared to have recovered and jumped out to open, then close it again, sending a group of goats scattering in the process. Not for the first time, Owen was glad Bernadette and John had fenced off the house. Otherwise he was sure the goats would have taken over.

'Hi, Fran!' Pia was seated on the veranda with a book, the two cats at her feet. 'Dad said he was picking you up. I suppose you're coming to this barbecue, too? You know these people?'

'Jo and Col? Yes. Jo's become a good friend. You've already met her, haven't you? She's rather a special person. I'm sure you'll discover that for yourself.'

'And the rest of her family – the ones I'm expected to be instant friends with?'

Knowing his daughter, Owen detected a note of bitterness in her tone. Hopefully, Fran didn't.

'I haven't met her daughter socially, but I have been in her shop. Eve has a boutique in town – quite upmarket.'

'She has three children *and* runs a business?'

Owen was pleased to hear a note of interest in Pia's voice. Maybe Pia's walk and thinking time had been fruitful. 'Good walk, honey?' he asked.

'I walked up the lane, past that burnt house. Did that happen in the bushfire you told me about?'

'Sure did. Magda, the owner, is an elderly lady. She's gone to stay with her son at the moment but plans to rebuild.'

Pia shivered. 'I don't think I could do that. Doesn't it worry you it could happen again, and this place could burn next time?'

'I think there's more danger of being run down in the centre of Sydney, honey. I love it here. I just hope I can find a place as good as this one.'

'Hmm.'

Owen could tell Pia wasn't convinced. But she didn't need to be. He had no expectation of her wanting to stay here. He knew she'd be off back to the city whenever… He wanted to know if she'd made any decision yet, but knew it would be wrong to ask. If she had, she'd tell him in her own good time, if not, then he'd just have to wait.

'Coffee?' he asked, to change the subject. 'I think we have time for one before we go to Jo and Col's. Tea for you, Pia, and Fran?'

'I'll have coffee, thanks,' Fran said, joining Pia on the veranda. 'Don't you just love it here, Pia?' Owen heard her say as he went into the kitchen and slid the door closed behind him.

*

'That went well,' Jo said.

The four adults were relaxing by the pool. Jo and Fran were enjoying a glass of wine, while Col and Owen nursed bottles of beer. The younger women and the three children were in the spa section of the pool, the children having fun splashing around, while the women looked to be engaged in serious conversation. Scout was in his customary spot at Col's feet raising his head from time to time when the shouts from the pool disturbed him.

'Thanks for kitting Pia out,' Owen said. 'She seems to be enjoying herself. I wasn't sure how she'd react to meeting your two – and the children.'

'It wasn't a problem,' Jo said. 'We always keep a few spare swimsuits around. And as to Eve and Sally – they're pretty easy to get along with. I did brief Eve about Pia. Hope you don't mind.'

'Not at all. It seems to have done the trick. The mood Pia was in this morning, I wouldn't have been surprised if she'd upped and left at any time.'

'Thanks for this, Jo,' Fran said.

'It's good to see you two together,' Jo said with a conspiratorial smile. 'I hope we're going to see more of you out this way.'

'You will if I have anything to do with it,' Owen said, taking Fran's hand. 'This lady has changed my life.'

Fran reddened and looked down at her feet.

*

'Thanks, Dad. You, too, Fran,' Pia said as they were walking back along the lane. 'I didn't expect to enjoy it, but Eve and Sally are okay. It was good to see little Emily Rose, too. I've never had anything to do with such a young child. It made me think.'

Owen held his breath.

'Sally suggested I get myself checked out, find exactly how pregnant I am, maybe talk with a counsellor. She says if I plan to go ahead and stay in Granite Springs, I should book into prenatal classes.'

Owen, who had an arm around Fran's shoulders, felt her tense.

So far, she hadn't made any comment to Pia about her pregnancy, but now, as if she couldn't help herself, Fran said, 'You're not considering you won't have the baby? Oh, Pia!'

Pia turned sharply. 'It's my body!' she said, then, perhaps remembering what Owen had told her about Fran, added, 'But I haven't decided yet. A counsellor might be a good idea. Sally said it might help me understand my options. Dad told me what you went through, Fran. So, I guess I sort of understand how you feel, but I'm not you. I need to work this out for myself.'

Fran didn't reply but Owen sensed her dejection. It must be hard for her, having lost her only chance at being a mother, to see another woman prepared to throw that chance away.

Pia disappeared to bed as soon as they got back, claiming exhaustion, even though it was still early evening, not yet sunset. 'Want to help me check the goats?' Owen asked Fran, putting on his gum boots and offering Fran a pair that must have belonged to Bernadette.

'Gum boots?' she asked. 'The ground's hard.'

'You never know what you're going to find out in the paddock,' he said. 'If the goats have messed up their water supply again, it'll be pretty muddy around their trough. You need to get used to life on the farm,' he joked. But his comment was only partly in jest. He already knew he wanted a future with Fran, and for him, that meant living on a property like this and, in all likelihood, raising animals of some sort. He'd had a good chat with Col today about the possibilities of a small acreage. Col was currently researching llamas and alpacas as a possibility for theirs. It had interested Owen. They sounded a better bet than goats, and friendlier.

All was well with the animals' water supply and as the pair wandered back toward the house Pia was on both of their minds.

'I hope…' Fran began.

Owen put a finger on her lips and pulled her around to face him, her face luminous in the growing dusk. A flock of red-tailed black cockatoos flew overhead their harsh cries echoing across the paddock. 'I know how you must feel,' he said, but did he? How could he possibly put himself in her shoes? 'But it's her life. She must do what she feels is best for her. If she does go ahead, and this thing between us goes where I hope it's going, we'll get to be grandparents.'

Fran gasped. He saw her eyes widen in surprise, whether at the idea of their relationship turning into something more, or the idea of becoming a grandmother, Owen wasn't sure. 'Anyway, there's nothing we can do about it. It's getting cool out here. Race you back.'

Any further discussion was lost as they attempted to run back to the house across the uneven ground, wearing gun boots which, in Fran's case at least were extremely ill-fitting. By the time they arrived they were both out of breath, their earlier conversation seemingly forgotten.

But Owen hadn't forgotten. He'd meant every word of it.

Thirty-six

It was late on Sunday evening when Fran left to drive home. She and Owen spent the day driving around the countryside seeking out suitable properties for him. It had been fun and shown her a different side of the man she was becoming attached to, a more serious side. She hadn't realised how much it meant to him to be able to have his own few acres. Could she be content on a property, if what they had together morphed into something more permanent?

Of course, it was far too soon to be thinking in those terms. His comments about becoming grandparents had taken her breath away. He had to be joking. But, for a brief moment, she'd toyed with the idea, before his suggestion they run back cleared it from her mind – and presumably his.

Now it re-emerged. Fran let the idea circle around her consciousness. A grandchild, not of her blood, but part of her family. Maybe a little girl with Pia's beauty or a boy who looked like Owen. How she'd love that. Her eyes misted over. Then she dismissed the images which arose. It would never happen. Pia might have her child – though even that was uncertain – but there was no guarantee it would favour her family. Boy or girl, it might take after the father – the unknown Darren who, according to Owen, was an arrogant scoundrel, to put it more politely than he had. And there might not be a future for her and Owen.

Stormy greeted Fran as soon as she opened the door, and she scooped the cat up before he could disappear again. As she cuddled the warm furry bundle Fran reflected that this would be the closest she'd get to having a child of her own. Why had she never thought to have a pet before now? Had she been afraid of being taunted by others? Though when had she ever cared what other people thought of her? She was well aware they were too wrapped up in their own affairs to give her a minute of their time.

Her phone rang, and Stormy leapt down, slinking off to find a favourite spot. Fran smiled in pleasure to see Owen's face on the screen. It was only around forty minutes since they'd parted.

'Missing me already?' she asked, slipping off her shoes, curling up in her rocking chair, and tucking her feet under her.

'I am.'

The sound of his voice sent a quiver up the back of her neck. Fran smoothed down her hair as if Owen could see her.

'But that's not why I rang. I've just had an odd call. From old George. He wants to talk with me before choir on Tuesday. Do you have any idea what it might be about? Did I mess up so badly on my audition, he wants to break it to me gently?'

'Absolutely not. You were wonderful.' Fran hesitated. 'Do you think…? He has been talking of retirement. He may be wanting to get your opinion on his replacement.'

'Hmm. Doubt it. Isn't that Ron's prerogative?'

'Perhaps. But I've often wondered why George hung on so long. Every Christmas we think it's going to be his last Messiah, then, come January, he's back again. He's still pretty hale and hearty. I think he just doesn't want to let go. It's been his whole life, especially since he retired from his legal practice.'

'Well, there was one more thing…'

'Yes?'

'After you left, Pia came back out. Seems she wasn't as tired as she made out. She went into her bedroom to call that idiot, Darren. After all she said about him.' Owen's voice rose so much Fran had to hold the phone away from her ear.

'She doesn't want to go back to him?'

'I don't know what she wants.' Owen exhaled loudly. 'Oh, Fran. I wish you were here with me. I need your calm thinking to get me through this.'

Fran wished she was there, too. She could picture Owen. He was probably sitting outside – she could hear familiar outdoor noises: the soft bleating of the goats, the not-so-subtle sounds of cicadas in the surrounding trees, and the gentle meow of one of the cats. It was a homely sound and one with which she'd like to become even more familiar.

'Did she say anything more about her conversation with Eve and Sally?'

'No. I guess they did all their talking in the pool.'

Fran bit her lip. It was none of her business, but she couldn't help herself. 'Oh, Owen, she can't have a termination. She'll regret it all her life. To think of that little life growing inside her.' Her hand went to her stomach, remembering.

If only things had been different.

Pia could almost be her daughter.

Thirty-seven

It had been a hectic day at work. This damned grand opening the vice chancellor wanted was proving to be a mammoth task. Fran was taking care of most of the planning, and preparing the invitations was a nightmare by itself. If it was left to him, Owen would have taken the students' name for the place and invited everyone to The Mad House, but even *he* realised that wouldn't be acceptable. He was beginning to regret he'd ever applied for this position. But it had brought him to Granite Springs and to Fran. He wasn't sorry about that. Maybe things would improve next year when the staff were in place and the students arrived. He hoped so.

Meanwhile, tonight was choir and the meeting with old George. He pondered what Fran had hinted at. Could the old man be thinking of asking him to take over? He'd love it, but there was Ron to think of. He'd already ousted him from one position he believed was his by right. How would the man react to losing another coveted role to Owen? And he had to work with the guy.

'Sure you don't want to come tonight?' he asked Pia, who was curled up on the sofa with her iPad, her two faithful companions at her feet. Oscar and Lucinda had found a kindred spirit in Pia and, these days, were usually to be found close to her. It was as if they sensed her vulnerability.

Pia shook her head. 'No thanks, Dad. It's not my scene. Last week was enough. You know I didn't inherit your musical genes.'

'I guess not,' Owen sighed. When Pia had been born, he'd hoped, assumed, she'd be a musical genius, perhaps even surpassing him. Throughout her childhood he'd tried everything to bring out the talent he knew was hiding in her, just waiting for the chance to shine. But after a series of unsuccessful attempts at lessons in piano, flute, guitar and violin, he was forced to accept that not one of his own gifts had been passed on. 'Well, better see what this meeting is about. I won't be late.'

'Don't hurry back on my account. I'll probably go to bed early. And give my regards to Fran,' she said with a wink.

Owen grinned. Pia and Fran got on well. He'd get no objections from her if he wanted to turn the relationship into something more permanent. But he wasn't sure how Fran felt. It was too soon to broach the subject. He'd sensed her slight withdrawal when he made the joking reference to their becoming grandparents, and backed off. But the idea had never left him.

It was another glorious day. Even though Owen knew the countryside desperately needed rain, he couldn't help rejoicing in the bright sunlight and dry days in the lead up to the end of the year. He wouldn't say Christmas. It was still only November, but he'd noticed the stores were already decked out in all the bells and whistles for the festive season, and the supermarket shelves were stacked with mince pies, Christmas puddings and other such festive paraphernalia.

Owen began to sing as he drove along, enjoying the sound of his own voice. He was glad Fran had introduced him to the choir. They were a good group, with a surprising selection of talent. It was years since he'd belonged to a choir, not since his student days. He'd become side-tracked by the band he and his friends had formed, then by his marriage, work, life. Now he felt he'd been reborn, in more ways than one.

Fran! Everything came back to her. Her image forced itself into the forefront of his mind – her calm appearance, her eyes, a smoky grey that seemed to change colour with her mood, her soft lips, her indifferent expression, even though he knew she wasn't as carefree as she pretended. Her very presence in the office brightened his day, and he was going to see her again soon. Maybe he could persuade her to invite him home with her after choir, though he knew she and Kay or Marie usually went off for coffee together after rehearsal.

He was still thinking about her when he drove into the campus, the trees lining the entrance road looking like ghostly sentries in the approaching darkness.

'Welcome, young Owen,' George greeted him with a handshake. The room was empty apart from the two of them. George gestured to a seat and took the neighbouring one. 'How are you liking our little town?'

So, the old man wasn't going to get directly to the point? 'I love it here. I'm glad I made the move. You've lived here all your life?'

'I have, never wanted to move anywhere else. Even though it was tough some years. But the choir has always been my saviour. They're a grand bunch of people, for the most part.'

'So, what's this about, George? You sounded very mysterious on the phone. Are you going to tell me I haven't made the cut?' Owen gave an awkward laugh.

'Far from it, my boy. You have the voice of an angel. But it's not your voice we're here to talk about.'

Owen felt a twinge of excitement. Had Fran been right?

'I'm not as young as I used to be and, for some time now, I've been thinking I should hang up my spurs and hand over the reins. But…' he pulled on one ear, '…the one member who's been champing at the bit to take my place isn't one I'd like to hand over to, if you get my drift.' He peered at Owen.

'Ron Harris.'

'That's him. You'd know him from the university. I understand you pipped him at the post there, too.' George chuckled. 'He's a good musician, no doubt about that, and has a fine voice. But… I'm afraid he does tend to rub people up the wrong way. I dread to think what would happen to the group if he was director.'

'I'm afraid I don't know the others well enough to be able to advise you,' Owen said, deliberately misunderstanding his companion.

George slapped his leg and laughed. 'Don't be more of a fool than you need to be. You know exactly what I'm getting at. When you walked into this room that night a few weeks ago, I felt you'd been sent to solve my problem. You're the man we need to take on the job.' He sat back and grinned. 'What do you say?'

Although Owen had been half-expecting this offer, he was still stunned. 'But I'm a newcomer,' he said. 'Won't the others object?'

George chuckled. 'I suspect the majority will be delighted. Oh, there may be a few – drinking mates of Ron's – who'll complain a bit. But I wouldn't let them worry you. They'll soon see sense. Ron's going to be your major concern. My guess is you've locked horns with him already?'

'I have.' Owens lips tightened at the thought of giving his nemesis one more thing to hold against him. But the prospect of leading this choir was tempting. 'Can I take a few days to think about it?' he asked.

'Take as long as you like. I'm not going anywhere in a hurry. I fully intend to see the group through our Christmas performance. But I would like to be assured that my successor is announced before then.'

The two men shook hands.

At that point, the door burst open, and Ron Harris pushed through, looking around wildly. Seeing the two men, he stopped in his tracks. 'Oh, I didn't realise anyone was here,' he said, walking towards them. 'Private meeting?'

'No, no, Ron,' George said calmly. 'Owen here was just filling me in on this new school of his. I think you said the students are calling it The Mad House, Owen?' he chuckled.

'I consider that to be most disrespectful. It should be stopped,' Ron said, glaring at Owen. 'It would never have happened if I…' He paused, evidently thinking better of what he was about to say.

The door opened again, this time a group of women entered, chattering as they came. The atmosphere immediately changed, and Ron was forced to readjust his expression to one of a polite greeting. The rest of the choir gradually filtered in, but by the time George called the group to order, Fran hadn't arrived.

Owen had managed to avoid any further conversation with Ron – or George – instead moving around the group in an effort to make himself known and to remember names of those he'd only met briefly before. Unlike Ron, who stood by the far wall, surrounded by his acolytes and glowering at the others, he was good at this. It was a skill he'd perfected in his early days at Sydney University, leading many to consider him a ladies' man, since most of the groups were women. All the while, he kept an eye on the door, waiting for Fran's arrival.

Everyone was in place and they were about to begin when Fran rushed in, mouthing a "sorry" in Owen's direction and taking her place, George's glare of annoyance forcing her to avoid eye contact with anyone else.

'What kept you?' Owen asked Fran, having managed to corner her as they were readying to leave. 'I need to talk with you.' He glanced over his shoulder to where Kay and Marie were obviously waiting for them to finish their conversation. 'Do you have to go with your friends tonight?'

'I…' Fran glanced at the two women. 'Give me a minute.' She went over to them, said a few words, and they left, but not before sending what Owen could only describe as a knowing look his way.

'Now they'll jump to all sorts of conclusions,' she said with a resigned air, as Owen steered her out of the building and into the car park.

'Let them. They'd be right. They're probably just envious,' he said. 'Can I follow you home? We can talk there.'

Fran nodded and unlocked her car, Owen doing the same with the Suzuki, his own yellow monster this time. He'd finally got rid of his old Mazda and found a second-hand Suzuki 4WD, almost identical to the one belonging to John Kelly.

As soon as they entered Fran's townhouse, even before she turned on the lights, Owen took Fran in his arms. 'I've been wanting to do this all evening,' he murmured into her hair, his hands encircling her waist, 'all day, actually.'

'I thought you wanted to talk,' Fran said, slipping out of his arms to turn on the light. Owen blinked in the brightness, and Stormy, at this sign his mistress was home, emerged from the bedroom, meowing.

'I do. You were right.' He ran a hand through his hair. 'About old George. He's asked me to take over the choir next year when he steps down.'

'I told you!' she said gleefully. 'You accepted, of course.'

'Not yet. I said I needed to think about it.'

'What's to think about? Oh!' she said. 'Ron.'

'Exactly.' Owen rubbed his chin. 'Ron. He arrived early and found George and me together. I think he guessed something was up. You should have seen his expression. Maybe I should let him have this one.'

'No! Absolutely not! It would be a disaster. Ron would have us all at each other's throats in no time. It would be the end of the choir. And George knows that. It's why he's stayed as long as he has.'

'You think?'

'I know.'

'Well then. Now, I had another reason for coming back with you.'

'Coffee?'

Owen shook his head.

'Wine?'

He shook his head again, moving closer.

'I can't think…'

This time he grasped Fran in an embrace that left her in no room for doubt as to his intentions. 'This,' he kissed her on the lips, 'and this,' his lips travelled down to her collar bone, 'and this.' He slipped one arm around her back, the other under her knees and carried her into the bedroom.

Thirty-eight

The morning sun shone in through the shutters wakening Fran. She stretched her arms above her head and looked at the man lying beside her. Last night she'd broken her golden rule, and he'd spent a weeknight here. It hadn't been her intention when they'd driven back from choir, but she knew that, in a tiny recess of her mind, she'd been hoping.

Last night, when they'd driven back together – one behind the other – she'd known there was more than just the need to talk on Owen's mind. It was on her mind, too. She couldn't believe how much her body longed for his. And yet, she was still wary of being hurt. She knew from Marie how feelings like these didn't always last. It had been safe with Richard – her innermost feelings had remained untouched. While with Owen, she was overcome with a tumult of desire – one that was met by an answering passion from him. She lay back, a smile playing across her lips.

Owen turned towards her. His eyes opened, those piercing blue eyes she'd become so accustomed to. 'Morning, sweetheart. Hell, it's a work-day, isn't it?'

'Wednesday.'

'What time is it?'

Fran checked her phone, lying on the bedside table. 'Just after six.'

'I'm sorry. I need to get home, check on Pia, shower and change. I guess I shouldn't turn up in the same gear I wore to choir last night.'

'There might be some raised eyebrows,' Fran agreed, chuckling and knowing she should care more than she did. *What was happening to her?* 'You don't want something to eat before you go?'

'Better not.' He was already out of bed and struggling into his clothes, which were somewhat creased, having been hurriedly thrown off and strewn across the floor the night before. 'See you in the office.' He dropped a kiss on her forehead and left.

Feeling suddenly bereft, Fran curled her knees up to her chin and wrapped her arms around them. She should get up, too. But it was comfortable here. The bed still retained Owen's scent. She closed her eyes and inhaled, remembering their night of passion.

When Fran reached the university campus sometime later, her eyes were still glowing with the memory of her night with Owen. She was unlocking her office door when an angry Ron Harris accosted her.

'What did your boss and old George get up to last night?' he blustered.

'I don't know what you're talking about. How should I know anything about Owen and George?' Fran's throat constricted. *What did Ron know? What had he guessed?* She and Owen hadn't made any attempt to be secretive about their relationship but had ensured they kept their interactions professional on campus.

'Don't think I don't know what you two get up to in here, all on your own.' He leered, pointing a finger at her, then at the echoing vastness of the empty building. He seemed about to say something more, when Owen appeared bearing the usual coffees and paper bag.

'Looking for me, Ron?' Owen asked pleasantly.

Ron didn't reply, only glared at them both before turning on his heel and leaving.

They heard the downstairs outer door slam behind him, then Owen turned to Fran. 'What did he want?'

'Oh, his usual bluster. He wanted to know what you and George were planning, then,' she shivered, 'he insinuated about what we might be getting up to.'

'Here? The man's a bigger fool than I thought. You're not worried, are you?'

'No…oo.' But Fran couldn't dismiss the fear that Ron would – what? What could he do?

'Then don't be. I'll give old George my answer today, then he can let everyone know next week. That'll settle Ron's petty ambitions.'

But Fran wasn't so sure. Owen hadn't seen the expression on Ron's face this morning, before he arrived. The man was out for revenge in whatever form he could get.

The day passed as usual, interrupted only by a call from Kay suggesting coffee mid-afternoon.

Banjo's was quiet when the two women arrived. Most of the students were in class or finished for the day, and the place looked as if it was about to close.

'How are you?' Kay asked when they were seated with their coffees. 'I was surprised to see you go off with Owen last night. We missed our coffee and chat. Is everything all right?'

'Yes…no. Everything is fine with Owen. We don't usually meet evenings mid-week, but he had something to tell me.'

Kay raised an eyebrow.

'You'll find out soon enough. Might as well tell you, George has asked him to take over the choir next year.'

Kay's breath hissed from between her teeth. 'He's finally decided to retire? Well, I'm not surprised. We've been expecting this, but Owen…? That'll really piss Ron off. Owen'll do a much better job, of course, but does he realise…?'

'I think he does. Ron doesn't know for sure yet, but he's guessed. He confronted me about it this morning, then stalked off when Owen appeared. I'm afraid what he might try to do, Kay. He made insinuations about me and Owen alone in The Mad House. What if…?'

'He'd be a fool to try to do anything along those lines.' But Kay frowned. They both knew Ron might stop at nothing to see his rival brought down. 'Anyway, it's good to know everything's going well for you and Owen. It is, isn't it?' she asked, seeing Fran's slight frown. 'Jo said you and he were at Yarran with his daughter on the weekend.'

'Yes, we were. Pia's a lovely girl. And we are getting on well. That's what worries me, Kay. It's all so good. What if… what if it all falls apart? I can't bear the thought of being hurt again.'

Kay's eyes softened. 'Oh, Fran, we've all felt like that at some time or another. It wasn't all plain sailing with Nick and me. I had all sorts of doubts. But Owen's such an open book, and you already know his daughter. I can't see you have anything to worry about. If it's fear of commitment, I know all about that. But, if you want my advice, I'd say let your heart guide you.'

Her heart? It wasn't her heart that had guided her last night. But Kay's words made sense. Maybe she was worrying needlessly.

Thirty-nine

'Brit! What the hell are you doing here?'

Owen couldn't believe his eyes. Granite Springs was the last place he expected to see his ex-wife. It was so far out of her usual environment. He looked around, expecting to see Rosemary with her customary curled lips, trailing behind her. But there was no one. 'On your own?' he asked.

'I'm here to see Pia.' Brit swept into the house as if she owned it, then stood in the middle of the kitchen and gazed around. 'Well, this is a bit different for you, isn't it?'

The cats appeared as if from nowhere and began to prowl around her.

'Cats? You really have gone into this whole country idyll, then?' she asked sarcastically.

'They come with the house. I'm housesitting for a couple who're doing the grey nomad thing. Pia probably told you.' Owen didn't want to waste time explaining himself. Brit hadn't come to see him or to comment on his lifestyle.

'Where is she?'

'Pia?' Owen decided to stall for time. Ever since Pia had said she'd told her mother about her pregnancy, he'd been expecting something, but not this.

'I've come to take her back to Sydney.' Brit sat down at the kitchen table, rubbing her hand across it absentmindedly. 'And a glass of wine wouldn't go astray.'

'It's a bit early for wine. Coffee do?'

Owen had come home early from uni to prepare dinner. He and Fran had fallen into the habit of dining here every Friday, then spending the weekend together. Hell! Fran! She'd be here in under an hour. What would she think if she found Brit here? His initial panic subsided. Fran knew he and Brit had been divorced for years. She knew she was Pia's mother. It was natural a mother would want to see her daughter at this time.

The trouble was, Brit was no natural mother, never had been. So, what was all this about wanting to take Pia back to Sydney? Pia wasn't an errant child.

'I suppose,' she said. 'At least I see you have a decent coffee maker.'

Owen chose to ignore the petty remark.

'Where is Pia?' Brit asked again, gazing around as if expecting her to make a sudden appearance.

'She went into town.' Owen knew exactly where their daughter was. Today was the first of the prenatal classes Pia had booked on Sally's advice. Although she hadn't discussed it with her father, it was clear to both him and Fran that Pia had made her decision to have the baby. The two women planned to have dinner together afterwards, Pia having welcomed Sally's support. He had no intention of sharing that with Brit.

'Town? You mean that one-street huddle of shops and houses I drove through from the airport?'

Owen almost burst out laughing. This was Brit at her most spiteful. 'Fair go,' he said. 'Granite Springs may not be the metropolis Sydney is, but it's a good-sized regional centre. It's a university town, not to mention…'

'Yeah, yeah,' she interrupted him. 'When will she be back?'

'Not till later.' He placed a mug of coffee on the table. Maybe he should have agreed to her request for wine. He could do with a glass right now. 'Where are you staying?'

'I thought…' Brit gazed around again as if assessing the size of the house.

Owen shook his head. No way was he going to have Brit stay here. It was untenable, even if Fran wasn't going to be here soon. He sneaked a quick look at his watch. He should be making a start on dinner. Instead, he sat down, pretending to be relaxed while seething inside. How dare Brit arrive out of the blue and expect everyone to fall in with her plans. But why should that surprise him? It was what she'd been doing all her life – and now she had Rosemary to encourage her – to egg her on. In fact…

'Did Pia know you planned to come here to – as you say – take her back to Sydney? Was it your idea or Rosemary's?'

Brit's expression said it all. Rosemary's!

He was about to tell her it was time to go. The cats had given up and slunk off, and through the window he could see the goats making their way towards the water trough as they did at this time of day, when there was the sound of a car engine.

Owen didn't get to the door fast enough. Fran's bright face appeared at the door, her smile of greeting fading at the sight of Brit sitting there as if she belonged.

'Well, well,' Brit said. 'It didn't take you long, Owen. I should have known you couldn't do without a woman in your life. Who's this?'

'Fran, this is…'

'Brit.' She rose to shake Fran's hand, eyeing her as if she was a piece of horseflesh. 'Not your usual type, Owen,' she said, turning back towards him.

'I'm sorry, Fran. This is Pia's mother. She arrived unexpectedly. She…'

'I came to see my daughter,' Brit said. 'Whereas there are no prizes for guessing why you've come to see my ex-husband.' She paused to let the full import of her words sink in.

Owen wanted to tell her to leave but knew Pia would be upset if she knew her mother had come, only to be turned away. But he couldn't face the thought of sitting here with both Fran and Brit till Pia returned home later in the evening. What was he to do?

Fran took the decision from him. 'I think I should go,' she said. 'You two probably have a lot to talk about.' She turned, almost tripping over the cats who chose that moment to dash to the door.

'Fran!' Owen hurried after her. 'Don't go. Brit won't stay long.' But he knew it was a lie. Brit had no intention of going anywhere till she'd seen Pia, maybe not even then. She'd know the house was big enough for there to be several spare rooms and it wasn't as if she hadn't stayed with him before – even after they'd broken up, divorced. Over the years, he hadn't been too fussy who shared his bed, and Brit had sometimes wanted to revisit old memories.

'Call me when you've sorted out your family,' Fran said in a broken voice, wrenching her car door open.

Owen watched helplessly as she drove off.

Forty

'Won't you listen to me, Fran? I had no idea Brit was going to turn up on Friday. She hung around till Pia got back, then I went to bed and left them to it. There were raised voices – not so unusual where those two are concerned – and she was gone when I got up.

'You didn't answer your phone all weekend. I brought your coffee,' he added, placing one, in its cardboard container on her desk, the Banjo's logo emblazoned on its side.

'Thanks.' Fran knew she was being unfair. It wasn't Owen's fault, wasn't anything he'd done, but Brit's words, her sly look, had made Fran feel dirty. What if she *was* just one in a long line of women? What did that make her? She'd lain awake most of the night alternately remembering how it had been lying there with him, and imagining Brit was right in her assessment of their relationship.

Now, she found it hard to face him, to resume their normal easy camaraderie. Instead of joining Owen in drinking coffee and consuming the croissants which sat there in their brown paper bag as if accusing her, she turned her back on him and fired up the computer.

'Looks like you're busy this morning. I know when I'm not wanted.' Owen picked up the bag of croissants and left, closing his office door behind him.

Fran wanted to call after him, to say she'd been mistaken, that she understood. But she steeled herself not to. It was better to stop now, before she became more involved, before it was too late. But was it already too late? Seeing him walk out like that, shoulders drooping, the customary spring missing from his step, almost tore her heart out.

She entered her password and was scrolling down her emails when she was interrupted by the phone ringing. Damn! Couldn't Owen let things be? It had to be him. Who else would call her at this time in the morning?

'Hello,' she said tersely, still scrolling through her emails with one hand.

'Fran, I'm so glad I've been able to catch you this early.' Sheila Allen, secretary to the vice chancellor, was the last person Fran expected to hear.

'Sheila! Yes, I'm always in at this time. What can I do for you?'

'Something has come to the vice chancellor's notice and Human Resources would like a word with you. Shall we say ten o'clock with Flora Richards?'

Fran thought quickly. What on earth could it be about? What could have come to Aaron Peters' notice to trigger a meeting with HR? But it wasn't possible to refuse. 'Ten o'clock. I'll be there,' she confirmed. She put down the phone and stared at it, the emails forgotten. What she dearly wanted to do was to pop into Owen's office to ask if he had any idea what it was about. But, given the way she'd dismissed him only a few minutes earlier, that wasn't a good idea. She'd have to stew on it by herself.

'Back around eleven,' Owen muttered as he passed her desk on his way out. Did he seem a little more subdued than usual? Was that her fault? She'd forgotten the faculty heads meeting this morning, so she'd have had no opportunity to share her fears about this meeting with HR anyway.

At a few minutes before ten, Fran presented herself at the reception desk in Human Resources. The girl sitting there was one Fran didn't recognise, but a couple of the older women in the office behind her called out greetings to Fran, who nodded her acknowledgment.

'Take a seat. Ms Richards will be right with you,' the young girl said.

Fran sat down on the edge of a chair. She'd dealt with Flora Richards many times over the years, most recently in connection with the recruitment of the school's new staff. It could be something related to that.

But she knew it wasn't. Any recruitment matter could be dealt with by phone or email. And for Sheila Allen to have made the call – her words that "something had come to the vice chancellor's notice" – was what alerted Fran to the fact she wasn't going to like what Flora had to say.

'Come in, Fran.'

Fran looked up to see Flora Richards at the open door. She led the way into the meeting room, a room Fran was familiar with. But in the past, she'd been there as part of a recruitment panel. She wasn't sure what this was but breathed a sigh of relief to see Flora was on her own.

'What's this about, Flora?' Fran asked, trying to subdue the butterflies that were creating havoc in her stomach.

'It's a sensitive matter, Fran.' Flora's expression told Fran nothing. 'I've been asked by the vice chancellor to have a word with you before...'

'A word about what?' Fran asked again.

Flora sighed. 'There's been a complaint and, although both the vice chancellor and I know you as the epitome of integrity, of your years of excellent service...'

She paused, and Fran flinched. What on earth was going on?

Flora cleared her throat. 'It pains me to say this Fran, but the complaint is about inappropriate behaviour.'

Fran gasped. Had she been brought in here about her relationship with Owen? That was a laugh as it was all but over, in her mind, at least. But, no, it couldn't be that – no one objected to Nick and Kay's relationship. What else might she have been guilty of?

'There has been a complaint,' Flora repeated, 'by a member of staff.' She cleared her throat. 'This is difficult for me, Fran. I've known you for years, but the member of staff is of long-standing too, and we have to take it seriously.'

Something in the back of Fran's mind began to put two and two together. Could Ron Harris have been so devious as to...?

'Can I ask who made the complaint?'

Flora checked a sheet of paper from a folder on her lap. 'I'm sorry. I'm not able to provide that information.'

'And what is this inappropriate behaviour I'm alleged to have engaged in?' Fran asked, her heart thumping.

Flora referred to the sheet of paper again. 'It's been alleged that you have acted inappropriately by engaging in sexual acts in the new School of Music and Drama building when you and Professor Larsen were there alone.' She looked up to meet Fran's eyes with a pitying expression. 'In view of this, I…'

Fran didn't allow her to finish. 'That's outrageous! It was Ron Harris who made the complaint, wasn't it?'

'I'm afraid I can't…'

'The rat! He's so annoyed Owen – Professor Larsen – was given the position instead of him. He's been bellyaching about it ever since the appointment was made. And he's just learned that he's been passed over for the director's position in the Granite Springs Choristers. He can't get at Owen directly, so he's doing it through me.'

'Calm down, Fran. Getting angry won't solve anything.'

Fran hadn't realised her voice had risen and could probably be heard in the outside office. 'What happens now?' she asked in a more subdued voice.

'Well, normally we'd look at suspending you immediately until we could source all the evidence. But I can use my discretion and, given you're such a well-known and respected employee, I propose we allow you to continue as before until we know more. We'll be speaking with Professor Larsen too, of course, and with Professor Kerr with whom you worked before, prior to your taking up your present position.'

'Is there anything else?' Fran couldn't wait to get out of there.

'You may go.'

Fran stormed out, ignoring the surprised looks from the office staff who had no doubt heard her outburst. She needed to let off steam, talk to someone. Her feet automatically took her to her old office in the education building where Kay was busily typing away. If she'd stayed here, taken back her old job, none of this would have happened.

Kay looked up when Fran appeared at the door, her eyes widening as she took in Fran's red face and wild expression. 'What's wrong?' she asked, coming around the desk to take her arm.

'Don't ask! That rat, Ron! I can't believe it.'

Kay gave a quick glance around. 'Banjo's,' she decided. 'Just a minute.' She turned off her computer and, taking Fran's arm, walked with the distracted woman out of the building and across campus to the café.

Fortunately, most of the students were in class at this time of the morning, only one group huddled in a corner.

'Now, tell me!' Kay said, when they'd been served with their coffees.

Fran was feeling calmer, though the memory of the meeting with Flora Richards still sat in the back of her mind like a snake coiled to strike. 'Ron Harris,' she said, then her throat constricted. How could even he have been so cruel?

'What's he done now?' Kay sounded resigned. In her time with the education faculty she must have had a few run-ins with him. He wasn't an easy man to deal with. Even before his disappointments and enmity towards Owen, he'd always seemed to harbour some grudge or other. Fran knew it had always been a curiosity to Nick how well he got on with the students.

Fran stirred her coffee aimlessly before replying, then she held the cup with both hands. 'Oh, Kay, it's beyond belief. Remember what I said he'd implied? Well, it seems he didn't stop there.' She filled Kay in on her meeting with Flora in HR, and on the episode with Brit on the weekend, finishing with, 'It's so awful, and I feel I can't talk with Owen about it. I don't know what to do.'

It was a few moments before Kay replied, and Fran thought she was going to tell her to get a grip. But what Kay said was, 'I think you need to take some time to yourself. I'm sure HR would understand if you requested leave – a week, or maybe two? Let them get this sorted out. *We* know it's all a storm in a teacup, but they have to come to their own decision. When they interview Ron, they'll soon see him for what he is – a sad, disappointed man who'd do anything to damage reputations in an effort to get what he thinks he's owed.'

'And Owen?'

'Let me and Nick deal with Owen. He'll still be in the faculty heads meeting. Leave him a note and get back in touch with him when you feel you can.'

Fran felt as if a load had been lifted from her shoulders. The thought of getting away from the campus, away from Ron, and yes, even from Owen, filled her with such a huge sense of relief, she almost hugged Kay.

'Thanks,' she said. 'I'll do it now.' Ignoring the still full cup of coffee, she pushed back her chair and stood up. She did give Kay a hug, muttering, 'Thanks,' again, before hurrying off to do exactly as Kay suggested.

It was when she was on her way home, her head filled with everything that had happened during the morning and cursing her own stupidity for getting involved with Owen in the first place, that she remembered Magda's words. "There's a light at the end of the tunnel. You need to be patient." Well, Fran felt she'd been patient for too long. There was no light, just an endless dark tunnel. But she could get through this, just as she'd got through everything else that had happened to her.

Forty-one

Owen was thinking of Fran when the phone rang. He'd been thinking about her all day, trying to work out why she hadn't returned his calls, what to say to her when she did, how to explain. When he got back to the office to discover her gone, he'd been worried something had happened to her. Then Flora Richards had called. He'd been ready to murder Ron Harris but had managed to cool down enough to speak to the man.

Now, he expected it to be Fran calling him.

'Owen?'

It wasn't Fran. The voice was unfamiliar. It took him a few seconds to recognise it. 'Bernadette?' he asked, wondering what she wanted. He'd been here two months and had been reporting regularly by text as they'd arranged.

'It's John,' she said. 'He's…' Owen heard her sharp intake of breath, 'he had a slight heart attack.'

'Oh, Bernadette, I'm so sorry. How is he?' Owen couldn't help wondering how this might affect him. There was no formal agreement regarding the housesitting arrangement, and he still hadn't found anywhere to buy.

'He's making a good recovery thanks, but it was touch and go for a while. We have to make some decisions about the future. John's still in hospital, but I'm planning to fly down for a few days.'

'Do you want to…?' Owen wasn't sure what he wanted to ask. 'Did she want to stay here? Did she want him to move out? When did they plan to return?'

'No need for you to do anything yet. I have a few things I need to sort out, a few people to see. But I would like to come out to the property and talk with you. How about Wednesday?'

'Sure, that would be fine. I'll be here after five-thirty. I'll expect you.'

Owen rubbed an eyebrow and pinched his throat. Poor John and poor Bernadette. They were just getting started on their trip. What a thing to happen. He'd been so stunned, he hadn't even asked where they were. He took a beer from the fridge and walked outside, taking a seat on the veranda. He guessed they'd want to come home as soon as John was fit enough. Where did that leave him? Surely he wouldn't have to resort to student residences again? And what about Pia?

*

'The place is looking good. You've done well.' Bernadette gazed around the property, the cats meowing their welcome and rubbing themselves against her ankles.

'Would you like tea, coffee, wine, beer?' Owen offered, feeling awkward. This was Bernadette's home. He was the stranger.

'A beer would go down well. It's been quite a trip.' She followed him into the house, the cats at her heels, and took a seat at the kitchen table, stroking it lovingly with her hand.

Owen remembered Brit doing that, only a few days earlier, but the way Bernadette did it was different. She was greeting an old friend.

'Thanks,' she said, as Owen handed her a bottle of Carlton Draught. She took a long swig. 'It's been a difficult few weeks.'

'It must have been.' Owen cradled his own beer, uncertain what to say, sure he was going to get his marching orders. 'When do you plan to come back?'

'Once John was over the worst,' she continued, ignoring Owen's question, 'we had a lot of thinking to do. The doctors say he'll make a full recovery, but will need to be careful, take things easy. We need to stay in Rockhampton for him to undertake the rehab they've recommended, then...' she met Owen's eyes apologetically, '...I'm afraid we'll have to sell this place, Owen.'

Bernadette's eyes misted as she gazed out the window to where the goats were engaged in their usual capers, a breeze was fluttering the branches on the fruit trees, and the ground was as parched as ever. She knuckled away the incipient tears. 'It'll be a wrench. We always thought we'd end our days here, but… John's health comes first.'

'You'll move into town?' Owen couldn't believe what he was hearing.

Bernadette shook her head. 'No. We've decided. We're going to make a clean break. The climate in North Queensland suits us. As soon as we have this place off our hands, we'll look for something up there, something smaller, maybe on the coast. We'll become beach bums,' she laughed. 'That's what I've been doing – talking to our solicitor, seeing the stock and station agent. He says there are always people looking for a small acreage, it shouldn't be difficult to shift.'

Owen took a deep breath. He could feel his heart pounding. 'Would you sell it to me?'

Forty-two

It was over a week since what Fran liked to call *the wrath of Ron* and, despite the predicament hanging over her, she was enjoying the break. There had been no word from the university, but she'd had lunch with Jo, visited her physio, and put in a few extra half-days volunteering at the hospital. On one of those, she'd been sent to the Maternity ward. In all the years she'd been volunteering, Fran had managed to steer clear of both Maternity and Paediatrics, fearing the reminder of her own failings in that regard would prove too much. But, to her surprise, she was able to cope without breaking down. Maybe, at last, she was getting over what had been a worrying phobia.

Fran was sitting in the sun watching Stormy's unsuccessful efforts to trap a tiny lizard when her phone rang. She sighed and checked the caller ID. Since the day she'd walked out of the office, she'd been bombarded by calls and texts from Owen. She knew what he wanted, but wasn't ready to talk to him yet, though knew she'd have to eventually.

It was a surprise to see Pia's number. What did she want? In two minds whether to answer – what if she wanted to plead Owen's case? – Fran accepted the call.

'Oh, Fran! Dad said you're on leave or something, and I need to talk with you. Mum's driving me mad. You're the only one who'll understand. Can I come to see you?'

So, Brit was still there. Was she staying at the property with Owen and Pia? Why would Fran understand whatever it was? Although tempted to refuse – Owen's daughter was none of her business – Fran found herself agreeing and they arranged for Pia to drop around that afternoon.

*

'What's with you and Dad? He's been mooching around like a bear with a sore head all this week. He says you're on leave?' Pia wrapped her hands around the mug of peppermint tea and cooed at Stormy who seemed to have decided to add her to his list of favourite people.

'It's difficult to explain, but surely that's not why you're here? You said…'

'No, but I wondered. You two were getting on so well until… Mum arrived.' Pia nodded as if something had suddenly become clear. 'She did it again, didn't she?'

'I don't know what you mean.'

'It's Mum. She didn't want Dad herself, and she and Rosemary are happy together, but she can't seem to help herself. Whenever she sees Dad being happy, she wants to spoil things for him. What did she say this time? No, don't tell me,' she added, as if sensing Fran's reluctance to discuss Pia's parents with her. 'I can imagine. She made some comment about your being one in a long line of Dad's women, or said something disparaging about you. It's not true you know. Oh, Dad has had a few women. Well, maybe more than a few.' She gave a wicked grin that reminded Fran so much of Owen, her heart turned over. 'So, not content with trying to ruin my life, she wants to do the same to him. You're really special to him, you know. I've never seen him so happy.'

Fran felt a warm glow at Pia's words, but could she believe her? 'There's some stuff at the university, too,' she said weakly.

'Oh, Dad's told me about that. Some arsehole's trying to stir up trouble for him. Dad says he's on the case.'

Fran gave a weak smile. That sounded so like Owen. He wouldn't let anything or anyone – especially Ron Harris – get the better of him. 'You wanted to talk to me,' she reminded Pia.

'It's Mum. She wants to ruin my life,' she repeated. 'She and

Rosemary. They have this weird idea they have the right to tell me what to do. They've decided I can't possibly bring up a child on my own and they're the only ones who can help. In their view, my only option, if I intend to have this baby – which I do, you knew that, didn't you? – is to go back to Sydney and move in with them. Then, according to Mum, I can continue with my career while *they* bring up *my* child. As if she did a good job with me!' Pia seemed to run out of breath. She took a long drink of tea and sighed.

This was all very interesting, and Fran could understand why Pia was upset, but where did she come in?

'Dad told me,' Pia said, 'about your accident, about your boyfriend dying. That must have been so awful. I can't imagine.' She shivered. 'He told me about the baby, too. I hope you don't mind. But it made me think...'

Fran was perplexed. What possible connection could Pia make between herself and Fran's loss of her baby?

'I wanted to know... If you hadn't lost the baby... How do you think you could have coped? I mean, as a single mother. How hard could it be?' She ran her fingers around the rim of the cup, avoiding Fran's eyes. 'I hope you don't mind my asking, but I thought you might understand. There's no one else I can talk to. Eve has her husband, and Sally's never been pregnant.' She raised her eyes to meet Fran's. They were filled with hope.

Strangely, it was something Fran had often asked herself in the weeks and months following the accident. She remembered the hours of agonising over what might have been, of what she would do if she could change things. She almost wept. 'I do. I gave it a lot of thought. I knew it would have been hard, but it would have been worth it. I'd have done anything if I could have held my baby, seen her grow up. She'd have been almost your age by now.'

Pia was silent for what seemed like several minutes, then she said, 'Thanks, Fran. I knew you'd understand. Mum and Rosemary may mean well, but they're really only thinking of themselves, and how to get one up on Dad. It was okay when Mum left. I was happy to move between Mum and Dad's, but it would have driven me mad to be with her and Rosemary all the time. I wanted to say no to her, but she kept insisting I couldn't manage on my own.'

'Will you go back to Sydney?'

'I still have to work that out. They're expecting me back at work, but I don't have anywhere to stay. After Mum's behaviour, I don't want to stay with her, not even on a temporary basis. Dad's been good. He lets me do my own thing. If I could find work here, I might stay on, at least for a while. You did.'

'I did, and I've never regretted it.' Then it all came back to Fran, threatening to overwhelm her – Brit, the way she'd treated Owen, Ron Harris and the business at the university. She had a few things to sort out, too.

'Dad doesn't know I'm here,' Pia said. 'You will contact him, won't you?'

'I will,' Fran agreed.

But, when Pia had left, she picked up her pet and cuddled him. 'I've behaved abominably, Stormy. What am I going to tell him? Will he ever forgive me?'

Forty-three

'You're buying this dump?' Brit's shriek of amazement echoed through the old kitchen, sending the cats for cover.

'I like it.' Owen gazed around the room with satisfaction. His visit to Col's friend, Ken Thomson, had borne fruit. A call to the stock and station agent from Bernie had ensured Owen was able to make an offer before the property was listed for sale. A deal had been done, and Owen was now the proud owner of the property he intended to name The Haven. That's what it was – his haven, the place where he could settle down for the rest of his life.

The one blot on his future landscape was Fran. What was happening with her? It was over a week since he'd returned to his office to find a note saying she'd gone home, taken leave, and would be in touch. Then – nothing. There had been a weird message from Flora in HR about a complaint they were investigating. He'd known right away who was behind it. Ron had backed down when Owen confronted him with it. Sex in the office? As if! Though there were times when he'd been tempted to throw Fran across the desk and have his wicked way with her, he'd had more sense. Not to mention his conventional Fran would have been shocked to the core.

There had been no answer to his texts and calls. Owen could only assume Fran was avoiding him, especially as it all happened immediately after her seeing Brit making herself at home in this very kitchen. Damn the woman! Why did she have to stick her nose into his life? He was forgetting it was actually Pia whose life Brit was intent on organising.

He gazed past Brit, out of the window to where he could see the goats climbing onto the edge of the dam, a couple of galahs swooping down to the vegetable garden, and a cheeky kookaburra on the fence post. It was all his – or would be as soon as all the paperwork went through. It was strange how different it all looked in the pride of ownership. Owen had agreed to take the goats too, putting paid to any ideas he had about llamas or alpacas, but he could live with that. Bernadette had promised to move out all of their furniture as soon as she could arrange it. She was keen to take the cats, too. Owen frowned. He'd become attached to Oscar and Lucinda, and they to him. But he supposed he could replace them. The only thing missing was Fran.

'You're not listening!' Brit's voice broke through his thoughts. She was still here? Owen thought he'd managed to erase her from his life when he left Sydney. Then she turned up here to hassle their daughter. Thankfully, she'd booked into a motel in town, but was out here at every opportunity. He was weary of it.

'Isn't it time you went home?' he asked. 'Rosemary must be missing you.'

'She is. But I'm not going without Pia. She must realise…'

'What must I realise, Mum?' Pia walked in, her hair a tousled mess on her shoulders, her eyes bleary with sleep. She was wearing a long white tee-shirt and looked beautiful. How had he and Brit managed to produce such a beauty?

Brit turned at her daughter's voice. 'Your dad thinks it's time I went back to Sydney – Rosemary does, too. We spoke last night. She has your room all ready for you and has plans for the nursery. It's time to go, Pia. You've hung around here long enough. This isn't real life. You need to get back to the city.'

'No!'

'No? What do you mean? I've gone to all the trouble to come down here. Rosemary has been rearranging our house to accommodate you and the baby – my grandchild.' Her face softened. 'And you say, "no"?'

'Mum, it's been good to see you and know that you care – you and Rosemary. But I need to stand on my own two feet. This baby isn't something you can take care of for me. I need to do it myself. I spoke with Fran and…'

'You spoke with Fran?' Owen couldn't believe his ears. While he'd been trying unsuccessfully to contact Fran for days, Pia was glibly saying she spoke with her. 'When?'

'What does it matter? You two need to get your act together.'

Owen's mouth fell open in surprise. What had Fran said about him to Pia?

Before he could ask, she continued, 'She understands. I wanted to know what it would be like to be a single mother.'

'But…'

'I know she lost her baby, but it was something she'd thought about – a lot. I know it won't be easy, but it'll be easier here than in Sydney. So, Mum, I'll be staying in Granite Springs. If it's okay with you, Dad, I'd like to stay here till I have the baby, then I want to find somewhere of my own. I don't want to feel I'm beholden to you or Mum. This is my life. Now, I need a cup of tea.'

Both Owen and Brit stared at their daughter as if she was a stranger. This was a different person from the distraught girl who'd been mooning around the house for the past few weeks. Owen was first to recover. He enveloped her in a warm hug. 'You know we'll support you in whatever you decide, and you're welcome to stay here as long as you like. Brit?'

Although clearly not pleased, Brit obviously decided to go along with him. 'I'm sorry that's your decision, Pia, but I accept it. I only hope you don't live to regret it. Rosemary and I will always be there for you. I don't know how I'm going to break this to her. She was so looking forward to having a baby to look after. She never had a child of her own.'

'Well, she can't have mine.' Pia poured boiling water over a peppermint teabag in her favourite mug and took it outside, the cats, who had reappeared with her arrival, following her.

Owen would miss them.

'Well,' Brit said, when she and Owen were alone again. 'I guess that's it. Who'd have thought our little girl would have the spirit to see it through on her own. You have to admire her resilience.'

And your about-face.

'I'll book a flight back today. And I wish you well with this…' Brit gave one more glance around and smirked.

'Thanks.' Owen didn't care about Brit's opinion. He hadn't since they were in the throes of first love – and how long ago that had been.

After she'd gone, he made himself a coffee and joined Pia on the veranda.

'So Dad. You're really buying this place?'

'Already have.'

Forty-four

Fran took a deep breath and picked up the phone. The call from HR had been reassuring. Flora had actually apologised for the trouble Fran had been caused. It seemed they hadn't even spoken with Owen. That annoyed Fran. Why was it always the women who seemed to get blamed for workplace improprieties, while the men got off scot-free? But Ron Harris had admitted he'd fabricated the accusation to get revenge on Owen who'd ruined his life. He was presently on leave without pay while the university decided how to deal with him.

But, now, she had to do what she'd been dreading. It had been lovely to see Pia, and flattering to be asked for advice. The conversation had made Fran realise that the past was just that – past, and the future was in her hands. Pia had been able to reassure her Brit had no place in Owen's life – her sole reason for coming to Granite Springs had been, in Pia's words, "to treat me like a child again", and to force her back to Sydney.

Pia's assurance that Fran was special to Owen and made him happy should have sent her to the phone immediately, but it hadn't. However, now she'd agreed to go back to work next week, she knew she couldn't face him in the office without some sort of reconciliation.

Maybe Pia had got it wrong, but Fran would never know if she didn't make the effort to find out. It was four o'clock on a Friday afternoon. Owen should still be in the office.

She picked up the phone.

Fran's heart was beating wildly as she heard it ring… and ring…

and ring. Finally, it rang out. Her eyes filled with tears. It had taken so much courage to make the call. Why couldn't he have answered?

She was still sitting there holding the phone, when Stormy began to yowl. 'What is it?' she asked the cat, who was scratching at the front door. 'You know you can get out through the cat flap at the back.' For once, the antics of her pet failed to amuse her. Why was he making such a fuss?

There was a knock at the door. For a moment, Fran hesitated, then went to answer it, some instinct making her check herself in the hall mirror on the way and stroke back a strand of hair which was out of place.

She'd known. She should have guessed as soon as Stormy started scratching at the door.

Owen was standing on the doorstep, his hands thrust into the pockets of a pair of faded jeans, his feet encased in his customary Nikes, and rocking back on his heels in a manner that was achingly familiar. But the expression on his face wasn't. He looked… unsure of himself. 'You're not answering your phone,' he said, his blue eyes fixing her with a piercing gaze.

'No, I… You'd better come in.'

Owen followed her inside, into the kitchen, where he stood in the middle of the room seeming to take up all the space.

Fran didn't know what to do. She hadn't expected him to arrive unheralded. She wasn't ready to face him – not yet. 'Wine?' she asked. She needed something to do with her hands, and a glass of wine wouldn't go amiss.

Owen didn't reply as she took two glasses from the cupboard and a bottle of merlot from the wine rack, while she tried to work out what to say, how to handle this situation. She was opening the bottle when Owen spoke again.

'Brit's gone. I'm sorry she was such a bitch. Pia said she'd spoken to you.'

He sounded so despondent, so unlike the spontaneous, boisterous Owen she'd come to know – *and love*, a tiny voice in her head said – that Fran knew she had to say something to ease his torment. Could Pia have been right when she said Fran was special to Owen?

She handed Owen a glass of wine, and before she could speak, he said, 'We need to talk. Can we sit down?'

Shutting Stormy in the laundry much against his will, but not wanting him to interrupt what promised to be a serious conversation, Fran silently led Owen into the sitting room and sat down on one of the two armchairs. He sat opposite her on the sofa, clasping the glass in both hands between his knees.

'I'm sorry.'

They both spoke at once.

'You first,' Owen said.

'I'm sorry,' Fran repeated. 'I may have over-reacted to Brit's comments, but she made me feel…' she gave a long sigh, '…dirty. I don't want to be one in a long line of women who…'

'You're not! Brit's… she's always been like that. And I guess I've always looked out for her, too – maybe even given her the impression she can still rely on me. She *is* Pia's mother.' He thrust a hand through his hair. 'Hell. I don't know, Fran. I've been all kinds of a fool. But I want you to know this isn't like other times, you're not like any other woman I've ever known. The thought of losing you, of having to go through the rest of my life without you… I can't…'

'Then there was the stuff with Ron,' Fran continued as if Owen hadn't spoken. 'Coming on top of everything else, it was too much so I…'

'Retreated into your shell,' he finished for her.

'Yes,' Fran said in a small voice, twirling her glass by the stem. 'I seem to be good at that. I had a call from Flora earlier. She said Ron's retracted his complaint. Did you have something to do with it? Pia said you were on his case.' She allowed a tiny smile to escape and stole a sideways glance at him.

'That bastard! I can't believe they took him seriously. They should have known you'd never…'

'But you would?'

'Well, given the chance…' Owen grinned, seemingly beginning to relax. 'But,' he said becoming serious again, 'he hasn't done himself any favours. I doubt we'll see him back on campus.'

'Mmm.' Fran swirled her wine around and took a sip. 'Pia said you…' Fran thought again about what Pia had said. Hadn't that been what Owen had just said himself? 'Did I hear you correctly? Did you say…'

'I think I'm in love with you, Fran Reilly,' he said, draining his glass and putting it down on the coffee table.

Fran felt a warm glow – it started in her toes and made its way right up through her body.

Owen held out one hand, palm upraised. 'Come here.'

In an almost involuntary motion, Fran put down her own glass and moved slowly but surely towards the sofa.

Owen pulled her down, his arms tightening around her. 'I'm in love with you,' he repeated. 'My God, I never thought I'd say those words again, but I never thought I'd meet anyone like you. You've turned my life around, you and this town.'

Fran felt his lips in her hair, on her neck. She surrendered to his embrace, her body yielding to his passion, all her fears forgotten.

Sometime later, they were still together on the sofa, Fran still in his arms. Owen leant his chin on her head

'I love you, too,' she murmured, surprising herself with the admission. She remembered Magda's sage advice "Accept what is given to you. Be willing to give in return". *Was this what the old woman had meant? Was she really some sort of a witch? Had she seen Owen and her together?*

Owen kissed her again and sent everything else out of her mind.

'One more thing,' he said, when they stopped for air.

'What?' Fran felt a small curl of fear in her stomach. Was he going to ruin everything – just when she'd taken the biggest risk of her life?

'The property. The Kellys aren't coming back. I've bought the place. Goats included. Do you think you could get used to living outside of town?'

Fran's eyes widened. To live in the country, on that property, with Owen?

'And Stormy, of course,' he added. 'I'm sure he'll love the goats.'

'Oh, Owen.' She took his hands in hers. 'That's exactly the life I want.'

THE END

Look out for the next Granite Springs novel,
The Life She Finds, which is Lyn's story.

When *Lyn Hudson* takes early retirement, she plans to fulfil a lifelong dream to travel the world. But news of her father's death forces her back to Granite Springs; the town she fled when she was eighteen. While she has fond memories of roaming the paddocks with her childhood friend, Ken, life on the land is definitely not for her.

Ken Thomson, cheated out of his inheritance in the family property after an argument with his father, has built up a successful business in Granite Springs as a realter and stock and station agent. When the son he intended to inherit his business returns to work on the family property, his plans for the future are shattered and family relations further strained.

Thrown together by circumstances, the pair discover the spark which they denied forty-five years earlier is still smouldering. But time has passed. They are different people.

Can Lyn find common ground and start afresh with Ken, or will she once again follow her dreams and abandon Granite Springs and her chance at happiness?

From the Author

Dear Reader,

First, I'd like to thank you for choosing to read *The Life She Wants*. Having spent seven years teaching university and living in an Australian country town, I've enjoyed writing a series with a rural setting and drawing on my experience of living in the country – with goats – and teaching in univerisity. This is the third book in the series set in the fictional country town of Granite Springs. I hope you've enjoyed meeting Fran and Owen.

If you'd like to stay up to date with my new releases and special offers you can sign up to my reader's group.

You can sign up here   https://mailchi.mp/f5cbde96a5e6/maggiechristensensreadersgroup

I'll never share your email address, and you can unsubscribe at any time. You can also contact me via Facebook Twitter or by email. I love hearing from my readers and will always reply.

Thanks again.

Acknowledgements

As always, this book could not have been written without the help and advice of a number of people.

Firstly, my husband Jim for listening to my plotlines without complaint, for his patience and insights as I discuss my characters and storyline with him, for his patience and help with difficult passages and advice on my male dialogue, and for being there when I need him.

John Hudspith, editor extraordinaire for his ideas, suggestions, encouragement and attention to detail.

Jane Dixon-Smith for her patience and for working her magic on my beautiful cover and interior.

My thanks also to early readers of this book –Helen, Maggie and Louise, for their helpful comments and advice. Also to Annie of *Annie's books at Peregian* for her ongoing support.

And to all of my readers. Your support and comments make it all worthwhile. I'm thrilled you enjoy my more mature characters, and love to hear from you.

About the Author

After a career in education, Maggie Christensen began writing contemporary women's fiction portraying mature women facing life-changing situations. Her travels inspire her writing, be it her frequent visits to family in Oregon, USA or her home on Queensland's beautiful Sunshine Coast. Maggie writes of mature heroines coming to terms with changes in their lives and the heroes worthy of them. Her writing has been described by one reviewer as *like a nice warm cup of tea. It is warm, nourishing, comforting and embracing.*

From her native Glasgow, Scotland, Maggie was lured by the call 'Come and teach in the sun' to Australia, where she worked as a primary school teacher, university lecturer and in educational management. Now living with her husband of over thirty years on Queensland's Sunshine Coast, she loves walking on the deserted beach in the early mornings and having coffee by the river on weekends. Her days are spent surrounded by books, either reading or writing them – her idea of heaven!

She continues her love of books as a volunteer with her local library where she selects and delivers books to the housebound.

Maggie can be found on Facebook, Twitter, Goodreads, Instagram or on her website.

www.facebook.com/maggiechristensenauthor
www.twitter.com/MaggieChriste33
www.goodreads.com/author/show/8120020.Maggie_Christensen
www.instagram.com/maggiechriste33/
maggiechristensenauthor.com/